PLEASE DON'T TELL

LAURA TIMS

HARPER TEEN
An Imprint of HarperCollinsPublishers

To every young person who has ever struggled alone with a
secret burden: I see you, and you're incredible.

HarperTeen is an imprint of HarperCollins Publishers.

Library of Congress Control Number: 2015956261
ISBN 978-0-06-231732-2 (trade bdg.)

Typography by Ray Shappell
16 17 18 19 20 CG/RRDH 10 9 8 7 6 5 4 3 2 1
❖
First Edition

ONE

October 1

I'M HIDING IN THE BATHROOM.

My hands are shaking, and I'm crying. I don't know when that started.

Preston pounds on the door again.

"Please open the door, Joy. So what if you blacked out last night? That doesn't mean . . . what you think."

It's the bathroom on the bottom floor of school, the only single-stall bathroom in Stanwick High. Nobody comes down here before lunch. Nobody'll hear these noises, but I muffle myself with my fist anyway.

"Just come out. I have something important to tell you. You'll feel better." He's pleading. "First period's almost over. It's nine oh one."

I flash briefly to last night. If anyone said "Call nine one one," they weren't fast enough.

Wouldn't I remember that?

No, because I'm more than hungover enough to throw up into the stained ceramic toilet beside my face. But I shouldn't freak Pres out. Shouldn't make him think I've completely snapped.

I take a deep breath, punch down a wave of nausea. "Right. Okay. Right," I whisper.

"Joy, please. Come talk to me."

But I don't move. I'm staying here with the bathroom graffiti until the world stops being messed up. Until *I* stop.

Names, insults, scarring the rust-orange paint. The only ones I read are two letters, scratched extra deep.

A.G. ♥ ♥

And then I do throw up. It's quick and not messy, but Preston clearly hears me because he thumps the door with both palms. "Joy! Seriously, unlock this so I can—"

So he can what?

How's any single person in the universe gonna fix this?

Outside in the hall, Principal Eastman's voice crackles over the loudspeaker for the third time this morning. In here, it sounds tinny, distorted.

"Just a reminder that any absences from class today'll be excused. The therapy room will provide grief counseling for anybody who needs it." Pres stops knocking, and I flatten my cheek against the cold tile. The hearts next to *A.G.* march past the toilet paper dispenser. It's not my sister's writing. Some other girl with some other life etched those. Did she cry at the news, or smile?

A week ago I'd've known which one I'd do.

Principal Eastman breathes over the loudspeaker, no idea what to say next. First time we've had something in common. It clicks off, and the silence gushes back into my ears and nose and mouth.

He was cute, Grace had insisted. I wasn't allowed to make fun of her, because he was cute.

Also according to her, he was sensitive, not a douche, for carting his Gibson guitar everywhere. What if he was lonely, living up there by the old bluestone quarry that his grandfather's one hit song made famous? He probably needed somebody to talk to.

But talking wasn't what he wanted from her.

Did I talk to him last night, before I killed him?

I finally get myself together and open the door. Preston pulls me close and walks me back into the land of the living. He grips my backpack, steers me down the hall. It makes me move like a killer: stiff, jerky. At least my legs work like a human's. Whatever I turned into last night, it's still wearing my skin.

"You gotta quit freaking out," Pres whispers. I barely hear him. "I have to tell you something once we're alone. It's important."

Nobody points at me and screams *You pushed Adam Gordon into the quarry last night!*—but nobody looks at me, either, even though Preston's awkwardly guiding me down the hall like a prisoner. His frizzy orange curls, his jeans that end an inch above the ankle . . . they always stand out, but not today. The bell's gone off, hallway's flooded, but no one rushes. They trade hushed information.

"It was his eighteenth birthday party."

"It's creepy that they found him in the quarry. Those lyrics to his granddad's song . . . 'Carry me down to the quarry . . .'"

"He was so drunk, it was dark, he fell in."

"See?" Pres says as he leads me toward the counseling room. "Accident. Not you."

Maybe . . .

Kennedy Brown flies out in front of us, sobbing, hurling herself into Sarah McCaughney's arms. My spine shakes apart.

The world isn't a fair enough place that Adam would've staggered drunk over the edge by himself. Not after all the time I spent imagining stabbing-shooting-crushing him. It must've been me.

Whether I was sober enough to remember it or not.

Ms. Bell, Preston's mom, is the school counselor. Clumped on her lumpy beige couches, underneath the loud mental health posters (Invest in your Life! Go for a Walk!) are Kennedy, Sarah, Ben Stockholm, some other artsy seniors. A couple of other juniors like me. Adam's people. I sit on the carpet by the door.

"We met at summer camp when we were kids." Kennedy

stuffs used tissues into her sweater pocket. "No one should ever die if you remember what they looked like when they were seven years old."

Sarah shifts, silky blond hair hiding her eyes. Flashes of last night: she and Kennedy were barefoot on the lawn, dancing together by the bonfire. But I was looking for Adam, so I went inside, pushed through music and bodies, deeper into the big slanted house on the hill. Passing the bar, I snatched a bottle of Four Roses bourbon for bravery. And . . .

Blurry dreams. This morning, in my bed, shoes still on, hair knotted, cotton mouthed.

And the guy I'd looked for, wanted gone—

"This is hard for you all. Very hard." Ms. Bell's pale under the burst of purple in her scarf, and the glass lily on a ribbon around her neck is orange like the hair she shares with Pres. She catches my eye, smiles small and sad. I'm special to her. The only one who hangs out with her son.

She'll hate me when she hears. But I gotta tell. My mouth's novocaine numb. I open it anyway. "I'm—"

But the door opens faster. Cassius Somerset—Adam's best friend—stands in the doorway and looks around. He has vitiligo, so his skin's like a map, continents breaking up the brown on his arms, neck, wide face. His hair's buzzed across his forehead in a ruler-sharp line. He's a broad person, but he's always trying to take up less space. There's a mark on his hip, hidden now, like a comet

5

trailing stars down his thigh. I think I'm the only one who knows about that.

Amazing how someone's presence can firebomb your skin, right up until it doesn't anymore.

He turns, sees me. He has a black eye. Cassius, president of the Art Club, vegetarian who speaks so quietly they turned the mic up extra loud during his valedictorian speech to the freshmen this year, has a black eye.

He gazes at me for a minute, shell-shocked. He walks back out of the room.

Kennedy rakes her fingers through her hair, whispers to Sarah. I swear everyone can sense it when two people've had sex. Like a ghost in the air.

But who cares about that now?

"I'm sorry," I say aloud, suddenly, crackly, useless.

It's weird, being the only one who knows what I'm apologizing for.

I'm not letting myself hide in the bathroom anymore.

Since the beginning of school last month, the cafeteria's been a war zone for me. I looked around corners with a mirror. Adam was a land mine, winning the battle he didn't even know was happening.

Now I've won, I guess.

I sit at the table closest to the garbage cans and do the bravest thing I've done all day: I check my phone.

Twenty texts from Grace.

It wouldn't be twenty if it were just about our fight last night. She's heard.

I sneak a gulp from the minibottle of Jägermeister in my backpack, stolen from the sample collection Dad has. It's an art—drinking enough that you can breathe again but not so much that people notice. One I've perfected in the last month. The alcohol burns my throat. It burned last night, too, on the way to the party, but it wouldn't have been enough to make me forget. What I drank after I got there was enough.

November sits down across from me, and I ram the bottle back into my bag. She's eight inches shorter than me, but somehow way taller. Her hair's in a zillion braids, half of them green. She probably wondered why I stopped begging her to dye mine, halfway through the summer.

"You okay?" she asks immediately.

"I'm always okay," I say without thinking.

She toys with her rubber bands. She's never explained why, but she always has at least ten on each wrist. "So. Adam. Damn."

Everything she and I did together over the summer feels like a movie I watched about someone else. The silence between you and someone you're supposed to love can get bigger and bigger, both of you feeding it, until you can barely see the person on the other side. And you wonder how long it's been since you looked.

"I went to his birthday party," I force out. "Got sorta wasted. I don't remember anything after his front door."

Her eyes widen. "Why the hell did you go? I told you to keep away from him."

People lie all the time. I can lie. *Just lie, Joy.*

Instead I start crying.

She moves to the seat next to me and sighs. She presses me into her chest, arms solid wire. A hurricane couldn't move her if she didn't give it signed permission. It fucks me up that she thinks I'm sad for him.

"I'll go with you," she says.

For a second I think she's talking about jail.

"To his funeral in a couple days. You know I hated that dick, but if you're crying you need to go, and if you need to go, you can't go alone."

If I see his body, maybe I'll remember what happened.

"Grace can come, too," she says quietly. I don't say anything. Empty noise fills me.

"I'm gonna head home. Principal Eastman said all absences are excused. Should take advantage."

She's already halfway up. "I'll drive you. My car's right at the front of the senior lot."

"No." I swallow. "I want to walk."

Stanwick, New York, has two claims to fame—the birthplace of the seventies hit "Carry Me Down to the Quarry" and the fact that the *Times* named it the third most walkable small town in America, like small towns aren't walkable by definition. I don't know anyone who lives farther than two miles from the high school. Even the elementary school playground and the shopping center with the Regal Cinemas are just a twenty-minute walk from my house. The quarry, Adam's house: half an hour. An easy trip, even in the dark, up that road past the tall black pines.

I'm halfway home when my phone goes off again and again. Preston, texting—he's worried.

Did you ditch? I told you I need to talk to you.

I text him back: **sorry. tell me now.**

Okay, listen: I know why you couldn't have done it. You left the party last night before Adam died. After you told me about your fight with Grace and quit replying, I figured it was where you went.

Was scared you'd do something bad. So I went to the party and looked everywhere (Everywhere) but you weren't there. Adam was definitely alive at that point. I know because he called me a fucking fag and made me leave.

I close my eyes and squeeze my phone until my knuckles ache.

I left the party before he died. It wasn't me.

I'm not going to jail. I'm not capable of it after all. I'm normal, thank God, oh thank God.

u r the most incredible friend in the world thank u so much

I sprint the rest of the way, even though it kills my head. I'm awake now. Now that Adam's dead, now that the universe is proving it does love us, maybe Grace'll wake up, too.

Mom and Dad are still at work—Mom at her law office, Dad at the gym. The only sound at home is a thudding underneath the floorboards. It's always there, like a heartbeat. She's on the treadmill.

I slam downstairs to the exercise room. The walls yell

at me, Dad's posters: You Are as Strong as You Want to Be! Push Through It! Breathe! I'm just going to talk to my twin, not jump into a pool of sharks. The only reason my legs feel like this is because I ran here.

Some people jog with their limbs flailing in what Dad calls a *disorganized unit*. Grace is an organized unit. She runs clean, elbows in, flat-ironed hair twined up tight, bangs pinned to her scalp. We're identical in the same way as a sketch and a painting. Same basic material, but only one of us is polished-perfect. Even in our fourth-grade gym relay races, she ran like that.

She hears me come in and hits a button. The treadmill slows but doesn't stop. Sweat studs her forehead, her waterproof makeup flawless. "You get my texts?" The words heave out of her.

She doesn't know about Adam. If she did, she'd be crying, laughing, hugging me, sliding back into her old self.

"He's dead," I blurt. "Adam. He fell into the quarry last night, bashed his head. Everyone always said how someone was going to fall in. It's like the universe was listening to us."

I stare at her with anticipation. She'll get off the treadmill. We'll step into the time machine, go back to the beginning of the summer, and redo everything.

"I heard," she says. She doesn't get off the treadmill.

"Do you feel . . . How do you feel?"

She shrugs. "Glad. I guess." *Thud, thud, thud.* "Maybe I'm still taking it in."

She's paler, wider than me, and I swear her eyes are bluer, but we both have the double sports bra boobs, the narrow upper lip, the stubby Morris thumbs from Dad.

"So how was the party?" she asks, throwing a spear through my chest.

"You know I went?"

"I heard you climb out your window." A weird cold silence. "You said we shouldn't go, and you went by yourself."

I laugh desperately. "It doesn't matter now, does it?"

"You didn't have anything to do with him falling, then."

"*No.*" I need her to believe I'm not capable of that. No matter what threats I've made, raging at my worst. "I thought I'd confront him or something. It was stupid. But I left before anything happened to him. The night's . . . blurry."

"You were drunk?"

Remember what happened the last time you got drunk there?

"I was scared," I say.

Sweat dyes dark circles under her armpits, on her chest. People always say twins can read each other's minds. I'm supposed to be able to read her mind.

"Are we still fighting?" I ask.

"I guess not."

"Can you get off the treadmill?"

"Can't. I ate, like, five hundred extra calories by accident."

Which is one of the things she says these days that I don't get.

Then she's silent forever, except for the pound of her feet on the treadmill. Silence is the worst thing someone can give you. Your mind fills it with every possible bad thing.

He's gone, but nothing's changed. What if this is just the way things are now?

"Joy?" She steps off the treadmill, finally. Her make-up's not so perfect after all, foundation-caked scabs on her forehead where she's been squeezing blackheads, eyebrows plucked raw. But her eyes are still a little bluer than mine.

"I'm fine," she's saying. "I'm fine with it. I've always been fine. Everything will be okay now."

TWO

October 3

I'VE NEVER THOUGHT ABOUT HOW BIG A coffin a six-foot-tall person needs. The lid's open and I can't see him from our spot in the back, but I can feel his ghost. Since it happened, any room he was in was on fire. This one's barely smoking.

November slouches beside me, her earbuds twisted around her wrist. "You okay?"

I make myself smile. "I'm always okay."

She nods. "So, Grace isn't . . ."

"No, she's not coming."

She nods again.

Above us, there's a dustless plaster Jesus on a glossy black cross, even though it's a funeral home, not a church. There's another service going on across the hall, smaller but with people crying louder. How many funerals does a town like Stanwick have per week? How often do people die?

I look around. Half the school's here. Even Principal Eastman sits in front, tall and straight so people notice he came. Ms. Bell, a beaded black scarf around her neck, murmurs to Ben Stockholm, quick hands illustrating everything she says. Cassius is in the corner, hunched like something's fighting its way out of his spine. I can't tell if I feel bad for him or if I want to yell at him.

And Mr. Gordon—Adam's dad—stands near the casket, fumbling to shake people's hands as they greet him. His alcohol stink battles the smell of all the flowers, makes the hidden bottle in my pocket burn. His hair curls in gray waves under his cheekbones, skin too taut over a jawline that probably cut through hearts like butter when he was eighteen. Adam would have looked like him.

"I don't care how famous this song is," Nov grunts. "It's creepy how they keep playing it on repeat."

Abe Gordon, Adam's grandfather, sings over the speakers: "And I'll carry you down to the quarry, once it's dark and there's no point sayin' sorry . . ."

Suddenly everyone is shuffling, taking their seats, and Mr. Gordon picks up the microphone.

"Adam was . . . my son." Mr. Gordon strangles the mic. His voice filters through gravel. "And he was . . . his grandfather's grandson. He'd've made it as far as my father, that's the musical talent he had. . . ."

Parents have no idea how little they know about the people they gave life to.

"Adam—"And then Mr. Gordon shakes his head, takes a deep breath, and pukes. The mic broadcasts the sound, the smell hitting us all at once. He staggers. An Asian guy I've never seen before—his hair gelled in short spikes and a T-shirt blazing orange underneath a too-small black vest—leaps up, catching Mr. Gordon's elbow. I can't hear what the guy says as he quickly steers Mr. Gordon past us and out the door, but his tone's low and comforting.

"Jeeesus," November mutters.

"Who's that guy?" I whisper. "Why's Mr. Gordon his responsibility?"

She shrugs.

Two funeral home employees clean up while Abe Gordon continues to sing about the quarry where the grandson he never met died. It used to be a love song, now it's a dirge. Sweat laminates my shirt to my back. I want to take off my skin.

There's whispers throughout the crowd. No one knows what's happening now. But then Cassius approaches the mic, his black eye puffed purple. The overhead lights wash out the paler parts of him. From here, it's like someone splattered him with paint.

"What's he doing?" November mumbles.

"I was Adam's best friend. . . ." he starts.

Cassius is the school artist. Adam was the school musician. The sweet-voiced daydreamer and the smirking

I 5

asshole. I grip the minibottle in my pocket.

"And I'm here to tell you he was a fucking prick."

An audible gasp sounds. A new kind of silence washes over the room. My throat seals shut.

I should have been the one brave enough to say it.

Cassius stares helplessly around the room. His eyes hit mine, and I fold into the bench. Then he drops the mic, tucks in his shoulders, and walks out fast, chased by glares and whispers.

"Someone's gotta go after him." November squeezes my shoulder, and then she's gone. I guess funerals mean taking responsibility for the sadness of people you barely know.

Everyone waits for some family member to grab the wheel, but Mr. Gordon was all Adam had. So after another awkward moment, people start rising. Slowly, a queue forms. Final good-byes. I stand behind everybody else.

The line moves joltingly, like an execution, a pause for each person to leap off the cliff at the end. Tears. Murmurs. Propped between pews is a photo collage of Adam through the years: A toddler with the ghost of his face mashes a toy keyboard. An eight-year-old reaches through reindeer wrapping paper for the fretboard of a guitar. Was this kid-version of Adam always capable of what he did? If something changed, what and when? Did he notice?

I step up to the casket and see that each hard, crisp tendril of his hair is arranged specifically on the pillow, arms bent over his chest, mouth locked, hidden stitches disappearing into his temple. There's no rush of memories from my missing night. If something had changed in me to make me capable of murder, I'd notice, right?

People look at bodies to understand how they're just empty houses, and then they're not scared anymore, right?

I hate him. I hate him so much I wish I'd killed him—

No! I dig my fingernails into my palms. I don't want to be scary. Or to wish for that.

But I am. And I do.

The funeral home bathroom is all fake elegance—fake marble sinks, plastic craft-store flowers in a plastic vase, a plastic doily underneath. But there's nothing realer than a toilet, or the things people write on the wall above one. Sharpie underneath the door hinge: *I still have your sweater.* This is grief, dirty and cold. It's hiding in a bathroom and doing your shameful things where no one else can see. Mostly it's the word carved in tiny letters above the coat hook: *please.*

Please don't let me be a girl who looks at a dead person and wishes she'd killed him. Let me be what someone peering in would see, a girl crying, too tall maybe, hair too wild, but nobody's nightmare.

Grace used to hide in the bathroom in kindergarten, as soon as Mom dropped us off. She'd come out only if I promised to hold her hand.

I take out my bottle, drop it. It clatters like the world's ending, but doesn't break. I swallow the contents. Breathe. It's my head, I'm in control of it, and Adam's dead, dead, dead.

Through the wall, there's the dry rasp of someone

throwing up in the men's room. Then a thud, a ceramic clonk, and a softly whispered "fuck."

I know what it is to swear hopelessly to yourself in a bathroom. So I gather myself and go next door.

I've never been in a men's room. It's the same as the girls', minus the fake flowers, plus a urinal. A man's legs stick out under the door to the only stall.

I step forward.

The stranger from earlier is looping Mr. Gordon's arm over his shoulders. He's shed his vest, his orange shirt flecked with puke. He braces himself against the tiles, face dimming with that kind of desperation people get when they have to lift something way too heavy for them.

"Can I help?" It comes out so normal.

He looks up, relieved. "Thanks, would you mind?" he pants. "I wanna take him to his car."

We maneuver Mr. Gordon up, his legs jumbling, suit ruined. This is real alcohol. An adult going to the store and buying a forty and drinking all of it.

The parking lot's cold for upstate New York in October, though the sunlight's laser sharp, the kind that always burns me and spares Grace, thanks to the SPF-30 moisturizer she puts on every day. We prop Mr. Gordon against his blue Mazda. He slouches semiconscious against the hood. The stranger wipes his forehead, smiles gratefully at me.

"Thank you so much. I'm Levi. You're the nicest person in the world."

It's like every word's tattooed on his heart, he's so sincere.

He's two inches shorter than me. Eyebrows, perfect. His upper lip's fuller than the bottom. If he combined with Grace and me, we'd have an even mouth.

"I had no idea what I was gonna do with him in there," he says.

We realize simultaneously we have no idea what we're going to do with him out here.

"You don't drive, do you?"

I shake my head. "I just got my permit. Sorry."

"Don't be sorry. " He rolls a shoulder, winces, crouches. Mr. Gordon grumbles nonsense. There's a special kind of shittiness about an adult whose life's a train wreck. I have time to fix mine. But maybe that's what he thought when he was sixteen.

My phone buzzes. It's November.

Giving Cassius a ride home. Lemme know if u need me to come back for ya.

People start filtering out, looking at the sky and the ground and every car in the lot except Mr. Gordon's. The easiest way to deal with a problem is to pretend it doesn't exist, as taught by my parents. Only Ms. Bell heads toward us. There're rules against staff touching students, but she hugs me. Levi, too. He hugs her back tight.

"You guys know each other?" I'm stuck on the mystery of who he is.

"Nope." Ms. Bell bends and shouts, "Mr. Gordon!" A

groan. She straightens. "Joy, I'm bringin' my car around, and I'm takin' him home. He won't get to see his son bein' buried, but if you ask me, I don't think he'd see it even if we plonked him down next to the minister."

It takes her three minutes to back her car up to us. We tip Mr. Gordon into the backseat.

After she's driven off, Levi says, "Thanks again. For helping, and for being the first person in Stanwick I've talked to. Makes me think all of you must be pretty nice."

He doesn't see the train wreck. But it's not as obvious on me, like a pukey suit and Jell-O legs. "I can't believe he got so wasted."

"It's not his fault. People do things to cope."

"People shouldn't need . . . that kind of coping."

"Everyone has something they use to cope." His eyes are wood brown, oak branches, sunlight. "Doesn't make 'em bad people."

I should ask how he knew Adam, but I don't want to hear that they were friends. Maybe he helped Mr. Gordon for the same reason November's giving Cassius a ride home.

"The graveyard's across the road," he says hesitantly. "Walk with me?"

I nod and walk with him.

Grace and I were seven the last time we came to the grave-yard. It was after some nameless great-uncle had a heart attack in front of *Antiques Roadshow*. I stole a daisy from someone else's grave, put it in Grace's hair, and cried when Mom snatched it back.

Now it's a summer graveyard with winter air. We surround the fresh pit, everyone silent. Adam'll lie here forever, neutralized. He won't follow me out.

The minister tells some nice lies about Adam, and then several men lift the casket and lower it into the open hole. I'll make sure they don't fuck it up. This is why the time machine didn't work yesterday—they hadn't buried him yet. Grace'll be fine as soon as he's covered in dirt.

Kennedy cries for real, heaving sobs over the dirt patter. Sarah clings to her back. I'm rigid. No girl should ever cry for him.

Grace never cried.

Then Levi's beside Kennedy, whispering gently to her. She quiets. Does he know her? Or does he just know what to say? If I were like him, I'd've found the right words to tell Grace in the exercise room. I'd've found the right words in the summer.

The shovel noise devolves from artillery fire to heavy rainfall. One foot of dirt. Two. The graveyard empties. The sun dips lower and the men work until there's a mound of clean earth.

But there's no magic text from Grace announcing she's okay. Nothing teleports me back to the beginning of the summer. I'm still here. He's still here.

He *is* going to follow me out.

"Joy?"

I turn. Levi's still here, too. I realize we're alone next to the grave. Everyone must've left.

He touches my wrist, and I yank back.

"Sorry," he says immediately. "Um."

I look away. Half the graves nearby have fresh flowers. Daisies. Grace's favorite.

"You must've cared a lot about him."

If dead people can make someone pay ten dollars for a bunch of flowers at the grocery store and drive here to drop them off, what else can they do?

"I hated him," I say.

"Oh." Sadness fits him worse than that vest.

"He—" The truth claws my throat. I choke on it. "Never mind. Fuck. I'm sorry. Shit. I don't mean to swear so much."

"It's fucking fine." He smiles a little bit. Even though the sun's setting, the graveyard lightens.

But his smile disappears when he glances at the grave again. It's clear he wishes Adam weren't dead. Which means he and I are fundamentally incompatible human beings.

I start to say bye, but instead, suddenly, I'm gulping. I can't control anything that comes out of my mouth, but I can control what comes out of my eyes. I'm *not* going to cry over Adam's grave. I take a deep breath. And then tears leak out anyway.

"Whoa, hey. It's okay."

Strangers say that like they know what's okay and what's not.

"Death is hard." He lifts his hands: *I'm not going to hurt you.* "Even if you didn't like him. Sometimes that makes it harder."

I don't want him to take responsibility for my sadness. But he's making me feel a little better. What doorway did he find into my head, and how can I find the same one into Grace's?

"How'd you get here if you don't drive?" I ask.

"Came with my, um. My dad." A cold breeze speckles his bare arms with goose bumps. He tugs a baseball cap out of his pocket, puts it on. It's bent, threads sprouting from the brim. It messes up his hair. "Looks like I'll be hoofing it."

I love that he says *hoofing it.*

"Lemme give you a ride." I text Mom. "You deserve a favor, helping out Mr. Gordon like that."

"Ah, yeah. I forgot it's not that obvious. Perils of being mixed race. My mom's Vietnamese. He's the aforementioned dad I won't be riding back with."

Levi is—Adam's brother?

"It doesn't feel obvious to me, either. Trust me."

I've been standing here talking to him like a friend.

"I haven't seen him since I was nine."

Nausea rolls over me.

"I swear our left pinkies are both crooked. Or they were when we were little. Meant to check if his still was." He stares at the grave for the hundredth time. "I forgot to look."

I betrayed Grace by smiling at him.

"Why'd you hate him?" he asks tentatively. "I had this idea of him in my head. I'm wondering how right I was."

Breathe.

Before I realize it, I'm walking away, hurrying toward the graveyard gate, abandoning Levi. He catches up to me by the curb. He smells like cinnamon and summer wheat. No more breathing, not while he's in a hundred-mile radius.

"Sorry if I said something wrong."

I look at him. There's no Adam in his angular ears, or in the earring I just noticed, a thin silver hoop. No Adam in his freckles, few but dark: three in a line from the edge of his left eye to his cheekbone, one underneath the right edge of his mouth, a faint one on the tip of his nose.

His Adam parts are hidden, which makes them more dangerous.

"I don't mind walking home." He backs away. "I'll see you around. Nice to meet you, Joy."

The Gordons' house is a half-hour trek, and he might not be used to walking, if he's not from Stanwick. The wind shoves his T-shirt against his shoulder blades. Some boys are so skinny it makes my chest hurt.

"Wait." The word tastes like guilt. "My mom'll be here any minute."

In the car, Mom's knuckles whiten more on the steering wheel with every hundred feet. She and Grace get those lines on their foreheads when they're holding something in.

"How was it?" she asks warily.

"It was a funeral, Mom. It was sad."

"Horrible accident, what happened." Dad twists in the front seat to face Levi, who's beside me in the back. "You a friend of Joy's from school?"

"Nah." Levi presses against the window. Is he doing it because he wants to get away from me, or because he knows I want to get away from him? "I don't know how long I'll be staying, though, so I'm enrolled at school here. Starting tomorrow."

How does he not know how long he'll be staying?

"You just moved here?" Dad's shirt says Just Do It! in awful red letters.

"I flew here from Indiana for the funeral, and I'll be staying with my . . . dad." He picks at his battered baseball cap. It's a little too small. "Adam was my half brother."

"*Oh.*" Mom fills the car with pity like steam.

Dad fires off an instant "I'm so sorry for your loss."

"Don't be. It's no big deal." He rotates the hoop in his earlobe. "I mean, it's a big deal, just for everyone else, since I never knew Adam. I mean, it's still a big deal to *me*, but other people . . . never mind."

He mutters something that sounds like *idiot*.

"Stay away from that quarry," says Mom suddenly. "It's dangerous how kids hang out there, just because of the song. Your father and I and some other parents are starting a petition to have the town fence it off."

Yeah. Seal it away.

We arrive at the house. It slants on the hill, like a claw that popped out of the earth, glass and wood. The lawn's blisteringly green. The night Grace and I came here together, the first night, *the* night, I tore off my shoes after the long walk and buried my toes in the grass. She kept hers on. Told me to hurry up, please, she didn't want to make him wait.

The night of his birthday party, I kept my shoes on. That's all I remember.

Levi gets out, thanks us for the ride, traipses up the steps. It takes him a while to open the door, like he's not used to the lock. It's hard to leave anyone here to this dark slash of a house, the quarry lurking past the trees.

But he's enemy territory.

Mom and Dad fidget on the way back. They're like twins, too, blond and tall, doing everything in tandem, always putting on ChapStick. I have no idea who they are.

"I know you'll run upstairs to your computer the minute we get home, so your father and I wanted to ask you something." Mom stops too hard at a red light. My head jerks. "Is something going on with Grace?"

They used to ask her about me. I'd hear them in the living room—*Is something going on with Joy?*

She's fine, she'd say. Because she was on my side. Because my job was to protect her and bring her out of her shell and their job was to get in the way.

I shove my toe into the front of my sneaker. "What d'you mean?"

2 6

"It's this independent project thing she's doing with her teachers," says Mom. "It's an amazing opportunity, and of course we want to support her academically."

"But we're starting to wonder if it's a good idea for her to be out of school for the whole semester," Dad adds. "Even if the principal okayed it and the teachers are working with her from home. She's in her room a lot these days."

They're worried about her grades.

"I hang out in my room a lot."

"But you and Grace have different . . . approaches," says Mom.

"Maybe she's depressed or something," I bite out.

"What would she be depressed about?" asks Dad, surprised.

"I don't think she's *depressed*," says Mom, like someone would say *I don't think she's a purple giraffe.* "Moody, maybe. I was exactly the same at her age."

"Does this have anything to do with that night this summer?" Dad wants to know.

I bend my toenail backward against the front of my sneaker until something cracks. But he's not talking about *the* night, he's talking about the night they picked us up at the police station. I forgot how many things went wrong over the summer.

"No. I'm sure she's fine."

Silence again. I stare out the window at the town, at the patches of trees, the small neat houses, the cracks in the sidewalk I've memorized.

They're not going to question me. We're twins. I know

Grace better than anybody else. If something were wrong, I would know.

But I do know, and I promised to stay silent.

My bedroom's built from fossils of me and Grace. Scattered plastic horses from our horse phase at age nine. Beads jammed between the floorboards from our jewelry-making phase at twelve, when she insisted we work in here because I kept spilling the beads. I papered the walls with every birthday card, every stupid drawing. It's a shrine to the way we used to be.

It was so much better, the way we used to be.

Now there's also Pop-Tarts wrappers, empty Gatorade bottles, crumbs in the bed. Sometimes I can feel Grace's younger self in here, being disappointed in me.

I bend to pick up a crumpled paper plate, but my phone buzzes with Preston's name.

How was the funeral?

mr gordon puked, cassius called adam a prick, I was accidentally nice to adams half brother

Adam has a half brother?

gonna ask u a thing on a topic that is not that. r u like sad? abt adam dying?

I didn't like him even before you told me what he did.

I thought maybe u should always be sad when someone dies no matter what

Im not sad and Im scared that makes me a bad person but Im always kinda worryin about bein a

bad person. idk
I hated him so much I didnt understand how he
could not feel it, and it feels kinda like I killed
him by hating him that hard even tho u say I left
the party before he died. sometimes I feel like I
have so much hate inside me and I have to spend
all my energy tryin to keep it from gettin out but
idk if Im strong enough to do it forever

I'm still typing, losing track of what I'm saying, my hands shaking, when my phone buzzes hard and loud. He's calling me.

"It was an accident, Joy," Preston says as soon as I pick up. "People always said how someone was going to fall in."

I roll across my bed, pull Grace's old stuffed tiger toward me. I rescued it from the trash after one of her yearly room purges. There's nothing worse than being something someone used to need. "You're right."

"Say it again, slower."

I need to be better at convincing people I'm okay.

"It's just a weird coincidence. But for every person who dies, I guess there's someone who wanted them gone and can't believe their luck." One of the tiger's legs is half-severed. "I just have to pretend to be sad about him at school for a couple days."

"How's Grace taking it?"

Maybe I can sew the tiger's leg. I rotate it and it comes off in my hand.

"It makes me anxious when you don't answer," he

blurts. "I start thinking I said something annoying and that I should stop talking and that maybe you don't like me anymore, and I know it's ridiculous but I can't help it."

People are always turning silence into a knife to stab themselves with. "I would never stop liking you, I promise."

"Okay. Thanks." Relief, embarrassment.

"I should probably go. I have a thousand years of homework. I'm still failing American History because I hate America and I hate history." Make another joke, show him I'm fine. "Also tomorrow's trash pickup day so I gotta go put myself out on the curb."

"Please don't say things like that."

Wrong joke. "Just kidding."

"You're the only person at school I feel comfortable around, and you're a very important friend to me, and I don't think you should call yourself trash."

"You always cheer me up every single time you talk to me, did you know that?"

I can feel him smiling.

"Don't stay up too late tonight, okay?" I tell him before I hang up.

I stare at my history book on the floor. Principal Eastman's brought me in twice to talk about American History. But I can't start the homework. It's not just a sheet of paper, it's the horrible black hole of my future.

I toss the broken tiger into my closet, go out into the hall, knock three times on Grace's door.

She doesn't open it all the way. "What's up, Joy?"

It's the way teachers talk to you when you go to them after class and they know you're gonna ask for an extension. That kind of weary readiness.

"I went to his funeral." Mom and Dad are watching football downstairs. The noise blares up to us. She still doesn't let me in.

"How was it?"

"It was okay."

"Uh-huh."

Let me in, let me in, let me in.

She tilts the door closed a little more. "I'm doing some school stuff. . . ."

"Yeah."

"So I kind of need to concentrate."

"Oh! I'll leave you alone."

She hesitates. "You okay?"

"I'm always okay." Now I need to ask it back. But what if she finally admits that she's not, and I still have no clue what the right words are—

She closes the door before I can find them.

We used to crawl into bed together and turn off all the lights and watch YouTube videos until we sobbed with laughter.

Back in my room, I check Adam's Facebook. His wall goes straight from thirty-seven happy birthday posts to fifty-eight death posts. He's got more friends now.

Maybe he reeled drunk through the woods to look

soulfully at the moon and think about what a fucking "art-ist" he was. And that last birthday shot caught around his ankles, and the wind carried him into the quarry.

The breeze drags a splintered piece of the overgrown oak tree branch against my window screen. Must've done that when I snuck out. The breeze rustles Grace's old drawings taped to my wall, crayon versions of us. She always drew me taller and gave me a sword.

I get up to close the window. But there's an envelope on the sill. Sealed neatly, thick. My name's written on the back.

A weird feeling settles in my stomach.

I tear it open, feel inside. Photographs, stiff and glossy, and a folded piece of paper. A letter.

Only the first few lines make sense to me before the rest blurs and my mind gets stuck and my hands stop feeling like anything.

To Joy Morris—

I was at the party. I was at the quarry. I saw what you did.

I saw you murder Adam Gordon.

THREE

June 7

Grace

"YALE." PRINCIPAL EASTMAN THROWS A PAM-phlet onto the pile on his desk. "Brown." Pamphlet. "Penn State. Even Harvard, Grace. I called you in here because your grades, your test scores, they are outstanding. The best in your class. Yes, it's only the end of your sophomore year, but you should be thinking about college."

Fourteen pamphlets on the desk. A mountain I have to climb every day. Schedule: study for three hours daily, minimum. Social life: nonexistent.

"A lot of students see summer as their vacation time, so this is your chance to get ahead. Volunteer work? Amazing on an application. And it's never too early to start SAT prep classes."

Schedule: study four hours a day, minimum. Two hours

volunteer work. SAT prep class on weekends. Two hours exercise—there needs to be less of me. Five hours for sleep. Makeup: two hours.

My phone buzzes on top of my backpack. I adjust my shirt, comb bangs out flat with my fingers, look down at the screen. It's my sister.

LAST DAY OF SCHOOL YASSSSS. ME AND NOV IN FRONT OF BUS CIRCLE, FIND US.

Principal Eastman leans forward, looking at me like I'm the best photo he's ever taken. "The Honors Club and the Environmentalism Club and the—what was the other one?"

"Art Club," I mumble, chewing the inside of my cheek.

"They've appreciated your participation this year. You ought to think about helping out with the school newspaper. To be honest, I'm a bit worried about the direction it's taken under November Roseby."

My phone buzzes. Her again.

big plans for this summer! gonna be v fun.

Eastman claps my shoulder. I'm dismissed. I get up, pulling my shirt down flat over my stomach.

GRAACEEEEE where r u?

She gave up on me being social during the school year. She's trying hard again, now that it's summer. Why does she want me so bad? What's there to have?

I text her back.

don't wait for me! i have some stuff to do! :)

I have to walk the hallway loop of the school twice

before I can go home. If I can do it in two hundred steps, I'll burn fifty calories and I won't disappoint anybody.

I start my lap. Lockers left open, empty classrooms. Around the corner of the science wing are the glass doors to the outdoor relaxation garden. Ms. Bell's idea, a place for students to unwind. One more way for Principal Eastman to claim our school's different, even though we're exactly like every public high school in every small town in every state. Nothing special here. Keep going. The city's that way.

I step into the little outdoor courtyard, full of cheap plants. The seeds in the bird feeder are moldy. It was only filled once. Even the birds are headed someplace better.

Ninety-five. Ninety-six. Keeping steps small so I don't go over. My phone buzzes twice in my back pocket. Two more texts from Joy, I'm sure, all in caps.

"You high?" someone says.

Startled, I turn. Adam Gordon, inches away. *Him*. Really cute junior. Sitting on the plaster bench, glossy acoustic guitar on his lap. I've looked at him all year, but he's never looked at me. I drop all my college handouts, so cliché it must have been on purpose. My future in the dirt.

"Did you even see me?" Adam laughs, not helping. I gather the handouts. Measure each movement. Must move smoothly, not awkwardly. He leans forward, his T-shirt crumpling at the waist. "You look so high."

What's being high like: stammering, heart racing? Maybe this is it. Wavy dark hair skims his cheekbones.

Dark eyes. Dark soul? Writes beautiful, sad music, plays it for talent shows, musicals. He has a way of looking at people like they're special. Like Joy does. Whenever I see him, I want to ask if he's okay.

"I thought you were a freshman." He gestures at the pamphlets.

"Sophomore. Or, I was. I'm a junior now, technically." I wince.

He taps his cigarette on the edge of the bench. His fingers are calloused. "Applying extra-extra early decision?"

"Principal Eastman wants me to look to the future." I. Sound. So. Ridiculous.

"He probably just wanted to look down your shirt." He smirks. A bad-boy smile, like the twenty-five-year-old actors who think they can play seventeen-year-old boys in teen movies. "Kidding. A guy with a telescope couldn't get a glimpse down there." He holds out a cigarette. "Want one?"

"No, thank you." Should have said yes. Was he just looking at my chest? I'm wearing two sports bras. "Does Principal Eastman look down shirts?"

"Yeah, he's a pedo." He shifts his guitar onto his other leg. "But some girls here are thirsty for it."

Is he joking? Do I joke back?

"If that's what you're into, wear, like, a button-down. Pop the top two before he calls you into his office. Easy." He breathes smoke and fire. "You freshman and sophomore girls. Half of you have no clue. Makes a guy wanna look out for you."

Sometimes I think everyone but me had a secret meeting about the way people are supposed to talk.

"Kidding." He coughs out an acrid smell. His eyes are foggy and rimmed with red. Meaning any mistakes I make might be ones he'll forget.

"Eastman's the worst," I venture. "I bet he hides in the girls' bathroom on his lunch break."

He snorts so hard his guitar slides off his lap and thuds against the bench. "Ladies and gentlemen, we have the world's only funny underclassmen."

I made him laugh!

"Monroe, right?" He's looking at me. Finally.

"Morris. Grace Morris."

"Oh yeah, right. One of the twins. The smart one and the obnoxious one. Which one are you again?"

I nervous-giggle. Joy hates that habit. I don't know how to stop.

"Kidding. You're supposed to be brilliant, right? Everyone else at this school is so fucking stupid." He yanks a book out of his bag. Ayn Rand's *Atlas Shrugged*. "Have you read this? I'm halfway through."

It's a terrible book.

"We should talk philosophy sometime. I can never find anyone who can keep up with me."

I have this fantasy where I finally ask if he's okay. Fantasy Adam says, "Nobody's asked me that in years. Thank you. No. I'm not okay." I say, "Me neither." And he says, "Maybe we can be not okay together."

God, I'm stupid.

In real life, he tilts his head to the side. Smirks. "You know, just from a guy's perspective, you'd be cuter with less makeup."

Mornings: makeup, two hours.

"I, uh . . ."

"Don't cover up your face," he says. "You should relax. Be more like your sister. She truly does not give a fuck." He laughs and adds quickly, "But not too much like her."

I die a little inside.

That night, Joy fights with Mom and Dad.

She cries like she lives, never making the sound of herself smaller. It fills the house. Downstairs: Dad banging dishes against the sink. Mom banging the vacuum against the floor. They always clean the house after they fight with her. But she stains.

If I roll this pencil between my fingers thirteen times before Mom stops vacuuming, Joy'll stop crying.

The vacuum whirs off immediately.

I should study. I should go for a run. Half an hour and I can burn three hundred calories. That cancels out lunch.

Downstairs: Mom, Dad, talking. We can always hear what they say in the living room. Either they don't realize, they don't care, or they want us to hear everything.

"I just don't get why she doesn't try as hard as Grace," Mom's saying.

I slip out into the hallway and through Joy's door.

Her room is inside out. She saves everything: birthday cards, handmade presents from first grade, memories scattered in the open. A monument to how dorky I used to be. Even stupider than I am now. Everything triggers a crystal moment of embarrassment. Moments that stay alive because of her. I wish she'd let things die.

She's splayed in the center of the rumpled quilt. Dirty clothes, stuffed animals. Her hair everywhere. Drowning her pillow. It's hard not to love somebody who hides nothing.

"Hey." Double-check to make sure I said it. "Hey." Around her, my volume turns way down. Sometimes my words don't make it out at all.

She flings herself onto her back. She's so tall. Six feet. I guess I'm the same height, but it doesn't feel like it. Her shirt hikes over her hip. Her stomach's flatter than mine. It sucks to be the chubby twin.

"So I told them that I'm sick of them treating me like their first draft, their screwup."

This is what she does: shocks people into silence, then takes it as confirmation she's right.

"See? You can't even deny it."

"That's ridiculous." I sound like I don't mean it. "Maybe you could try being a little less . . . honest about what you're thinking all the time?"

"I have to be honest," she says angrily. "It's the only way I can get anything from them. They're like robot parents. Sometimes I can get an actual human being to look at me for a second, and then the overlord takes back over and it's beep-beep, we-are-the-parents, beep, we-don't-need-to-explain-ourselves-to-you, beep, talk-to-us-when-you've-calmed-down. Except to them, I'm never calmed down."

Because she never does calm down. She slams around the house. Taking her mood out on kitchen cabinets. The fridge door.

"It doesn't matter if I make a good point. All that matters is the tone I make it in," she says.

"They just don't like it when you accuse them of favoritism."

She props herself up on one elbow. "Because that's what it is! They're obsessed with you, and they're sick of me being a fuckup. Which is fair! I am a fuckup! But they should at least admit it."

My face warms. "You're being unreasonable."

"Ugh." She throws her head back. Her hair springs all over the place. "You don't know. Sneeze and they're like, wow, Grace, best sneeze ever, A freakin' plus. I could construct a twenty-foot-tall statue of them out of toenail clippings and they'd still be all, your sister could have done a better job."

Her anger is always a weird soup of humor and self-loathing. Which is why it's so hard to deal with. "I don't have it easy, either."

"You've always liked their attention."

She tosses out words with no idea how much they sting. "You never used to be like this."

"Oh, hush about what used to be. You don't know."

"You're trying to get a rise out of me the same way you try to get a rise out of them."

"And you're analyzing me and taking their side and you never *used* to be like that."

"You've always liked their attention, too." When we were little, she was the kid everyone recorded in the hopes she'd go viral online. She was so loud. When we stood at separate ends of the playground and called for our parents at the same time, they'd go to her. They never heard me.

"Wow, okay. I'm being obnoxious. I am aware that I'm being obnoxious. I'm sorry, Grace." She nudges my arm like a cat. "I know I'm being impossible and you're so patient and nice and ugh."

"You know I'm not mad." I nudge her back. "I'd never be mad at you."

"Remember when I buried all your Halloween candy in the yard and you didn't get mad?"

"Because I was crying about not getting that much, and you thought it'd grow into candy plants."

"You still should have been mad."

If I got mad at her, I wouldn't have anyone else.

"Change of topic. You're in here now, we're hanging out now. Let's play the secrets game," she says, like the last time we played it was yesterday and not five years ago. She sits up, grinning. I try not to want to run away. "Me first. You're gonna die about this. I had a sex dream about Cassius Somerset last night."

The president of the Art Club, the quiet boy with the

skin condition. Adam's best friend. Since when does she have sex dreams? Should I be having sex dreams?

"Your turn," she says.

She hates Adam because November hates Adam. They make fun of his guitar, his band T-shirts, his hair. She'd point out all his flaws. Ruin him. I'd never see him again in any way but hers.

I don't say anything.

My real secrets now: I'm afraid of everything. I don't ever want to get out of bed. I hate school. I'm fat. I'm not good enough. I want to be her.

She thinks I never used to be like this, but I've always been like this.

"Jeez, Grace. You gotta open up more. Like me!" She laughs. "But not too much like me."

FOUR

October 3

Joy

To Joy Morris—

I was at the party. I was at the quarry. I saw what you did.

I saw you murder Adam Gordon.

I want you to post the enclosed photos all over the school. Do it early in the morning before anyone can take them down. Slip them into lockers. Hide them in classroom desks. Don't bring them to the police.

Speaking of the police:

If you don't do what I say, I'll tell the police what I saw.

I'll tell them what you did.

This is impossible.

Nobody saw anything; there was nothing to see. Preston said I left the party before Adam died.

I crumple the letter and throw it into a corner of my room, not even looking at the photos in the envelope. I turn off the lights, crawl under my blanket. My own breathing echoes harshly back at me. I need Grace here with me, I need—

It's a dream, I try to convince myself. *I'm going to go to sleep now. When I wake up, this will all disappear.*

Instead I tremble for long, dark hours. I pretend my breathing is Grace's. When we were kids, she'd get nightmares, bad ones, and I'd climb into her bed and tell her nothing bad can happen to someone who's under a blanket. I pull the covers over my head and pray that's really true.

When the sun rises, the letter and envelope are exactly where I left them. Okay. So it's a fucked-up prank. I'll take it to Principal Eastman. Or Ms. Bell. Somebody'll recognize the handwriting.

But when I get up to look at everything in the light of day, I realize the note's typed, not printed.

   I saw you murder Adam Gordon.

I didn't, I didn't. I wanted to, but I didn't.

I scatter the pictures on the carpet. There's three, four. But they aren't photographs of me shoving Adam into the quarry. They're images of Principal Eastman, his thick hair, jutting chin, the ridge of his naked shoulder, the rest of him naked, too—

Just like the girl he's with.

I've seen her in the halls. She's a freshman. Young. Too young for his hands to be crossed pseudoartistically over her stomach, over—

This is illegal. This is wrong. Principal Eastman papers his office walls with portraits of himself with students, but none like this. I think of all the hours Grace has spent in that office.

I'm dizzy. I have to call the police.

Don't bring them to the police.

I have to tell somebody.

   If you don't do what I say, I'll tell the police what I saw.

But what did he see? My lips tingle, my blood slows in my veins. I try to put the photos back in the envelope and drop them twice.

Could I tell Mom, Dad? Jesus, no. November—no, no, she has to think I'm okay. Grace? I can't show her these pictures. What if they trigger—

What if she believes what this person's saying? That I murdered—

I bend over and breathe with my head between my knees for a few seconds.

Preston. Pres'll remind me how I couldn't've done it, how he looked for me, how I was gone before Adam died. I just need to hear him say it again. Then I'll take the photos to the police and get Principal Eastman arrested.

I get dressed, force myself to eat something. Mom's on the phone with a client on the drive to school. It's not until she pulls up to the curb, so early that only one bus is here, that she covers her phone with her hand and mouths, "Are you okay? You're pale."

"I'm fine."

I'm fine. The envelope is in my backpack. Grace is still sleeping, probably. She sleeps later and later now.

"Your father and I work today. I'm at the office until six and he's training a new client. We can't pick you up if you're sick."

"I'm fine, Mom."

She stares for a minute, brow furrowed, while I rearrange my face. Finally she nods and lets me go.

Pres always hangs out downstairs before the bell. I go past the gym and the double doors that lead to the auditorium, I turn in to the hallway that leads to the art room, and I stop. There he is, at the end of the hallway, walking toward me, not noticing me yet. He always slouches, which hides the fact that he's one of the few here taller than me.

Four freshmen trail him. Three are guys I've seen getting high in the relaxation garden after school, so proud about it. They're tiny, loud, they throw stuff in the cafeteria. One, a girl, lags—

The girl from the photos.

Her name . . . Sahara, or Savannah. She's shy. I get the sense she hangs out with the guys for the same reason I hung with Grace's study group—because I wasn't attached to anyone else.

I don't want her here at school. I don't want her anywhere near Principal Eastman.

Then one of the freshmen calls Preston the f-word.

Pres looks up, sees me finally, his face red. The freshmen slow. In the back, Savannah bites her lip, ties her hair to the side, and unties it again. People do not normally bully Preston. This is because, in the second semester of our freshman year, I gave the captain of the lacrosse team a bloody nose for calling him a retard.

"What the fuck do you want?" The freshman sniggers at me. I stare at him. Adam wore that exact Jim Morrison T-shirt.

And then I punch him in the face.

★★★

All the photos are still on Principal Eastman's office walls. In the one next to the window, he's with Savannah, his arm around her shoulders while she looks at the floor. In another one, he's with Grace. I'm gonna throw up.

"I know Adam Gordon's death affected many of us strongly." Eastman talks slowly, heavily. Is it him or is something wrong with my ears? Are his photos that blurry or are my eyes messed up? "But after this morning's display of violence, I'm seriously considering suspension, Ms. Morris. And Mr. Fennis tells me you're still failing American History. What's going on with you, Joy?"

Don't talk to me, don't look at me, I want my sister.

I turn my hands over, like they'd've been stained if I'd pushed Adam. My mind spins. Was Preston wrong about me leaving the birthday party early? Or is someone using me to try and humiliate Principal Eastman? Someone who knows I blacked out that night, that I had a reason to want Adam dead? But the only people who know about that reason are me and Grace and Pres and a dead person.

Eastman leans forward across his desk, puts his hand on my knee. I yank back so hard my chair nearly tips over—

"Principal Eastman?" someone says.

Sunlight pours into the room. Levi's in the doorway. Levi, Adam's half brother, from the funeral.

"You are?" Principal Eastman squints.

"Levi Pham. I'm just starting today. You wanted to meet with me," he says cheerfully. "Adam Gordon's half brother, remember? I have my mom's last name."

Go away, go away.

Eastman winces. "I'm dealing with a situation. Please wait outside and I'll call you in."

He stares at my leg, the one Eastman touched. "Actually, I thought you might want my input, since I saw what happened. I was in the hallway."

He's lying. Why's he lying?

"Preston was getting bullied," he continues. "Joy stuck up for him."

"Yes, thank you," Eastman says irritably. "But that hardly excuses violence."

"Everything I heard about this school stressed the no-bullying environment. I thought it was impressive. Joy told me how important this school's reputation is to her."

"She did?"

The walls, my lungs, they're shrinking.

"She was the first Stanwick High student I talked to," says Levi. "Told me all about how the principal makes it so nobody's singled out."

Eastman's nodding calmly and I have naked photos of him with a freshman in my bag and Levi's chattering all eager in the doorway and someone says I pushed his half brother into the quarry. I'm losing my mind.

"She stood up for the school's principles," Levi finishes. "So I think the school's principal should stand up for her."

I wasn't standing up for anything. I snapped. If that's what I do when I snap—

What if I snapped at the quarry?

Eastman adjusts his mug that says PRINCI *PAL*. "I'm going to use that for the website. 'Stand up for Stanwick High's principles, and Stanwick High's principal will stand up for you.' You're a smart young man. Just like your half brother."

Levi lights up.

"You ought to meet Joy's sister sometime. She's working from home this semester on a special independent research project. We allow our students to spread their wings here, if they prove themselves." Eastman quits smiling, turns to me. "Though we still need to address your American History grade, Joy. There will be a need for consequences if you can't pull it up."

His words fizz in my ears.

"I can tutor her," Levi offers.

My vision goes even weirder. There are two of him now. Twins, like me and Grace.

"Excellent!" Eastman actually hits the table. "The more capable leading the less capable, that's what Stanwick High stands for."

I'm not breathing normal, my body isn't *normal*.

"Joy, you're in for detention this week, but you're off the hook for suspension. On the condition that Levi does, in fact, tutor you in American History. And you raise your grade to at least a C."

I gasp out, "I have to go to the bathroom."

I run down the hall, ignoring everything and everyone around me. I find my way upstairs and into the girls' bathroom. Everything I look at bounces slightly, like there's an earthquake. The toilet water jumps in the bowl, shaking along with my hands and the walls and the air. I manage to unzip my backpack and pull out a tiny bottle, swallow twice, and cough, hard. This is the upstairs bathroom, people will hear these sounds.

The bathroom door swings open. "Joy?" Levi's voice.

Go away, please, I'm dying.

His shoes stop in front of my stall. "Are you okay?"

"This. Is the. Girl's bathroom," I wheeze.

"That didn't stop you yesterday when it was the men's room."

I didn't lock the door, and he opens it, and then he's crouching in front of me, holding something up. "Breathe with this. You'll be okay."

There's a GIF on his phone, a trapezoid unfolding, inflating, collapsing again. I squeeze carbon dioxide out of my lungs as it shrinks, suck oxygen back in as it expands. My fingertips quit tingling. It's my head and I'm in control of it. They're my lungs.

"Am I dying," I choke.

"No." The sunlight from the bathroom window glints off his earring. "Panic attacks suck."

I sit on the floor for a minute before I say, "Why'd you follow me?" I have enough air for words now.

"You started hyperventilating halfway out the door. Your douche principal didn't notice."

I need to talk to Preston, I need to figure out what to

do about the note. Levi—Adam's half brother—is the enemy. "You should be in class."

"Two seconds ago you asked if you were dying. I'm not leaving you here by yourself."

"I'll go to the nurse's later."

"Do you want me to get a friend for you? That redheaded guy? The girl you were at the funeral with?"

"Pres'd freak, and Nov—" My stomach disintegrates. "Don't tell November. Okay? Don't say anything to her."

"I promise." He reaches for my wrist, snatches his hand back. "Right. You don't like that."

I'm shivering. He shucks his sweatshirt and drapes it over my shoulders.

If he knew what the note said, he'd be calling the cops. I need to call the cops. Those photos are sick. It's sick of me not to bring them to the police right now just because I'm scared that this person is telling the truth. That *I killed*—no, enough. I grab Levi's phone and stare at the trapezoid again.

"I know I've apparently inherited your hate for my half bro," he's saying, "and that's fine, and you are within your constitutional rights to tell me to get the fuck out of the girl's bathroom, but . . . what's going on?"

I can't remember that night. I can't prove anything.

"Joy? You don't look . . ." He falters. "Is someone at your house who could pick you up? Your parents? Your sister?"

If the cops got involved, what Adam did would come out. And then Grace'd hate me forever. She said she'd hate me forever if I told.

I make words. "I'm okay."

"I am very sorry this shit is happening to you."

I want him to know I'm a bad person so he'll stop being so nice to me. "When I was eight years old I was mad at my sister, so I filled her ant farm with water. They all drowned. But she didn't get mad at me."

"Okay," he says like I'm not croaking nonsensically. He waves a hand. "I hereby absolve you of that."

"That's what murderers do when they're kids, right? Kill bugs and animals?"

"Everyone does stuff when they're little." He doesn't take his eyes off me. "I also think people generally believe they're capable of a lot worse than they actually are."

Maybe he doesn't have any Adam parts. "Why are you helping me?"

"You gave me a ride home after a shitty couple of hours of my life." He shrugs shyly. "And you helped me in a bathroom. Now it's my turn."

"You lied to the principal for me."

"I didn't lie. I was here early this morning, signing up for classes. I was on the stairs and I did see you. You looked exhausted, but the second that asshole opened his mouth, you were on him. Like sticking up for your friend was more important than whatever else."

My friend. Preston. I remind myself that Pres will know what to do about the note, once I tell him. The knot in my throat loosens slightly.

Levi's smiling at me again.

"You can't tutor me," I say. "I'm not smart. I don't understand things, you'd get frustrated. I'm just going to fail no matter what and I've accepted that."

"I'm—"

"Thank you for helping me with Eastman. I know I'm being an asshole, but I can't be—friends with you. I can't tell you why. So you and me alone in a room, it wouldn't work."

"I get it," he says. "I'm not gonna tutor you."

Duh. He was lying and I gave him a speech.

"I'm going to help you cheat. You can copy my homework, and I'll sit next to you on quiz days so you can look at my answers."

He says it like I'd be doing him a favor by saying yes.

"What?" He rotates his earring. "What's the look for?"

"I'm just surprised. You didn't seem like the type to condone cheating."

"Seriously? The earring, the hair? The whole point is to look like the type. Girls love the type."

I start to smile, but the bell for second period rings out in the hall. In seconds, everyone'll swarm the bathroom.

"Sometimes there's stuff going on that makes grades impossible. That doesn't mean you should be screwed," he says. "I would suck at tutoring anyway. I think your principal's assuming I'm gonna be this straight-A Asian stereotype. Plus I owe you. I was weird to you at the funeral."

"You weren't weird. I was weird."

"Look, I'm gonna go before I make my big first day impression as the guy who chills in the girl's bathroom. But, real quick. My first day impression of you is that you're a badass. You picked up my dad, you punched an asshole. Whatever's going on, you got this."

He picks up my backpack, passes it to me. The side pocket's all unzipped and my heart stops—the photos are half sticking out. For a millisecond, I swear he looks. I grab the bag, hold it close.

But he doesn't say anything else. Just gives a little wave and leaves.

It's not until he's gone that I realize I'm still wearing his sweatshirt. I reach into the front pocket and there's his old baseball cap, folded in on itself.

Preston's not at lunch. He has Chem Club meetings every day. And he's not by his locker when school finishes.

When I get home, there's mac 'n' cheese powder on the kitchen counter, a pot and two plates in the sink, cereal flecking a bowl by the toaster. Grace does this sometimes. Hits the kitchen and eats everything in sight and vanishes five minutes later. The beat of the treadmill pulses through the house. She'll be on it all night.

I reach for chips and know immediately that food's not going to work out. So I go to my room. Nothing on my windowsill.

I text Preston, praying he's around and not at another nerdy club meeting.

hey I know this is hypocritical since I was all flakey the other day but I rly need to talk to u. come over?

I lie in bed and stare at the screen until my room darkens, my eyes burning. My mind's stuck on him: Preston. Preston will fix this.

An hour later, there's a tap on my window. I bite my tongue so hard I taste blood, but—it's only him, one leg swung over the oak tree branch, twigs in his hair. He raps on the glass again. I let him in.

"I am not aerodynamic enough for this." He brushes leaves onto my carpet.

He's here, he came, he'll fix it. I turn on the light. "You could have used the front door."

"I will literally scale oak trees to avoid uncomfortable and undesired familial social interaction. What did you need to talk to me about?"

I reach for the letter and envelope. I hear him sigh through his front teeth.

"Are you mad at me?" I ask, turning around.

"Mildly." He picks at a chin zit. "I want you to stop hitting people who make fun of me, because then everyone hears about it. It's like putting a big spotlight on the fact that I'm a freak."

"You're not—"

"I don't like the way it makes me feel, either." His words are practiced. He rehearsed this. "Like you think I'm helpless."

"You're right. It's bad, I'm trash—"

"You're not trash! You make it very difficult to talk to you sometimes."

I sit on my bed. How can I ask him for help now?

"Mom told me I should be honest with you about this." He sucks in his bottom lip. "Please don't decide to stop being my friend. I'm not that mad. Not end-of-relationship mad."

"I dunno why you always expect me to stop liking you."

"I don't know why, either." He rubs his forehead violently, sits next to me on the bed. "I'm sorry for being this way."

I take a deep breath. "When I was a kid, my parents were always like *you're the big sis, you gotta look out for the small sis* even though I'm only eighteen minutes older than Grace. But then she stopped needing me."

"So what, I was your replacement protectee?"

"At first," I admit. "But that's not the only reason I became your friend! You're fun to talk to and we like the same stupid shit and you're really helpful with figuring things out."

He tries to hide a smile. "What did you need help figuring out?"

Right. Okay. Back to this. I take the envelope out, slide the photos and the note onto his lap.

"Oh my God." He blanches. "That's Principal Eastman."

I dig my nails into my wrist as he reads the note. When he's done, his eyes glaze over, his mouth slightly open. Then he shakes himself, lightly hits his own cheek. "We are not going to panic."

"Okay," I whisper.

"We are definitely not going to do that."

"Right."

"Say it again, slower."

I breathe out. "Right."

"Obviously we need to find out who this is." He crumples the edge of the envelope. His eyes are still glassy. "It must be someone who was at the party. You must've been drunk enough where they knew you wouldn't remember it. And they must know why you hated him so much you might believe someone who said that you were the one who killed him."

Pres is a problem solver. I'm safe. I have him. I'm going to be okay.

Unless I actually did—no don't think about it.

"You and me and Grace are the only ones." I say it quietly, even though the treadmill's still thumping down in the basement, loud enough for me to hear even from up in my room. "Grace doesn't even know you know."

"She must've told someone."

"There's less than zero percent of a chance she did that."

"Then we have to assume Adam told."

Told someone, maybe. Bragged about it, maybe. My gut clenches.

"Which means that this person, the blackmailer, was friends with Adam." He's zoned into his thought process. "And obviously not a big Joy fan, if they're doing this to you. Here is my theory."

"You have a theory already?"

"We can't assume Adam's death was an accident anymore."

My hands go numb. "So you think I—"

"No! God, no. Look, there's only one reason someone would try to pin Adam's death on you when everybody thinks it's an accident. That's if somebody *did* kill him. And they're scared people'll find out."

"You think the person who wrote this letter is a murderer."

"It's the clearest motive."

"You think a murderer climbed the tree outside my window and left me this and, like, knows where I live."

"I didn't say it was ideal."

I put my head between my knees and imagine the trapezoid, breathe with it.

But Pres is in problem-solve mode. "They must have figured out a way to frame you, so nobody finds out what they did. But first, since it's convenient, they're going to use you to get revenge on someone else they hate— Principal Eastman. Two birds with one stone."

This still doesn't fix it. But he's getting there. He's got this.

I scrape myself together. "It's like everything that was jumping around in my head all panicked is lined up neat in a row now."

"I'm good at this sort of thing," he says. "And I think I have a pretty good guess as to who the blackmailer is."

I'm okay, I'm safe, he solved it. "Who?"

"Cassius Somerset."

"What?" *No way.*

"You saw his black eye? Cassius got in a fight with Adam at the party. I was there. He tackled Adam, and Adam punched him in the face." He's getting excited now. "It makes sense."

"Cassius was Adam's best friend."

"That's what I'm saying. He fits. Adam did something to make Cassius so angry that he'd attack him at his birthday party. Maybe even drunkenly push him when he was standing next to the quarry. Adam must have let slip what he did to Grace." Preston smooths out the note again and again. "So he panicked. He knew you were blackout drunk that night. The only thing I'm hung up on is that Cassius has no reason to hate you this much."

I dig my nails again into the inside of my wrist. I saw Grace do it in middle school. She said the pain zapped her back to the present.

"I never told you this because I hate thinking about it now," I say slowly. "But Cassius and I hooked up over the summer. Maybe he has weird feelings toward me because of that."

"Joy."

"It's Cassius, though. He protested the frog dissection in bio."

"Joy," he repeats. "You do know that's his little sister in the photos with Eastman?"

"What?" I grab the photos. They don't look alike. She's slim, no trace of vitiligo.

"Savannah Somerset. She's a freshman this year," he says. "That explains why Cassius wants Eastman to be publicly humiliated."

I want to believe him, I want all of this to be over before it starts. But it feels wrong. "If that's his sister, he wouldn't have me put these all over school."

"Maybe he's mad at his sister, too."

"What are we even gonna do—confront him?"

"We need a plan. If we're right, he killed somebody. He's dangerous."

"*I'm* more dangerous than Cassius Somerset."

"Quiet people, Joy. You can't see into their heads."

I remember how I tried to get to know Cassius over the summer, how little he spoke when I did.

"In the meantime, do you need help putting the pictures up tomorrow morning?" says Preston suddenly.

I shrink away. "What?"

"We have to assume Cassius has something to back this up. Some way to make it look like you killed Adam. It wouldn't be hard for the police to figure out you blacked out that night. You could be tried as an adult and sent to prison. Until we figure this out, we have to play along. This is murder, Joy."

"You're sure—you think there's no chance he's telling the truth—"

I said it without thinking: I'm *more dangerous.*

"You are not capable of something like that," he says firmly.

I'm so exhausted. "Either way, I can't spread these around. Imagine being Savannah, coming to school, seeing these pictures everywhere."

"It's not ideal. But it's better than *you going to prison*."

"I can't, Pres. I need to take the pictures to the cops no matter what the note says." My fingertips tingle again. "That is some creepy disgusting child porn shit."

"No, no, no." He scratches convulsively at the zit on his chin. "You have to do it. Joy, please. You can't go to jail."

I shake my head. "It isn't so easy just to frame someone for murder, you know? Maybe the cops could investigate. Like look at fingerprints and crime stuff. And then, if it was me, they could tell me."

"*Joy!*"

"And if it was, maybe I do deserve to go to jail," I mumble. "That's where they put people so they can't hurt anyone."

"Stop it. Grace needs you."

"She barely talks to me lately." I touch the rip on the side of my quilt. It's been there since fifth grade, since Grace and I made sock monkeys and her scissors snagged in the fabric. She cried over it, she felt so bad. "We're not the way we used to be."

He makes a weird noise that isn't a word.

"And my parents think I'm a failure anyway. I'm not going to college, Pres. I'm basically fucked after high school. Prison wouldn't be so bad." I'm dizzy. "They'd feed me and—I'd know what the rest of my life would look like."

"Forget about Grace, then." His chin's bleeding. "I need you."

"Pres, it's okay."

"It is *not* okay." He's half yelling. I flinch. Downstairs, the treadmill noise stops. "I rely on . . . before I met you, it was horrible. I don't need much. I just need one person. It's stupid."

"It is not stupid."

"It's stupid how I am. If something happened to you, I don't think anyone else in the world would want anything to do with me."

My heart splits wide open. "You'd find a new person."

"I don't want to."

Suddenly Grace opens my door, a microwave popcorn bag in her hand. "Hey."

Pres shoves the photos under his thigh. They trade panicky nods. They've always been alarmed by each other.

"Mom called and wanted me to tell you she and Dad are both going to be home in like fifteen," she says carefully.

If she moved the blanket just a little bit, she'd see the envelope.

"Okay," I say. And then a moment of awkward silence.

"Whose sweatshirt is that?" she asks, accusatorily, pointing to my chair across the room.

I turn and see Levi's sweatshirt, the baseball cap jutting out of the pocket.

"Nobody's."

"Is that a guy's sweatshirt?"

"It's mine."

She looks around my room for a second, all the pictures of us, all her old drawings. She crumples her nose, goes back out into the hall, and closes her door.

"If your parents are coming home, I should go," says Pres thickly.

"I promise I'll think about what to do," I whisper.

He takes the photos from under his thigh, shoves them back into the envelope so quickly I barely see him do it.

"You okay?" I ask.

"No."

"Preston—"

"I'm going to go now."

"Wait," I say, but he's already halfway across my room, climbing out into the night.

I spend the night awake, facing the window, a knife under my pillow, remembering every night I slept in Grace's room so she wouldn't be afraid of the dark.

"The tree branch outside my window is rotten," I tell Mom in the car to school the next morning. "The big branch. The one on the tree that Grace fell off when she was a kid and sprained her ankle. It's dead. Can Dad saw it off?"

"I don't know what all this is about trees, Joy."

I leave the car without saying good-bye.

The photos are in my bag. I'm not—I can't—do this. I'll take them to the police station after school. Or talk to Savannah myself.

Those are the good-person things to do.

I'm early again. Preston's always early, too, since he comes in with his mom. But I can't find him. The last place I look is the art room. Eastman hangs the decent still lifes and the landscapes upstairs, to show them off on Parent Night. Down here, it's bloated self-portraits, angry scribbles, a painting of someone in a bath full of knives. Art that makes adults uncomfortable.

Something catches my eye by the sinks. There's a painting of the quarry. But it's nothing romantic. It's a wound in the earth, blood splashing the trees. I squint. The name in the corner: *Cassius Somerset*. His art's always been upstairs. Pastels, clouds, not the kind of thing a murderer would paint. I used to sneak extra minutes in the hallway after school to look at them.

This bloody quarry, it's the kind of thing a murderer would paint.

I've dreamed about that night with him twice, muscle memory, his skin setting fires on mine. My cheeks ache with how hard I was smiling and then I have to curl up, digging my thumbnail into my palm, half-moon marks, because it should be a nightmare, not a dream.

Kissing someone doesn't mean you know them.

I wander out of the room. The buses'll be here in a few minutes. Pres vanishes when other people are around.

I turn the corner, nearly bang into Levi.

"Joy." His expression's weird. "I was looking for you."

"I forgot your sweatshirt at home," I say, tired. "I'll bring it tomorrow."

"It's not that. I looked in my locker."

"For your sweatshirt?"

He holds up a grainy printer-paper black-and-white copy of—

No. No, *how*?

"You were so messed up yesterday, and I didn't even know for sure what I saw . . ." He kind of hugs himself. "But this photo I found in my locker—it was in your bag yesterday, wasn't it?"

I wrench open my backpack, find the envelope, grope for the edges of the photos and count. One's missing.

Preston. He took one last night, he made copies. He was so afraid I wouldn't do it.

How long would it take to slip one through the slats of every locker in the school?

"This is the principal. Is this real?" Levi holds the copy away like it's poisonous. "Did *you* put this in my locker?"

I can't speak, can't move.

Upstairs: the echo of the bus arrival stampede, everyone piling inside, shedding jackets. I start to walk, run. Have to find Savannah, have to get her out of the school—

"Joy?" he asks, but I'm down the hall, fighting through the masses.

And then a hundred locker doors open at once.

FIVE

June 30

Grace

"ONE STRAWBERRY SOFT SERVE, ONE VANILLA with rainbow sprinkles." Joy glances at me eagerly.

One childhood, two children: extra large ice-cream cones. Strawberry for her. Vanilla for me. "I don't want one."

"Grace, seriously. Stop it. You're not fat."

Which is something people always say to confirm that, yes, being fat is as bad as you think it is.

"One small," I tell the girl behind the counter.

We sit in our old corner booth. The red pleather is peeling now. There's more gum wadded to the underside of the table. When we were little, Joy would steal the cherry on Dad's sundae and hold it out to me, but I'd shake my head. I could always tell when she wanted something for herself. Sometimes they'd give us free ice cream for never ever fighting.

Joy bites into her ice cream with her front teeth. "Remember that time we were spitting sprinkles and nailed that bald dude's head?"

"That was just something you were doing."

She doesn't hear me. "And he wanted Dad's phone number to get us in trouble, and I gave him the number for that sex hotline? This place is the best."

My ice cream's melting. Dripping on my thumb. I tear open a pack of sanitary wipes from my bag. When I told her I needed to talk, she insisted we come here.

"Remember when they had that sundae-eating contest, like if you could eat the whole thing, you wouldn't have to pay for it? And Mom and Dad were freaking out because they thought we wouldn't finish, but then I did?"

She's the hero of our childhood. The best part of every story. The knight in every game we played. I was the princess, and the point of me was to be afraid of dragons. But what does the princess do while the knight is having adventures? Nobody sees her.

"Do you know how many calories are in that?" I ask.

She shrugs, her ice cream half-gone already. "What did you want to tell me?"

Soon I'll have to eat mine or throw it away.

"I have a thing for this guy," I mumble.

"Oh my God, Grace! What guy?"

I brace myself. "Adam Gordon."

"Him? That guy is such a dick."

I shrivel up. "Please don't tell anyone."

"Duh." She tosses back her hair. Curly and wild. I flat-iron mine straight every morning. Forty-five minutes.

"You're not always so good at secrets."

"I am too! Well, no, I'm not. But you're the only person I'd get better for." She crunches cone. "Can we go back to him being a dick, though? Nov hates him."

"So?"

"I trust her taste in people."

My stomach is a hard rock. "November hates everybody."

"She doesn't hate me," she says a little smugly.

"You're so special."

"Why are you so weird about her?"

"She's the weird one." I don't like what I'm saying, but I say it anyway. "She was out of school for her whole sophomore year and nobody knows why. Supposedly she was into drugs."

"So?"

"It's just—November, and Preston, they're both . . . kind of . . . What was wrong with our old friends? Lily and Cat? And Brodie?" I ask.

"Those were *your* old friends."

"You liked them in middle school."

"They stopped talking to me when I didn't get into your honors classes. And then I noticed, surprise, I didn't even *have* any of my own friends, because I always hung around with yours. So don't be weird about Nov and Pres."

How did I not know any of this?

"You wanna know how I met Pres?" she asks. "He hates gore, right? And one day I see Adam waving some gross picture of guts from a bio textbook in his face. So I yelled at Adam. Like, what the fuck?"

"You hold on to things," I say, but what do I really know about Adam? Just stupid fantasies. Nothing real, other than that five-minute conversation.

"I don't forgive people for fucking with my friends. So that's why it's a big deal that I'm gonna give Adam another chance."

My stomach uncoils. "Really?"

"You're my sister. If you like him, I like him." She smiles at me. "Or I'll try, anyway. That'll be important for when we make him like you. I guess it's kind of perfect! Adam and Cassius. We'll have that whole twins-dating-best-friends thing."

Could I trust her with more than just this? I'm trying to find the right way to start when her eyes widen. I turn and look over my shoulder. The warmth disappears. November Roseby has just walked into the Ice Cream Palace.

"Quick," she hisses. "Do I have stuff on my face?"

"You're acting like you have a crush."

She shushes me and jumps up, waving and hurrying over to November. Apparently we're not talking about Adam anymore. I get up and throw my ice cream away while she's not looking.

November moseys over like she's too cool to move any faster.

"You got my text," Joy's crowing.

She invited her? I told her I needed to talk, and she invited November?

"I got your text." November casually steals a lick from the bottom of Joy's cone. She hasn't taken off her sunglasses. She has one of those haircuts where part of her scalp is buzzed. Several of her braids are dyed green. She has three holes in each ear. Rubber bands on each wrist.

What's so great about her?

"So what's up?" Joy sits down with her. Loops her arm over the back of the booth, then takes it back. Adjusts her masses of hair. I have a feeling November likes how hard she's trying.

"Arguing with my asshat dad, as usual." November yawns, but her shoulders are rigid. "*Officer Roseby* was bragging about his old arrest record. I pointed out that America has more prisoners per capita than any other country. He told me I'm turning into one of those sassy black girls."

"Are you kidding me?" Joy yells. "I hate him so much. God."

She doesn't weigh her words like I weigh mine. But all her words are light, no matter what they are. They soar out of her. Mine are always so heavy.

"He's like a hoarder," says November. "He has a copy

7 |

of the arrest record of everyone he's ever arrested. Like a serial killer keeps trophies."

If I tap my knee on the underside of the table twenty times before Joy finishes her ice cream, November will go away.

"He's so white," Joy says. "He probably wears salmon shorts when he's not in uniform. And spends, like, half his paycheck on fancy cheese."

"Joy, you're white," I say, just to keep from vanishing.

She turns pink. November laughs. Slow. Warm. She tips her sunglasses down. "I like you."

It's like a decree of approval from the universe. Joy beams.

"You're supersmart, yeah?" November says. "Heard you get these wild test scores."

I am now officially present and accounted for in the conversation.

Though my test scores should be better.

"I dig your makeup," she adds.

There's too much of it, Adam told me.

Joy gives November her special look that she's only ever given me. The *you-are-perfect* look. Makes you want to do anything to keep from shattering that illusion. But I'm not perfect, not on the inside, so November can't be, either.

"You're my two favorite people in the entire world, you know that?" Joy says. "And now we're all hanging out. We gotta hang out more this summer, the three of us. I'd invite Pres, but he hates people. *Oh!* I just had the best idea."

Oh no.

November knocks Joy's shoulder with her fist. "Yeah?"

"I think the three of us should make something out of this summer."

What's wrong with the *two* of us?

"I think this should be the summer of misdeeds," she keeps going. "Grace, you've been studying forever. We need to do some exciting stuff. Like getting you drunk, Grace, for the first time. Or maybe trying, like, weed. Doesn't matter. But seriously, we're going to be juniors. You need to loosen up or you're gonna regret being so flawless in high school."

"Corrupting you will keep me from getting too bored," November offers.

"Yes! You can find us cool parties to go to. We'll find the boys to make out with." She winks at me. Apparently we *are* still talking about Adam. "It'll help with all your stress."

"I don't know, Joy." She loves being the one who slashes through the jungle with a machete. Forging a path. Pulling me on.

"She doesn't have to do anything she doesn't want to do," says November.

"Right." Joy's eyebrows dive down. "Sorry."

Two possible summers. One spent listening to her window open across the hall, the sound of her slipping away while I'm in bed by nine. More distance between us. Or I can become a girl who gets high test scores and sneaks out at midnight. Who reads philosophy books and does drugs.

The kind of girl every musician boy wants. An *interesting* girl.

I sit up straighter. "No, it's fine. Maybe. The drinking, I mean. Possibly. We could try."

"Yes!" Joy punches the air. "Mom and Dad are gonna be so pissed that I'm leading you into a life of sin."

Is this just a way for her to get back at Mom and Dad?

"And you'll have stories to tell Adam on your first date with him—"

I stare at her. So much for secrets.

"What's the look?" she adds, then gasps. Mimes zipping her lips. "Sorry. Sorry."

"You like Adam Gordon?" November hardens.

A beat. Then I shake my head.

Pathetic.

But November doesn't soften. There's an awkward silence. Then she stands up. "Actually, I was only swinging by for a minute. Gotta pick up a prescription."

"That's fine! I'll text you!" My sister's a puppy, bouncing all over her.

The bell above the door rings as November leaves. Then the air's less intense.

"I'll make up for that." Joy grabs my arm. "I'm gonna personally make sure you and Adam hang out this summer. This is your first crush. It's important."

She hooks her ankle behind mine and tugs my foot. She's always touching people without thinking. Trying to drag them into her world.

Maybe this summer I'll let her.

★ ★ ★

A week later, it's the three of us again. I've only been to the quarry once before, during the day. It belongs to the town, even though it's close to Mr. Gordon's property, but everyone knows he doesn't mind. Mom and Dad took us for a picnic once when we were nine. They talked about the first time they kissed here, under the moon. That was before everyone started saying how someone might fall.

Now, at night, it's so dark that you can't see the bottom. The quarry is an inverted sky without stars. People took what they wanted from the earth, and this scar is still here, even though they're gone.

"Grace, come here!" Joy's sitting with November on a blanket scavenged from the back of her car. Close to the tall dark pines.

"Are you scared?" She laughs at me. "Remember how you used to be afraid of the dark?"

"Shhh!" I hiss.

She pokes my cheek as I sit on the scratchy wool. "I'll protect you, baby sister. The dark doesn't scare me."

"This was all I could steal from my dad's cabinet. Fair warning, it's gross." November pours a tiny glass of liquid. I can't see what color it is in the dark. She holds it out to me. "Youngest first. I'm not drinking, I drove here. And I want to be very sober in case one of you pukes."

"She's not gonna puke." Joy wraps her arm around my shoulders. The breeze tangles her hair with mine. "Try it, Grace. It's not that bad."

"Have you ever had it?"

"Well. No."

How many calories are in this? I drink it. It sears my throat and I cough. Joy laughs and the quarry swallows the echo. The aftertaste stings hard.

"You like it?" She jostles my shoulders. Throws her legs over mine. She's touching me so much tonight.

A normal girl would like it. "Sure."

She shrieks in delight.

"Don't scream, you maniac." November glances at the pines.

"Whatever. The Gordons can't hear us." Joy grabs the bottle and swigs. It looks badass until she gags and sprays liquid all over the rock.

"That's what you get." November stretches out on the blanket and pops one earbud in.

A normal girl wouldn't have to like it. Everything Joy does is what a normal girl would do.

I stop drinking before she does. She keeps it up until she's sprawled out on the blanket, cozied up to November, all her insecurities that I didn't know existed leaping off her like rats off a sinking ship.

"It's not gonna work with me and Cassius. I know that. I'm too much, I think. Way too much for any guy to want to deal with."

She's not too much. I'm not enough.

"I'm not hot," she says. "Not being hot is fucking annoying."

Does she ever look at her body and hate every part of it, too?

"Bullshit." In the dark, November looks like her older sister. "You're gorgeous."

That's all it takes, and Joy's smiling. What's the point of being smart, if I can't think of the words to tell my sister she's pretty? Why don't they have a class in how to say the right things to people?

"You're sooo cool, Nov." Joy's babbling. "You're like my cool big sis. Did you know that? You're the coolest person ever. God."

I stop existing.

"I'm not so great," she murmurs, and I'm the only one who hears. Even though Joy's closer to November than she is to me.

I wander away from the two of them. Closer to the quarry. If I take three steps, she'll like me more than November. Four steps and Adam will like me more than anybody.

Fantasy: I fall into the quarry. Adam comes down here in the middle of the night. Finds my broken body. Writes a song about me.

Suddenly Joy's shouting my name. I blink. The darkness retracts. She's up, a blur, yanking my arm. We both trip backward into the dirt.

November's up, too, shepherding us away from the edge. "From now on we stay over here by the trees."

"Oh my God. You almost fell." Joy clamps my elbow. "You were right on the edge."

"I didn't think I was that close," I mumble.

"But I got you. I saved you. Remember that time when

we were little and I made you climb that tree outside my window? You fell and I didn't grab you and you sprained your ankle? But I grabbed you this time. Right out of the air. *Whoosh!*"

"How long do you think it would take to hit the bottom?" I ask.

"A million years. Don't ask me that." She stumbles, collapses drunkenly against my side. "Grace. I love you sooo much. Did you know that? You are just. Sooo perfect. Oh my God."

My sister is an idiot and I love her.

She fumbles with my hands, examining them in the dark. Splaying them out on the blanket. "You have to stop biting your nails."

"I hate the quarry," November says suddenly. I forgot about her.

Joy abandons my fingers. "Because Adam lives up there?"

"No. He never comes down here."

How does she know that? She catches me staring.

"Guys," Joy says. "Guys. I'm so drunk. I'm hallucinating that Cassius just showed up."

I follow her pointing finger. Cassius Somerset is hanging back in the tree shadows, the strange patterns on his skin silver in the moonlight. Did he come down from Adam's house? Is Adam here, too? But no one else is moving in the trees.

"Hey, friends," he says. Even though none of us are his friends.

"Holy shit." Joy finger-combs her hair. Her hand gets tangled in the mess. "Hi. Hello. Did you hear us?"

He flinches at her drunk shouting. "I was leaving Adam's. I heard a scream."

"That was me! Wow! You should definitely hang out with us for a while, probably. We have whiskey. Can he drink your whiskey, Nov?"

"Cassius, I would be utterly delighted if you would come and drink my whiskey so there's less for this fool." November sighs.

He just stands there in the shadows, hands in his pockets.

Joy's wobbling. "Okay. I have to pee. Grace. Come with me."

She grabs my arm, not November's. She drags me away into the woods. Trees close over our heads and the night fills with crunching as she splinters every branch.

"Do you think we're far enough away where he won't hear any splashing?" she whisper-yells after a minute.

"Try to pee quietly?"

"How am I supposed to control the volume of my piss hitting the ground, Grace?" And then she's giggling frantically in dark, fumbling. I wait, facing the other way. Grinning in the dark.

"I need your help," she slurs as soon as she's done. "Cassius . . . is . . . beautiful and perfect, and I . . . am . . . drunk, and I love him, and I love you."

"Do you even know him?" I ask.

"I know that he's beautiful and perfect." Joy hiccups. "Help."

She's asking for *my* advice. "Just . . . be nice."

"Nice," she repeats. "Right."

We struggle back through the trees to our blanket. Cassius and November are sitting slightly apart. Talking quietly. They stop when they see us.

"Hello," Joy declares. About to be nice.

Instead, she vomits absolutely everywhere.

November springs up, businesslike, seizing her arm. Stabilizing her. I should be doing it, but I'm frozen. I didn't expect this. Neither did Joy, because she's looking openmouthed at the puke on her shirt like someone else put it there.

"All righty then," November says wearily. "It has been a night. Nice talking to you for the first time, Cassius."

Joy moans. Her face glows pale. "I don't wanna go yet. Cassius came all this way. He walked *forever*."

"Everyone walks everywhere here," November mutters.

Cassius folds his knees to his chest, pulls his sweatshirt sleeves over the patchy skin on his hands. Trying to make himself smaller. I can tell because I do the same thing. Joy takes up a lot of space. It's hard to fit when she's around.

"I'm at least taking you to my car to change. I have clean gym clothes in the back." November disappears with my sister into the woods. And I'm alone with the guy Joy has sex dreams about.

He doesn't seem like the kind of guy anyone would have

sex dreams about. He seems like the kind of guy people should be tucking into bed.

"You and November never talked before?" I'm not usually the one to break a silence.

"Not really . . . we were just talking about—it's funny—we were just talking about how we both resented how everyone thought we'd be friends, since there aren't a whole lot of black kids at Stanwick. So we avoided each other. But it turns out she's cool . . ."

Everything he says trails off at the ends. Like periods are too harsh for him. If Joy's words fly out of her, and I have to pry mine out, his drift from him like summer clouds. He stares dreamily at the moon, tapping the bottle of whiskey with his pinkie. His fingernails are curved and delicate.

Awkwardness stacks up, bricks of it. Does he expect me to say something? But he's not looking at me. He's lost in his own thoughts. It's hard not to feel soft toward somebody when you watch him watch the sky.

After a while, the silence stops being awkward.

"The quarry creeps me out," he says eventually. "It's supposed to be this romantic place . . . but it's just evidence of people screwing up the earth for their own gain."

It always catches me off guard when someone says something out loud that I was thinking. I always assume nobody else has the thoughts I have.

"I don't like that you can't see the bottom at night," I say.

"Me neither."

And suddenly I realize I'm talking casually with Cassius Somerset. Something Joy can't do.

"It feels like, um," I try. "Like it's pulling at me."

"Same." He nods, and that's it. He's not always unspooling the contents of his brain like Joy does, filling so much space with the things in her mind that there's no room for the things in mine.

"This is our first time drinking," I confess.

He smiles, not in a mean way.

"We're doing this, uh. Summer of misdeeds. She's trying to break me out of my shell or something. It's silly."

"It's not silly . . . it sounds like fun."

"It feels like everyone else is always already in on this stuff." The words unstick from me easily for once. Maybe it's the whiskey. "I don't even know how to talk about drinking or smoking or, like, which words are normal to use."

He plays with the edge of the blanket. "Me neither, really . . . I don't know if those teen parties in the movies with red Solo cups even exist. Sometimes Adam and I steal his dad's beer and drink in the basement and play Mario Kart. That's about it."

I should ask about Adam while this new passage between my brain and my mouth stays open.

"I'm sorry about my sister," I blurt instead. "She's . . . a lot."

"It's okay . . ." He rubs a heart-shaped splotch of lighter

skin next to his temple. "Loud people just kind of make me feel like I'm disappearing."

Yes.

That.

"You're not hard to talk to, though. Usually I have a harder time with strangers," he explains. "And don't worry, I understand sisters being a pain. Mine's a freshman next year, and she picked the worst kids in middle school to hang out with, and I don't want her coming to high school and getting in trouble and making everyone think I'm like that."

"Joy's a mess, and that doesn't make anyone look down on me."

"No, I mean . . . at a school like this, it's like a black kid represents every black kid. If Savannah does something bad, I might as well have done it." He shrugs. "I just think she needs consequences."

"Joy gets away with things, too."

"Adam also does stupid stuff. But he does it to cope."

"Cope?" Something in my chest yanks. "Cope with what?"

"His dad wants Adam to be a famous musician like his grandfather."

"Pressure sucks," I burst out. "It's like you can't screw up. Because all that matters is that you do the one thing you're supposed to be good at. Even if you're scared, or miserable, or hate the way you look . . ."

"Do you hate the way you look?"

"No," I say too quickly.

"I do. I hate the way I look. This skin thing. I hate it."

"But it's beautiful," I say without weighing it first. "You're like a work of art."

He lifts his chin from his knees and looks at me for a long time. "A work of art?"

"It's like people don't only look good when they look like a magazine." I'm drunker than I thought. "People can be aesthetically beautiful in the way sunsets and leaves and things are."

"Nobody has ever said anything like that to me in my entire life," he says.

Could I have this effect on Adam, if I told him he's beautiful?

"You are really not like your sister," he adds quietly.

"I know. I'm sorry."

"I'm glad."

Nobody's ever said anything like that to me, either.

Do people tell Joy to be like me as often as they tell me to be like her?

"Sometimes I think we were meant to be a whole person, and we would have been okay that way, but we got split up and now we'll never be . . . right. Technically, I mean medically, I guess we were supposed to be one person."

"Can I paint you?" he asks suddenly.

"Are you joking? Why would you want to paint me?"

"I like painting interesting people."

"You should paint Joy."

"I want to paint you."

He gives me a special look, like he's already painting in his mind.

If I spend more time alone with him, maybe I can get him to be interested in Joy. And maybe I can ask him more about Adam.

"Okay," I say. "You can paint me."

SIX

October 5

Joy

THE COPS DRAG PRINCIPAL EASTMAN OUT of school by 10:00 a.m.

Or he escapes through the fire door, or he breaks a window in his office. Depends who you listen to. But everyone agrees that Savannah ran out five minutes into advisory. They didn't even have time to call her to the office.

I did this to her. A freshman girl, and I ruined her life.

I'm the person who hurts people, the girl who destroys other girls. The failed knight. If nobody'll exile me, I'll exile myself. I hide from Levi for the rest of the day. I don't look for Preston. I spend detention writing apology letters I won't send and shredding them into thin piles of paper. After school, I make the ten-minute bike ride to Preston's house.

The Bell house is a healthy kind of messy, the furniture and nineties wallpaper in different floral shades. Preston's first step, first birthday, first ice-cream cone, it's all documented on the walls. He says he hates constantly looking at his past.

There's a zillion notes on his bedroom door: *Do not enter. Do not touch my things. Do not clean.*

"Pres, I'm coming in."

"Don't," he replies, muffled.

"I'm not mad at you for putting the photos in everyone's lockers. But we need to talk."

A long silence.

"Someone told me that Savannah girl is taking the rest of the semester off," he says.

"It's not your fault," I say desperately. "You just didn't want anything to happen to me."

He opens the door, slouching more than usual. His curls corkscrew like he just whipped a blanket off his head. His shades are shut as always, the dim light deepening the circles under his eyes.

"Last night, all of it felt like something from Sherlock Holmes. It didn't feel real. But now I'm panicking. And I think I wrecked someone's life because I was scared about someone wrecking yours."

Which one of us is gonna be the strong one?

"I'm the one who got the envelope. I'm the one who showed it to you." I try to smile.

He hugs me. Pres *hates* hugs. It's stiff, uncomfortable, and it's the best hug I've ever had.

"It's Adam and this blackmailer person," he says. "Not you."

It'd be so much easier if that were true.

"Have you heard anything else from the blackmailer?" he asks.

"No. I watched the window all night."

"You can't sleep there."

"I'm gonna stay awake in case he comes back."

"You can't stay awake forever."

"What if he comes through my window, goes to Grace's room?" The knife under my pillow won't be enough. "I stay awake or I tell the cops."

"No cops." He's agonized. "Please."

"Maybe now that Eastman's arrested, it's done with."

"We have to talk to Cassius. Tonight or tomorrow."

"I can't believe Cassius would do that to his sister. And if I ask him about it, and it wasn't him, what if he realizes the photos were because of me?"

Outside, a car gravels into the driveway. Pres shrinks back into his room. "I can't talk to Mom when I'm—she can always tell."

"I'll distract her."

"Text me if you get another envelope."

"I bet I won't," I say for him. "I bet it's over."

I hope it is. But I'm getting a sharper knife and setting my alarm for every ten minutes tonight.

I shut his door and head downstairs, tripping over Ms. Bell's shoes and scarves, scattered like she sheds accessories on her way to her room every night.

"Hello, Joy. Visiting Pres?" Ms. Bell is wearing a simple

blouse and a high-waisted skirt. No bright lipstick, no ten-cent craft store flowers in her ponytail. "Long day. Staff meetings about . . . those photos."

She beckons me to the kitchen, which is cluttered with spices and mismatched plates, and fills a bright purple mug with water. She sticks it in the microwave, finds a box of hibiscus tea. I bite my tongue. There's no way to wish someone else was your mom without feeling guilty.

"How's Pres? He good?" she asks.

"Fine," I say all quick. "Doing homework."

"Every single student comes to me with their feelings except my son." She takes out a sleeve of Thin Mints, shakes out three, rolls the rest to me. "I doubt there's anyone who's not feelin' a bit shaken right now. Adam's death, now this. Whoever it was ought to have just reported those photographs to the police."

I crumble the edge of a cookie in my fingers. "Maybe they wanted to humiliate Eastman."

"That's exactly what that man deserves, but not the girl. I have a meeting with her family tomorrow. Don't imagine she'll be comin' back to school right away."

There was a movie Grace and me watched once, about a man who accidentally killed anybody who got near him thanks to a lab experiment. He spent the whole movie running around oblivious, everyone within a mile falling over dead. If he'd just stayed still, they would have been fine.

"Good men are hard to find." She dunks a tea bag in her mug, splashes the counter. "Sometimes I think about findin' a father figure for Pres, and sometimes I think, screw it. The last one he had was no great shakes. I ask you, what does it tell a small boy when his own father doesn't want him?"

Everyone in school trusts Ms. Bell because she talks to us like we're people, not kids. She sucks in a deep breath and pushes it out again. "Sorry. Something like today makes you so mad, you start getting mad about everything else in the world there is to be mad about. How are you doing, Joy?"

I want to bury my face in her shoulder. But all I say is "I'm okay."

She nods sadly. "Were you at Adam Gordon's birthday party?"

It doesn't feel safe to say yes or no, but she keeps talking so I don't have to answer.

"You know, I'm holding a group counseling meeting next week, for everybody who went. You're welcome to join."

Preston said the blackmailer was probably at the party. If I locked eyes with him at this meeting, would he stutter, slip up?

"Do you remember the first time you came over here? Pres made me hide all the pictures of him." Ms. Bell listens so much that when it's her turn to talk, she never stops. "You picked him up a Diet Pepsi, and the can sat on his dresser for weeks. When I tossed it, he moped all day. He'd saved it because you gave it to him."

I've dragged Pres into this mess with me.

"A forty-year-old woman can't smack a bully when he's a teenager, can she? And she shouldn't want to. And I officially do not condone violence, but thanks for sticking up for Pres the other day. You're a good girl."

I push my knee into the table leg until it throbs.

My phone buzzes and I pull it out of my back pocket. It's Mom.

> When R U coming home? Could use U to help with Grace.

My blood freezes. What does that mean? I bolt up. "I have to go."

"If you need a ride—"

But I'm already out the door, not thinking, biking home, twice as fast as I did to Preston's. They've never needed help with her. Grace never needs help. Did the blackmailer break in through my window, did he hurt her—

When I get home, aching, sweating, Mom's on the porch, her head in her hands. She attempted to hide that she was crying with makeup, but it didn't work.

"What's wrong with Grace? Where's Dad?" I pant.

"Your father's at work." She fixes a smile on her face. "I tried to talk to her about maybe going back to school. I'm not used to fighting with her."

Only with me.

"You girls talk about everything." She holds open the door for me, an apology in her eyes.

I nod and go inside. Everything's meticulously clean in

Grace's room, except her desk lamp, which I painted for her at arts and crafts camp when we were ten. It's one of the only sentimental things she's kept. Now it's cracked in two.

"The fight wasn't a big deal. Honestly," she says, curled in bed, before I even open my mouth. "It's just the way she looks at me. Like she's searching for someone else. Some other version, smarter, prettier . . ."

"That's not true."

"Don't lie." She muffles herself with the blanket. "She's sick of having me around. *I'm* sick of having me around."

"Nobody's sick of you. They're scared you're a hermit now. A really brilliant hermit."

Long silence. Our conversations used to tie us together like ropes. Now they're shimmering threads, always about to break if I move too fast.

"I'm sorry the lamp fell," she says.

Longer silence.

"You could come back, now that he's gone," I say cautiously.

"I know I won't see him again," she says to the underside of the blanket. "And I know that the whole reason I started the independent project was so I wouldn't have to see him."

She's talking to me for real. Finally.

"I was supposed to stop dreaming about him." Semi-casually. "But he keeps coming back."

"I saw his body at the funeral," I tell her. "He's gone. Even though I know that doesn't cancel out . . ."

The absence of a word hangs in the air. What am I allowed to call what happened?

She peeks out from under the blanket. "Just because someone's dead doesn't make them gone."

SEVEN

October 12

IT TURNS OUT THAT WHEN YOU DON'T sleep at night, you sleep in class. And it turns out that when your principal is under house arrest, there's nobody for your teachers to complain to. Even if you do it all week.

Time slides by without me getting involved. The men's choir puts on a memorial performance for Adam. Savannah doesn't come back. Cassius isn't in school, either. Grace acts like she never said anything. Levi pokes me awake in American History long enough to copy his quiz answers, but he doesn't ask again about the photos, and I don't explain. I spend the weekend half-conscious on Preston's bed while he brainstorms ways to safely ask Cassius if he's, you know, blackmailing me and also possibly a murderer.

When you don't sleep, things stop being real and you

don't have to worry about them as much. Until Sunday
night, when there's a new note taped to the outside of my
nailed-shut window and I have to go out in the dark and
climb the tree to get it.

To Joy Morris—

Good job.

I go back to my room and kick my bedside table so hard
that the drawer splinters.

"Joy?" Grace's voice comes suddenly from the hallway.
"Are you okay?"

"Yeah. Just stubbed my toe!" I holler back, crumpling
the note.

I've got four minibottles left from Dad's sample pack-
age. I drink two, until my throat's numb, and my head
is—

Fuck this.

I grab a piece of paper and a black Sharpie and scrawl:
LEAVE ME ALONE. YOU DON'T HAVE ANY PROOF.
I tear out the nails with Dad's hammer, grunting, yanking until I can open the window wide enough to trap the
note beneath the frame. Then I pull up my chair, lay my
kitchen knife on my lap—the big cleaver, Mom's been asking where it went—and wait.

Could Cassius really balance on that branch? He lives

down the street and around the corner. I could go there right now, knock on his door, bring my knife, make him tell me the truth.

When you don't sleep, you think about these things.

Mom calls me for dinner and I claim a stomachache. Grace is in her bedroom, Dad in the exercise room, Mom in her office. We spend the night in our individual holes. Pres hasn't been sleeping well, either, so I don't text him about the new note.

I wonder how Savannah's been sleeping.

I tilt back in my chair, and Levi's sweatshirt slides to the ground. I forgot it was there. I almost forgot about him. Why hasn't he gone back to Indiana yet?

To distract myself, I open Facebook, search his name. His profile's public. He already has more friends from Stanwick than I do. His smile's so bright in his picture. It isn't fair for one person to have so much sunlight.

My window's still dark and empty.

I google his full name and the Indiana town listed on his profile. Apparently he was on the tennis team in eighth grade. He volunteered at an animal shelter. I skim the second page of results, the third. The first link on this page is a blog, captioned: *dear adam*. Shivering, I click it.

> so you're gone now. i guess that means you'll never read any of these.

> when i got the call, i remembered this blog right away. it's been three years since I posted. i don't

know what i thought it would accomplish. i'm the only
one who knows about it.

I shouldn't be doing this. It's a personal blog. He probably
didn't think anyone would find it.

I open the archives, clicking the very first post, from
years ago. Middle school?

this is for my creative writing class! we're supposed
to write a bunch of letters to somebody we look up
to. mr hendrick probably meant famous people, but i
decided to write to my half brother. he's going to be
a famous musician someday, so maybe that counts.
also, he's impossible to get in touch with, so he's like
a famous person that way, too.

The posts continue, around one every month. He kept
it up way after he passed in the creative writing assign-
ment.

adam, do you remember that baseball cap you gave
me for christmas when I was 9? this is dorky, but
i still have it. it's too small for me now but I wear it
anyway.

it's kind of nice having you for a half brother. you
don't talk to me, so I get to make you up.

The baseball cap in his sweatshirt pocket is still in my closet. If Adam had ever read these when he was alive, he would have laughed. Levi deserves to be related to someone better.

But Grace does, too.

> i had this stupid daydream the other day about what would happen if you replied to my emails and we actually talked. i think it would be nice.

I feel so weird reading this. Stop. I'm gonna stop.

There's so many of them, rambling, raw. All this yearning for someone who never really existed. Adam'll live on in his head as some wonderful person, a missed relationship. It's the kind of thing people regret on their deathbeds.

I want Levi to know. I grit my teeth and dig my nails into my wrist.

But of course he can't.

I read until the words blur, until everything inside and outside the house is quiet and the sky outside my window starts getting a little bit lighter.

The next morning, I wake up slumped in my chair, laptop battery dead, my mouth dusty, someone knocking on my door.

"Joy, I need you to come downstairs right now."

Mom's voice is razor thin. Am I late for school? I check my clock. I don't have to leave for another half hour. I hide the knife under a corner of my carpet and close my laptop. In the daylight, it feels a lot slimier that I read Levi's blog.

Mom's footsteps retreat. My note's still on the windowsill. The blackmailer didn't come back. Maybe his last note was the end and I'll never have to know who he is.

Downstairs, Officer Roseby is in our living room.

"Sorry for coming so early. Was hoping to catch Joy before school started," he says, clearly not sorry at all. A cop in uniform looks larger than life, like he should be in a video game, not in my house where my sister's sleeping. He's pale in the morning light, his blond hair scraped back over his scalp. "I'm asking around about the night Adam Gordon passed away."

I'm awake down to my toes.

"I thought that was an accident," Dad says. His socks are mismatched, and Mom's shirt is misbuttoned.

"The department believes so. But his father asked if I'd talk to a few kids who were at the party. Sort of as a favor. Just to be sure. We ought to know how much of a factor drugs and alcohol were."

I'm shaking. If he was here because I'm a suspect, he'd say so, right? If he searches my room—the notes, the knife . . . What if Grace comes downstairs?

"Joy was grounded that night." Mom side-eyes me. "She didn't go to this party."

"It's not like your daughter doesn't have a history of rule breaking, ma'am."

I'm on his bad-kids list. If I called the cops on the blackmailer, he wouldn't believe anything I said. I think of him finding out what happened to Grace, asking skeptical questions in our living room.

"Did you speak to Adam at his birthday party?" he asks me.

"No," I say before I realize I just accidentally confirmed I was there.

Mom stares at me, silently filling the room with poison.

Roseby looks at our walls. Grace took down all the pictures of her, like she untags every photo of herself on Facebook. "What about your sister? Was she there?"

"No, and she's asleep. She doesn't want to talk to you."

"Watch yourself, young lady. Especially after I was kind enough to let you go with a warning this past July."

I'm boiling over.

"I have my own teenage daughter. You have to watch them round the clock," he says to Dad, then turns back to me. "Were you involved in any drugs at this party?"

"Since this is just a 'favor' for Mr. Gordon, Joy doesn't really have to keep answering your questions. And I'm afraid we're late for work." Mom's a dragon. I want to hold on to her. The urge is so strong I'm amazed to discover how much of me is still a kid.

"Of course," he says ironically. "Thank you for your time."

The minute he leaves, Mom breathes fire.

"Really, Joy? I can't believe you snuck out again after we

picked you up from the police station this summer."

My eyes sting. I mash my toe into the carpet.

"Especially to go to a party near that quarry," Dad agrees. "What happened to the Gordon boy could've happened to you."

"You're grounded on weekends for the next three weeks." Mom grits her teeth. "I thought you were trying."

"I am trying." Don't cry.

"If you were, you wouldn't be failing American History," she says like she's explaining basic math. "You wouldn't have detention every other week and police wouldn't be in our house."

Go through my room, then. Find the notes. Tell me what to do.

"Do you ever consider the possibility that stuff is going on in my life that makes it hard to focus on school?" I say.

"It's just homework, Joy." Dad sighs. "It shouldn't be that hard."

I can't explain how homework zaps me with a panic that gets bigger and bigger until it feels like I have to either put it away or stab myself.

"If anything's going on, you can tell us. You know that," says Mom.

"You're just as smart as Grace," Dad says quietly. "You ought to be able to do as well as her."

I hate how furious I am. "I'm not as smart as Grace. We're not good at the same shit, so quit holding us to the same standard."

"Language," Dad snaps. "Go to your room until it's time for school."

"Do you realize what a ridiculous punishment that is?" I'm barreling down the tracks. "I spend all my time in my room. What is the point of sending me there?"

"Just . . . go get dressed," says Mom. "Perhaps tonight we can have a mature conversation about this."

I storm upstairs, slam my door. Grace is probably awake and hiding. She hides from fights and that's why I have to be the fighter.

I open the window, snatch my untouched note back from the mangled sill. I'll burn all the notes tonight. Outside, the tree branch bobs infuriatingly in the morning sun. I unfold it, and my heart slices in half. Beneath what I wrote, *you don't have proof*, there's something printed in blocky, unrecognizable handwriting.

DON'T I?

EIGHT

July 16

Grace

THE FIELD BEHIND THE MIDDLE SCHOOL IS wet, but that doesn't stop anybody from sitting on it. Kennedy, Ben, Sarah: three out of the five artsy seniors. Cassius isn't here and neither is Adam. I've never talked to them before, and they don't seem interested in starting. They've barely said a word to Joy or November either, even though November's in their grade.

The middle school road is dark, except for the pool of yellow light from the streetlamp. It's a bad idea to do this in the open.

"Quit checking the road. The cops won't come," Joy says confidently. Like she's smoked weed (bud? pot?) under the stars with the seniors before. Like I'm the only one doing this for the first time. She's wearing November's too-small sweatshirt. She rocks back on her knees, watching the seniors poke grassy stuff into a little glass pipe (bowl? bong?) and pass it in a circle.

I miss the trick to what they're doing. November exhales smoke, holds the pipe to me.

"No thank you," I say like a kindergartner.

"No problem," says November kindly. She turns to Joy. Moves her like a doll, adjusts her hands around the pipe (bowl?). Lights it for her. Murmurs instructions. Joy's eyes cross. I blush for her, but Kennedy-Ben-Sarah aren't watching. They're on their backs, arms tangled up like they're not conscious of their bodies. What's it like to not be conscious of your body?

Joy coughs. Hard. Forever. November pats her back.

"Fuck middle school," Kennedy says. "It's like a crypt of bad memories."

I wish I could say it: fuck middle school. Anything I don't like, just: fuck it.

"Remember what a bitch you were, Ken?"

"Remember all the shitty anime I watched?"

"I was sooo depressed in eighth grade. . . ."

There's no way they, too, were balls of silence and fear back then, or ever. Kennedy has pastel-pink hair. Ben's wearing a tie. Sarah's shirt quotes *The Great Gatsby*. They're like teenagers in books, and movies made out of books, with deep thoughts, quirky hobbies. They fall in love and it fixes them. They're interesting.

I'm never going to be broken in a way that makes someone

fall in love with me. My sadness will never be interesting. I'm not a girl who makes a good story.

Joy makes a good story.

"I don't know if it's working," she keeps saying. She rolls around in the grass. Getting soaked. "Grace, remember our lunch table by the stairs in middle school? I wonder who sits there now. What do you think Cat and them are doing tonight? Making out with an SAT prep book?"

I haven't seen my old friends since school ended last month. Maybe that means they're not my friends anymore. Strange how it can happen, just like that.

"You know that Halloween-themed fair they have every year on this field?" she asks. "We didn't go last year. We went every year before then. We should go this year."

Everybody in our whole town goes to that fair. Teachers, doctors, they all make the twin comments wherever they run into us: how we look the same but *they* can tell us apart. Like we're theirs because they can see the difference.

Joy faces November. "Did you like middle school, Nov?"

"The people who liked middle school are the reasons why everybody else hated middle school." November's got one earbud in again. She's apart from everyone.

"How come you were gone our sophomore year?" Ben asks bluntly. There's something aggressive in his expression. "I always wondered."

She plays with the rubber bands on her wrists. There's a long silence.

Finally Joy says, "Do you guys have any more weed? I don't feel anything."

Everyone reassures her: they didn't feel it their first time either, don't exhale right away. She nods, mimes taking notes. She's always been able to turn herself into a project.

"Remember how you punched me in elementary school for making fun of your sister's paintings?" Ben asks her, grinning. "I was a grade above you, too."

"I did!" She's delighted.

I lie on the grass. There's peace in being forgotten. This would be a good moment to think some profound thoughts about the stars. But I'm too anxious. I want to go home.

I close my eyes. I hear the lighter flick on. Joy coughs again. Then the darkness glows behind my eyelids. Headlights. I shoot upright, but it's not cop lights.

"I invited Adam," Ben says. "Hope that's cool."

Oh no. I have to fix my shirt. Have to fix my hair. I'm wearing too much makeup. Maybe he won't notice in the dark. Of course he'll notice.

And then Joy's arms fall over my shoulders. "Oh my God, this is your chance." Her eyes are red.

By the road, Adam hops the little fence. His guitar case bounces against his back with each step.

"'Sup, all," he says once he reaches us. Does he see me?

"Help us out with this." Ben hands him the pipe. Adam lights it easily. He knows. I have to pretend I know. He inhales smoke and holds it out to me, ignoring everyone else.

He does see me!

"I didn't know you knew Ben and them," he says.

I shrug. Cringe. "I don't. Not really."

"Don't make me smoke this alone." He sits cross-legged. Next to me. "There's a shit ton in here."

I look at him. He looks back with his dark eyes, darker at night. He lights the bowl for me. Does he know this is my first time? His chest brushes my shoulders. I do what everyone told Joy to do: breathe in, take my thumb off the hole, don't breathe out—

"Hey, you wouldn't do it with *me*!" Joy's next to me suddenly, upset. I breathe out the smoke too early.

"Can you two get a ride home?" November says to us. She's glaring at Adam. "I feel like going to bed."

"Oh, let me guess," he groans. "In the last two seconds I've managed to do something that contributes to the worldwide oppression of women, gay people, and everyone else probably."

"Or sometimes people just want to go to sleep," she says coolly, but her eyes are knives.

"Fine." He fake salutes. "Night. Miss ya already."

"You are such an asshole."

His eyes get darker. Kennedy-Ben-Sarah clump together, useless. Joy's normally the first to join a fight, but her gaze is unfocused.

"Can you not?" I say to November.

Adam grins at me. My stomach swoops. November scowls hard. She whispers something to Joy, hugs her quickly, turns to go.

"What, I don't get a hug?" Adam teases.

"Die."

Her hate is so pure that I'm amazed Adam doesn't bleed.

"Do you guys have any idea what her problem is?" he asks once she's gone. "Hasn't she always been a bitch to me, Ben? Pretty sure she just hates me because I'm a straight white guy."

"She used to like you," says Ben, smirking.

Joy stares after November as she walks alone across the field.

"Thanks for sticking up for me." Adam gives me a brief tight squeeze. I'm warm everywhere. Blossoming.

Joy scoots toward us. She pulls me aside, down into the grass, away from Adam.

"Nov said to make sure we didn't go anywhere with Adam alone," she whispers.

"She hates him." I feel brave. "It's like she hates every guy. It's stupid."

"Nov's our friend."

"She's *your* friend," I say. She blinks at me. I sigh, murmur, "Joy, I like him."

She rubs her eyes. "Just be sure you don't put him before us."

I don't think she's paying attention to what's coming out of her mouth. "You've been putting November before us."

"Are we fighting? I'm confused."

"You said you'd give him a chance. You've never even talked to him."

"Fine. I'll talk to him." And then she's wobbling back toward the group. "Where's Cassius tonight?" she asks Adam, like a challenge. My scalp gets hot.

"Fuck if I know." He's stretched out, shirt riding up. "I need a break from him sometimes. Guy has a lot of weird thoughts."

Next week is when he wants to paint me. I haven't told Joy—she wouldn't understand that I'm doing it for her.

"Don't say that about your husband!" Sarah chirps. "You guys are so married."

"He's not my type."

He looks at me and smiles!

After awhile, Joy brings out a whiskey bottle—how she had that in her bag I don't know. But now we're drinking and the night's blurring.

"Okay, everyone. I have an announcement to make." Joy struggles to her feet. "I hate secrets. Secrets are shit. Can we agree on that? Oh, wait." She bends over, takes off her shoes, and throws them several feet away before continuing. "Secrets keep people apart."

Kennedy-Ben-Sarah crack up. Adam grins. I grin, too. My dumb cute sister.

"So in the interest of that, all of you should know . . . wow . . . Okay, this grass feels amazing. All of you should take off your shoes right now, and then after that, you should know that she"—she points at me—"likes him." She points at Adam. "And you, Adam, you be good to her, or I'll kick your ass."

I freeze.

I'm dying.

I hate her.

"Aw," Sarah coos into Kennedy's shoulder. "That's so cute."

I can't look at Adam. But I feel him sidle up.

"So you like me?"

"She's high," I say weakly. "She doesn't know what she's saying." Except she does. I don't get why she always screws things up for no reason.

But he's not laughing. Not reassuring everyone he only dates thin girls. He's still looking at me. And it's really nice to have him look at me.

I'm sorry, I tell Joy in my head. She's picking at blades of grass, giggling. *I don't hate you. I'm not mad. Not ever.*

"Talk to me, Grace Morris." Adam brushes my shoulder. "Tell me your story."

I don't have one.

"I'd rather hear yours," I manage.

"I'm still writing mine. It's going to be a good one. There's a lot I plan on getting done in this life. You ever thought about what you want to do?"

Get good grades. "I don't know. Be a doctor. Help people, I guess?"

He rolls his eyes. "I'm not one of those people who talks about wanting to *help others*. That's very naïve. They're doing it to make themselves feel good. I want to get famous for my sake, and I'm going to be honest about that."

I wish I hadn't said anything.

"Not one single person who lives in this town is interesting," he says.

Don't disappoint him. Be interesting.

"It's like we get held to a different set of standards . . . because we're smarter," I say. Cringe. I'm not smarter than anyone, not in any way that counts.

But he says, "Fuckin' right."

If I can curl and uncurl my fist thirteen times before anyone stands up, I won't screw up the next thing I say, either.

"I'm having these assorted losers over my house at the end of the month," he says. "You should come. Raise the average IQ. There's not enough smart people in my life."

My stomach leaps. It takes me a second to recognize it: happiness.

"I'll show you my bed. It cost, like, two thousand dollars. Tempur-Pedic." He pushes his shoulder into mine and winks. "You'd look good in it."

It's so hard to tell when he's joking. Would a normal girl be annoyed or flattered? What would Joy do?

"I wanted to tell you, um," I start. Bad transition. "You . . . you should never feel like you have to live up to your grandfather. That's a lot of pressure—"

"What are you talking about?" He laughs, but it's mean. "What do I care what music some old dude made a billion years ago? He's dead and irrelevant."

His warmth is gone. I ruined it.

He looks around restlessly, glances at Joy's goofy smile. He mean-laughs again. "Is this her first time?"

"It's mine, too," I say defensively.

"Don't get all November on me. I like you sweet." He looks at me more closely. "Lemme pack another bowl."

This time, when he lights it, I suck in hard, determined to do it right. His face, so close: "Don't breathe out yet." I don't. A fire builds in my chest. My eyes water. I cough loudly. Can't stop. He pays no attention, takes a long hit, holds the pipe out to me again. I don't want it. I take it anyway.

My thoughts are tangled. I'm wearing too much makeup. Gross. I'm gross.

"Quit hiding your face." He pulls at me. No. Don't look. Even if someone saw what's inside me, they wouldn't want to help.

Adam disappears at the end of a long tunnel. Then Joy's with me. In the grass. "Grace?" She's the sky. I'm underground. She's so tall. My eighteen-minute-older sister. Protecting me from monsters. But the real monster's in me, and while she's waving her sword, it's eating me.

I'm vanishing. She presses her forehead to mine, giggling, and I'm still vanishing.

Then, suddenly: bright, bright lights.

"Oh shit!"

Noises. Everyone getting up. Joy's yanking at me. "Grace. Graaaace. Come on." Adam's running. I watch him, sideways. His guitar bouncing on his back. *Write a song about me.* Shouting. Flashlight beams. Crackling voices. Joy, panicking. "We gotta run, come on!"

I'm in a cage, Joy. I can run in as many circles as I want. I'm still not going anywhere.

"I can't believe this," Mom keeps saying. "I just can't believe this."

She drives fast, jerking around each corner. Stanwick shuts down after ten p.m. Everyone else in the world might as well be dead.

Joy's balled up in her seat, shoeless. It's been—two hours? Three? Everything's still furry-edged.

Officer Roseby's chin jutted out when he spoke to Mom and Dad, like he'd done something honorable for the world by putting us in the back of his police car. It was his daughter who got us high in the first place.

"Teenage girls. I'm telling you," he said, but he didn't explain what he was telling us. I've never heard someone say *teenage girls* without disdain. What's wrong with us, that everyone hates us so much?

Mom and Dad are murderously quiet. Guess what! I'm not perfect after all! I got high! I broke a rule! I snort. Joy shoots me a terrified look.

"You're both grounded for the rest of the summer," Mom hisses.

But Adam invited me—

Then she says, "I expected better from you, Grace Morris."

Joy freezes. I freeze.

"Both of you," Mom amends quickly. Dad rubs the back of his neck. "I expected better from both of you."

But it's already settled into us forever. Joy tucks herself against the window. A tear breaks down her cheek.

Rage fills me, hot and bloody. How dare anyone hurt her?

"You are so lucky Officer Roseby decided not to press charges," Mom continues. "It would have gone on your record. Your college applications, down the toilet. Your futures . . ."

I'm not listening to her anymore. I don't belong to her. I belong to my sister and she wants me out of my shell.

So I'm coming out.

NINE

October 13

Joy

THE SENIORS SQUEEZE FIVE TO A COUCH IN the counseling room. Kennedy-Ben-Sarah, a few others. People who were at the birthday party, but nobody talks about that.

"Principal Eastman's going to trial."

"That girl, Savannah Somerset, her mom pulled her out for the semester."

Guilt and nausea are almost the same thing. They both overwhelm me.

"Remember, people," says Ms. Bell, "we're here to talk about what happened."

I stare at the faces around me. Nobody stares back. I thought I'd feel the blackmailer's presence, like an alarm going off.

Ben's hollow eyed; Kennedy looks like she hasn't showered in days; Sarah's usual eyeliner is gone. They're like this because they loved their dead friend, not because any of them are blackmailing me.

They should have known Adam better. They should have warned Grace.

"Officer Roseby interviewed me yesterday." Kennedy hugs her knees. "I guess Mr. Gordon'd wanted him to find out about, like, alcohol."

So I wasn't the only one interviewed. Maybe the blackmailer didn't send Roseby to my house as a threat after all. But finding that note right afterward—it's too much of a coincidence. He's threatening me. Telling me he's not afraid to get the police involved.

"Adam lived next to that quarry his whole life." Grief has turned Ben hard. "He wouldn't fall in, drunk or not."

My head is full of a thick fog. When was the last time I ate? How long I can keep doing this?

"It feels like everyone forgot about Adam." Sarah's eyes are blank. "Because of Principal Eastman and Savannah. Nobody cares anymore."

"Adam's half brother does," says Kennedy quickly. "The new kid. He asked me all these things about Adam. I told him about that thing he always did with his car, and how he brought doughnuts to math class twice. . . ."

Levi's sweatshirt and the baseball cap are in my backpack. I almost threw the cap in the trash.

Sarah starts, "If this thing with Savannah hadn't—"

The door opens, and Cassius walks in as his sister's name is dissolving in the air. It's the first time I've seen him all week. His black eye's mostly faded, but there're bags under both eyes now. Grief or guilt?

I'm not scared, I'm a fighter—

His steps stutter when he sees me, but he doesn't leave. He sits on the last free couch. It groans beneath him despite the weight he's lost. A tree branch would snap.

But if it's not him . . . it's somebody else, faceless, scarier, someone capable of murder.

Then November follows him in. What's she doing here? I tap the spot next to me, but for some reason she sits beside Cassius. All the rubber bands on her wrist are gone.

"Let's go around the room, share our memories of that night." Ms. Bell faces November, who's closest to the door.

"I was only there for a second. So I don't have much to talk about." She doesn't look at me.

A little fire kindles in me. I pull out my phone and text her.

u went to adams birthday party?

She reads my message with her brow furrowed, and starts typing.

It was a bad idea.

That doesn't explain anything. Then something occurs to me.

did u see me there?

No you must have gone early and left early. I showed up late.

how come u didnt tell me u went?

Are you kidding? Don't act like you're entitled to information about my life when you've completely shut me out lately.

The fire in my stomach zips out, leaving me cold.

I hesitantly shut my phone off. "My biggest memory of that night is how Cassius punched Adam in the face," Ben says suddenly.

The silence is acidic.

November stands up. "What are you trying to say?"

"All I'm pointing out," growls Ben, "is that Cassius assaulted Adam, and that same night he ended up dead."

"Rumors and accusations are not welcome here," Ms. Bell says sharply, no trace of her usual lilting tone.

Even Sarah quits wiping her eyes long enough to glower at Cassius. I guess Preston's not the only one who suspects him. I try to be afraid of Cassius but I can't. There's no way he's capable of murder when he can't even sit up straight.

"When they arrest you, I hope you resist." Tears bud in Ben's eyes. "I hope they have to shoot—"

November launches across the room and slaps him in the face.

"*November!*" cries Ms. Bell.

Cassius's expression contorts. He rushes out of the room and Nov follows him out. Ben bark laughs, clasps his cheek. "I mean, come on! After what he said about Adam at the funeral? You're all thinking it. Mysterious guy, never talks—fits the profile, right?"

Nobody pays attention to me leaving.

The halls are deserted. Everyone's in class or in the cafeteria for lunch. I don't realize I'm running until the echo of my footsteps bounces back at me. I slow down near Grace's old locker, where I used to slip her notes and drawings.

I don't see November immediately. I hear the splashing first. I stop and look up. She's scouring the outside of a locker with wads of wet paper towels, her shoulders trembling with effort.

"Nov?" I say.

She jumps, knocks over her water bottle. The word on the locker in black paint is blurry but readable. KILLER.

"Don't you dare tell me you think it was him, too," she says fiercely.

"That's Cassius's locker?" I whisper. "Where is he?"

"He left school. Saw this and ran. Not sure where he went." She squeezes the paper towels. "Help me get this off before the bell rings. I don't want anyone else to see it."

We get more soap and water from the bathroom. With our arms moving up and down in silence, the letters vanish fast.

I inhale. "I didn't mean to shut you out—"

She pauses, then hugs me unexpectedly, a November hug, tight and calm. "Everyone blames him because he called Adam a prick at the funeral. But calling a spade a spade doesn't make him a murderer. He's a scapegoat—he only moved here a couple years ago, he stands out. And he's a big black guy—that doesn't help," she adds bitterly. "Meanwhile he's fucked up over his sister. He doesn't have anyone else right now."

"You don't suspect him at all?"

"I suspect everyone of everything, except for him. All you have to do is look at him."

"You're right," I breathe. "There's no way."

"My asshole father thinks it was him. I swear that's why he's interviewing people. Investigating alcohol, yeah right. Mr. Gordon knows there was booze. He probably enlisted my dad to hide the fact that he bought it. It's the first chance my dad's had in this town to play real cop again and he's going to find a murderer if he has to make one out of Play-Doh."

"I thought there wasn't a formal investigation happening?"

"There isn't. Everyone else at the police department thinks it was an accident."

Even if it wasn't Cassius, it wasn't an accident. It's someone else. Someone watching me who knows where I live.

"Are you okay?" she asks.

November's smart. She could help me.

"Joy?"

The bell shrieks and the classrooms hemorrhage people. The moment's passed. I gotta stay the girl that she knows, carefree, no darkness. What would the old Joy do?

"I'm always okay."

★ ★ ★

It's quiz day in American History, the scary hush of test taking, pencils on paper. I don't know a single answer.

"Here," Levi whispers and slides his test to the side, double-checking that Cat Olsen's back blocks Mr. Fennis's view. I copy his answers quickly. I'm not sure why he's still helping me—he thinks I put those photos in everyone's lockers.

Adam had failed American History his junior year and they were making him retake it. He sat in the back and burned up the room and that's why I was failing. There are flowers on top of his old desk, like a shrine. A few of his friends sit around it. Levi stares at it when he thinks nobody's looking. The longing in his eyes hurts me.

I need to give Levi his sweatshirt and baseball cap, need an excuse for why those photos were in my backpack, need a way to tell him Adam was bad without explaining why.

Mr. Fennis collects the tests, shuffling them like nobody's died or been arrested recently. Except for the desk and the memorial in the relaxation garden—a photo of Adam, flowers—his death is disappearing. Everyone's sucking their sadness back inside so they can do their homework.

I have other things to do. I set up a baby monitor by my window, the one that Mom and Dad had when Grace and I were babies. Next time the blackmailer comes, he can smile for the fucking camera.

After the quiz, Mr. Fennis starts lecturing. He calls on me. I shrug, he moves on. Cat murmurs something exasperated to Levi. He glances up, catches me looking. Shit.

He tears off an edge of notebook paper, writes something, tosses it onto my desk. I expect him to ask for his stuff back, but instead it says:

id still really like to talk to you about what i saw in your bag.

also i hope you're doing okay.

I gotta explain or he'll tell somebody. I write:

ok. we can talk after school.

I grip my pencil hard. I'm sick of being alone with the truth.

and i found your blog, with your letters to adam, maybe we should talk about that, too.

This is so stupid. Adam's dead, there's no point, I have the blackmailer to deal with.

I skim it across his desk anyway. He unfolds it and all at once, his sunlight vanishes. He shoves it in his bag without writing anything back, and doesn't look at me again.

The bell rings. As everyone pushes back their chairs, I reach for his arm, but he bursts out into the hallway fast.

He's freaked out that I internet stalked him. Of course he is. Why did I write that?

In the hall, there's only five minutes to get from one class to the next—go to your locker, switch out your books, go to the bathroom, get a drink, sprint to the other side of school to sit down before the bell rings again—and there's no spare second to find Levi's spiky-haired head. But Pres's orange curls bob up. I weave toward him, grab his shoulder.

"It's not Cassius," I whisper quickly. "Nov vouched for him."

"I—"

"I'm not scared of him. I don't feel it."

"Let's—"

"If we keep focusing on him, we'll never figure out who it is for real—"

"Okay!" he bellows. Two freshman girls snort. He drops his voice again. "Okay. We can think of others. I made a list of everyone I saw at the party. We'll start there."

"I think the blackmailer might've sent Roseby to my house," I say quietly. "He showed up there yesterday, and then there was this new note—"

"I thought you said you put up the baby monitor!"

"I put it up right after."

"Oh, God." He nearly walks into a locker. "Why didn't you tell me earlier?"

Before I can think of an excuse, noise interrupts us. There's a crowd by the plastic art display case. Something crashes and someone yells, "Get off!" I shoulder to the front, Pres behind me, just in time to see a flushed, heaving Ben bang his fist off Levi's mouth. His lip bursts in a crimson spray.

"Don't," Pres hisses, but I leap forward anyway and wrench Ben off.

"None of you give a shit that Adam's murderer goes to our school!" Ben jerks away and opens the art display case, tearing out Cassius's paintings, one after another. He rounds on Levi.

"You—you're supposed to be his half brother. You're pissed at me for not wanting his murderer's art on the walls? What the hell?"

Levi stops gathering the paintings.

"Break it up!" It's our regular security guard, with Officer Roseby. Sometimes Roseby hangs out by the water fountain when there's been a drug scare or a threat, side-eyeing people who take too long in the bathroom. Most everyone scatters, including Pres. Ben scowls, wincing when it hurts his swollen eye. Levi must have gotten in at least one punch before I showed up.

"You two couldn't think of a better way to behave, with all that's going on?" growls Roseby.

"That pathetic loser started it," Ben growls back.

"A pathetic loser who can kick your ass," Levi points out politely, cupping his hand under his chin to catch the blood.

"Look in a mirror, asshole."

"Joy," Roseby grunts. I tense, but he's barely looking at me. He gestures at Levi. "Take this boy to the nurse's office. And you, Stockholm, you look shipshape enough to get to class. In light of the recent tragedy, I'm going to let this slide."

More like in light of the fact that we don't have a principal anymore. And our vice principal has no clue what to do. The security guard nods helplessly. Ben glares, but flees. Levi still doesn't look at me.

Someone stumbles into me. It's Cassius. He stares at the torn paintings, despair fogging his face, before kneeling and gently gathering the undamaged ones. He clutches them to his chest.

No, he didn't murder anybody.

"And how are you involved here, Mr. Somerset?" Roseby's voice gets sharper.

"He wasn't," says Levi. "Someone was vandalizing his work."

Roseby ignores him. "Seems like you're at the center of everything that goes wrong at this school lately."

It's like Cassius thinks that if he stays hunched, predators won't see him. When was the last time I heard him speak?

"Because it makes total sense that he'd throw his own paintings on the floor," Levi says, frowning.

"What are you doing here, Dad?" Nov's finally found us. Her voice is glacial as she steps between her father and Cassius.

"Stay out of this, Annabella."

I always forget November's not her real name.

"Sorry, *Jacob*, I don't really want to," she says. "A police officer's job is to protect people, yeah? That's who needs it, right in front of you. He's being harassed. Yet you still see him as the criminal. I wonder why that is?"

"You're making a scene."

"Sometimes scenes need to get made."

"Go get in the car, young lady," he grits out, pointing down the hallway toward the doors. "You're coming home early."

"You can't talk to me like some little kid who doesn't know anything." She snaps a new rubber band on her wrist, her hand shaking. "I know lots of things." She pauses, then mumbles, "Like the real reason we moved here from the city."

Officer Roseby's face gets ugly. "We will have this discussion at home." He grabs her arm, hauls her away. She rolls her eyes over her shoulder at me, but it doesn't make me feel better.

"You're an incredible artist," Levi tells Cassius, all friendly.

"Thank you . . ." Cassius takes one step away from me, then another.

"You were Adam's best friend, right?"

There's so much hunger in the way he says it. Tell him, Cassius, tell him what he didn't hear you say at the funeral. But Cassius just collects his paintings and rushes away down the hall.

Levi wipes his mouth, streaking red across his cheek. "My social skills in action," he says uneasily.

"He was your half brother. You have a right to . . ."

To know.

"I don't have a right to anything." He touches his cut lip. "The people here, the ones who knew him, they have a right."

I find tissues in my bag, press them to his lip. He grimaces, his gaze fixing somewhere on my feet. He hasn't mentioned my internet stalking yet. I'm aching to shake the truth about Adam into him.

"That picture you saw in my bag, I found it in the copier," I lie on the way to the nurse's office. "I thought it was Photoshopped."

He nods, accepting it with an easy relief.

"Thanks for saving that dude from me. He was in imminent danger of some Levisceration." His jokes are half nonsense. He walks faster than me. When I speed up, he does, too.

"That makes the second bully I've seen you knock down," he adds. "Is there a belt you put notches on?"

"You're sweating."

"Sorry."

He's this nervous because I read his blog?

"Here's the nurse's office." He stops. "You can tell because the door says Nurse's Office. See you—"

"I want to talk to you about what I read," I blurt.

"Is this about you hating him?" he asks.

The truth is not an option. I'm silent.

"Okay. Let me buy you something cheap and greasy after school, and we can talk. Or not greasy. Not greasy is fine, too. Or not cheap. Also fine." He shuts up and mouths the word *idiot* underneath his tissues.

"There's this place, the Ice Cream Palace, at the shopping center, but in the fall they serve pizza, too," I say. His nervousness drowns out mine. "I have detention after school, but I can meet you there at four."

"Four. Okay. Four."

He disappears inside the nurse's office.

The versions of people that live in everyone's heads are powerful. Adam doesn't deserve to be remembered like that. It pisses me off. And if I'm pissed off, if I'm thinking about Levi and his blog and his stupid baseball cap, it's five seconds to not think about other things.

After detention, Levi's late to the Ice Cream Palace. I wait for him on the bench outside. It's cold. Behind the window, there's light and laughter, a kid dropping his pepperoni on the floor, his brother tossing it out for him, replacing it with one of his own. When you have a sibling, you take care of them without thinking. As long as you can do that right, you're worth something. You're made for them.

I'm supposed to made be for Grace, and the blackmailer's distracting me from her. I need to focus on her. I need to figure this out, end it, figure her out, sleep again, eat again. . . . Sometimes it feels like I'm not a person anymore, just a collection of different types of fear.

Pounding footsteps. Levi hurtles around the corner. His heel hooks on the curb and he crashes into the prickly leafless bush next to my bench. I leap up, but he stands by himself, blushing violently behind his freckles. With the split lip, he looks spectacularly beaten up.

"That bush is made of nails," he says. "I'm suing this establishment for putting a hazardous nail bush by their door."

He's still making the panicky jokes. If it were last year, if I were the old me—I think I'd laugh. "Why were you running?"

"Because I was late," he says, like it's the silliest question ever.

We buy our sodas and slices, pepperoni for me and vegetarian for him. It's a coincidence that he heads toward me and Grace's booth. The one with the chip on the corner, the jagged hole in the upholstery that I picked at one year when I was ten. I steer him to the other side of the restaurant, as far away from our booth as possible.

We sit in silence. I have no idea how to do this.

He shreds a napkin. "How'd you find that stupid blog?"

"I googled you." My face burns. "Kind of in depth."

"Did you find my discography and my bestselling romance series under a pen name, too?" he says, then groans. "I make awful jokes when I'm nervous—it's annoying. Sorry."

"You were calm in the bathroom when I was freaking out."

"Bathrooms have a deeply calming effect on me. It's like Superman and kryptonite, but the opposite and also not."

He inhales. "Sorry. Again. You know how when other people freak out, you stop freaking out?"

Like how Pres and I keep trading off who's panicking more about the blackmailer.

"About Adam," I say.

"Can we just," he says, "just for a minute, I mean, not yet. Tell me things about you first."

Our pizza congeals in front of us. "About me?"

"You read my weird stupid secret ancient letters to my half brother who I barely knew, which means you know way too much about me, and I don't know anything about you. You have strong arms and were upset in a bathroom once. That's it."

"There's nothing to know." I'm currently being blackmailed by someone who wants to frame me for his half brother's death, I fucked up with my sister, I hurt everyone I love.

"You look like there's stuff to know."

"My name's Joy. . . ." I shrug. "My sister's name's Grace, she's smart as fuck, she's out this semester for an independent project—"

"I want to know about you, not your sister. It's cute that you immediately start talking about her, though. You guys must be close."

I'm not going to cry.

Things to tell him? I haven't cleaned my room in two months. My dad thinks his alcohol sampler got lost in the mail.

Sometimes you don't understand how broken you are until you put all the pieces together, cutting your fingers on them, realizing that enough shards have disappeared so that you'll never fit together like you used to.

"I'm a mess," I say lightly.

"What kind of mess?" There's a yearning in him like there was when he asked about Adam—not the same, but similar.

I drain my grape soda and crush the can.

"It's scary, the idea of a stranger knowing stuff about you," he supplies.

"That's probably how you feel about me reading your blog." I wince. "Sorry."

"Most people would pretend they never read it."

I can tell he's wishing that's what I'd done, and asking why I didn't.

He points at our plates. "Maybe you're not eating because you're just as nervous as me—I don't know why you would be, you're way cooler than me—but I've heard your stomach growl like three times, and food generally helps with that."

What does he mean, cooler than him? I pick up my slice. It's like chewing glue.

"Are you doing okay?" he finally asks. "After your panic attack?"

The hardest thing is kindness when you know you don't deserve it. I want to deserve it. I want it so bad.

"You're trying to find out stuff about Adam, right?"

"I gotta say, I'm scared to ask." He wipes his hands on his lap. "Coming from a girl who hated him. But I'll take anything at this point. The trouble with asking people who liked him is that I don't want to make them sad."

He's so hopeful.

I can't kill Levi's Adam.

"I wanted to give you this back." I unzip my backpack, pull out his sweatshirt and baseball cap. I'm not prepared for how much his face lights up.

"That's where it went! I thought I lost it! The baseball cap, I mean, not the sweatshirt, I don't care about that. I forgot I left it in the pocket." He takes it, runs his thumb over the brim like how I touch Grace's old stuffed animals. "Adam gave it to me last time I came here. I think he was weirded out by me. One time I went with him to his friend's birthday party and he wouldn't tell anyone we were related. My mom and Mr. Gordon never married, it was the first time I stayed with them."

He looks down at the baseball cap again. "But this one time, Mr. Gordon—uh, my dad—was drunk, yelling at nothing, scaring the crap out of me. Adam took me down to the quarry until I stopped crying. It's cool, an older sibling, like someone's assigned to you. It's nice. How old's your sister?"

"We're twins," I whisper.

"Oh, cool." He shifts. "Well, I think I hit my daily quota of embarrassing stuff to say to cute girls I barely know. I left out wetting the bed at summer camp and everyone calling me Pee-vi. We'll save that for our next date. Oops. I just told you. Spoilers."

He's weird and nice and quick and he's trying to put me at ease. He should be talking to somebody else.

"I should probably ask why you hated him," he says. "But I'm not sure if I want to know."

"We just . . . didn't get along," I rasp.

"That's not so bad, then. Although I don't get it. You're pretty cool."

He looks shyly down at the table.

"Can I have your number?" he adds. "The homework for American History, I'll text the answers to you. That way you won't have to copy before class."

Right. That's all it is. I write my number on a napkin, slide it to him. He puts it in his bag along with his baseball cap.

"By the way." He fiddles with the backpack zipper. "I don't think you're a mess. You do good things for other people."

"Don't think that about me." I let it slip out.

"Why not?"

"It's not true." My face burns.

"When I think good things about other people, I try to say them out loud. People never know how liked they are, you know?"

"You don't worry about sounding weird?"

"I operate under the assumption that I always sound weird. It's the only way I ever have the courage to say anything."

"What if it's something you can't fuck up, though?" I insist. "Something you have to say right."

"I don't think there's a right way to say anything. If you know that, it takes the pressure off."

He's wrong. I just haven't found the right words for Grace. I'm not smart enough.

"Man," he says.

"What?"

"Talking with you is like . . . confusing. I always feel like you're asking me about something specific but you're not telling me what."

"*Always*," I repeat. "We haven't talked all that much."

"True. This is a personal failing of mine."

"There are lots of people at Stanwick for you to talk to."

"There are," he says. "None of them are you."

I'm sitting here doing this despite the blackmail. But he's a force field that pushes all those things into the background. Right now, they seem unreal.

"Sorry. That was such a bad line. I do the ironic flirt thing. It's annoying," he says. I realize how many times he's told me he's annoying. "It's just that I don't have anybody here. It's hard to make friends when everyone's sad. You're the closest one I've got and I'm trying to impress you by saying funny things and then weird semi-advice things and also creepy compliments and none of them are working very well."

He talks so much. "You want to be my friend?"

"It's very first grade. Will you be my friend, let's do

finger paints, et cetera."

"Just don't hit on me. That's never ever going to work." I swallow. "Not with you or anybody else. Not for me."

"You are mysterious as hell," he says. "And that's not the only reason to talk to a girl."

"I can be your stand-in friend," I mumble. "Convenience friend. Until you meet someone better."

"I hate that thing you just said," he says softly.

I used to be so easy. Everything I said was easy. "Apparently I will also be your issues friend."

"Everyone's got issues."

"Not my issues." It's an obnoxious thing to say. But normal people have normal issues. Normal people worry about sounding weird or that they're annoying. If I start to think for real about my issues, I can't breathe and then I have to stay up another night until my head's too foggy to think, or drink until the world blurs.

"It's okay, you know?" he says. "It's okay."

But I'm not distracted anymore. The blackmailer feels real again. I have to check the baby monitor and see if there are any new notes and . . . *Breathe.* "I have to go."

"Gotcha. I'll just sit here and wince thinking about all the annoying shit I just said."

"You're not annoying," I tell him, and leave before he can smile at me again.

TEN

July 20

Grace

I NEVER REALIZED CASSIUS LIVED SO CLOSE. It only takes me a few minutes to walk to his house. It's an unassuming blue one, tucked behind the hedge that the old neighbors used to trim early on Monday mornings, waking up the whole neighborhood. The new mailbox is brilliantly painted. Clouds and winding vines and birds of every hue. I never noticed before.

Joy doesn't know I'm here. Today I'm taking a path she didn't forge for me.

I'm on the porch, about to knock, when Cassius opens the front door.

"You were watching from the window?" I ask.

"Nah." There's a dab of paint in the middle of a moon-shaped patch of lighter skin on his forehead. "I just felt you here."

He leads me inside. It's clean, but not spotless like our house. Not a neurotic clean. Taylor Swift blasts from upstairs.

"My sister," he explains. "I work downstairs."

There's no car in the driveway. I'm at a boy's house with no parents around. A trial run for when I go to Adam's.

The basement isn't like any other basement in the world. The walls are covered with paper, big thick endless sheets from the rolls you can buy at craft stores, and they're full of sky. People and animals move from cloud to cloud.

And all the people are naked.

"I like painting the human figure," Cassius says openly, no creepiness to it, as he ties a paint-splattered apron around his waist and sets up an easel. "Not for school paintings. Adam would give me too much crap. But for paintings nobody sees. No one else comes down here."

Just me.

I step closer to the wall. The bodies aren't like any naked bodies I've seen before. A lot of them are fat, but it's not an ugly fat, exaggerated for a joke. They're grace-ful. Comfortable.

Did Cassius want to paint me naked?

"I don't think I can—" I burst out at the same second he goes, "You'll keep your clothes on, obviously—"

We both stare at each other and giggle.

"How do you want me to be?" I ask.

"Yourself."

I sit on the ratty tan couch, being myself.

"Hmm." He traces a line on his blank paper with the

wrong end of his brush. "The way you sit, you ball up . . . People are easier to paint when they're looser. Broad strokes, not all congested like a highway. I'm not that good yet."

I stretch the nerves out of my legs. How would Joy sit? I sling my arm over the back of the couch, kick up one leg.

"You're good at art," I say to distract him from how ridiculous I look.

"I'm not that good yet. But I will be."

I'm not that brave yet. But I will be.

He outlines the pattern of me over his paper once more before he starts his pencil sketch. The silence grows between us, but it doesn't fill with bad things. I can look at him when he's looking at the paper. I can see why Joy thinks he's so beautiful. He's a good combination of hard and soft: the clean edge of his jaw, his warm eyes, his gentle mouth. It's too bad he can't model for himself.

Joy would be so jealous. My stomach twists.

"Joy likes art," I blurt. "When our family took a trip to D.C., it took her like three hours to leave the art museum."

That was because she got lost and we had to look for her, but I don't say that.

"That's nice." He looks up. Catches me staring. Cringe.

"She's really great," I plow on. "You could paint her in loose swishy strokes, no problem. She's not congested."

"It's just hard with the clothes bunched up," he says, concentrating.

I try to smooth out the hem of my shirt.

"Oh, shoot." He sits back. "Now the lines are all new."

"Sorry!" I whip my hand away. "I knew I'd screw you up."

"I'll start over. It usually takes a couple tries. I always make mistakes the first time."

A couple tries. But I only get one shot with Adam. What if I want to take my clothes off in front of him? I don't want to make mistakes.

I don't want to hate my body forever.

A ridiculous thought: Could I take off my clothes in front of Cassius?

A trial run. No romance, no expectation. Even Joy couldn't do that.

Maybe I don't have to just be as brave as her. Maybe I could be braver.

"Cassius?" I say. Ridiculous. Ridiculous.

"Hm?"

A normal girl wouldn't do it.

But an interesting girl would.

"Do you think I could . . . I think I could try the nude modeling thing, if you want."

He puts down his pencil. He probably thinks I'm an exhibitionist.

"I mean, it's okay if you don't want to, that's under-standable, I'm not some beautiful model—" I stammer.

"Grace." His face shines. "If you'd be comfortable with that, I would love to paint you that way."

Is this actually going to happen?

"I don't mean to sound like a creep. I just suck so much at clothes." He scratches his cheek with the other end of his paintbrush, embarrassed. "Nudity is not that big of a deal to me . . . it's how we were born. Everyone is naked all the time under their clothes. Plus, people look softer that way. It's harder to be intimidated by them."

This is the girl I'll be: a girl who gets drunk, gets high, models nude, dates musicians.

"Can you maybe turn around while I take them off?" I whisper.

"Are you sure you're okay with this?"

"Yeah . . ."

"You positive?"

"Yes. I want to do this."

He covers his eyes and turns around, bumping into his easel.

Clothes are strange. They're flimsy, but they shield you from so much. I'm wearing a yellow T-shirt with a faded rose print. I've taken it off in my room so many times. Just shucked it over my shoulders. I try to mimic that motion now. It's difficult in a different way.

My bra is an ugly white. There's a tiny ingrown hair next to my belly button. Gross.

"Let me know when you're ready," Cassius says gently.

You have to do things that scare you to become someone new. Someone capable of doing those things.

I reach behind me, unhook my bra, and unzip my shorts before I can change my mind, balling them up so he can't see how big they are. I lie on my back. People look best on their backs. I cross my legs. Suck in my stomach. Fold an arm over my breasts. Make sure everything is smoothed out and arranged.

Will I be able to do this with Adam? Keep track of how he's seeing me, every angle?

"Ready," I croak.

Cassius turns around. I can't look at him. I look at the ceiling instead. He probably sees the ripples my heart-beat makes on my skin. How all my blood is trying to escape.

I wait for him to give me a rating. Good or bad. Acceptable or not. But he doesn't. I hear the scrape of him pulling a stool to his easel, sitting down, and then the scratching of pencil on canvas.

I'm doing this!

I work on relaxing my muscles, one by one, as he paints. Arms. Shoulders. After a while, my stomach aches from how hard I'm sucking it in. I let it go, a bit at a time. Does he notice? He's completely focused. I think I trust him not to notice more than I want him to.

"Have you ever done this yourself?" I say, tiny.

"Done what?" He's barely here. He's not judging my body, he's just taking it in. I relax a little more.

"Modeled, like . . . nude."

"My skin's too hard to draw," he mumbles. "I don't want people making me into some dalmatian."

I'm not sure if I'm supposed to giggle or not. I do. It doesn't feel wrong. He smiles. None of this feels wrong.

This would be a romance cliché. The artist and the

model. But I'm not in love with the artist, I'm in love with the musician.

"Have you ever been in love before?" I ask. I'm naked. It's not like things could get any weirder between us.

Cassius misses a stroke, frowns at his mistake. When he's spacing out he's so relaxed, but startle him and he tucks himself in right away.

"You ask a lot more questions without clothes on," he points out.

I'm bolder without clothes on. This is the new Grace Morris. A girl with no shell.

"Who do you think is hotter, me or Joy?" It slips out. I should take it back. I don't, even though I know the answer. We're twins, but there's too much of me. Girls are supposed to be sleek like glass slippers.

"I don't get questions like that," he says, after a long time. "To me, bodies are . . . I guess when you're an artist, and you have to break things down into shapes, see how they fit together, how harmonious and functional it all is . . . all bodies are beautiful. Not in . . . a sexual way. They just work."

He's trying to say nicely that I'm not hot.

"People talk about themselves and their bodies like they're separate," he keeps going. "But people are their bodies just like they are their brains. I can't think someone is a beautiful person without thinking their body is beautiful."

His dreamy tone slips and so does his gaze, to the

bottom of the paper. "I think you're beautiful, Grace."

I feel like he's holding me, but he's not touching me. I'm definitely not ready for someone to actually touch me naked.

"It's hard to like yourself," he murmurs.

I take a deep breath. "I never liked myself before, but I think you just have to make yourself into something you can like."

He paints for another few minutes. Talking to Cassius means giving him time to think.

"What if you're not sure who you want to be?" he says finally.

"Then think of a person you like." I brush my thumb against the mole on my thigh. Joy has one in the exact same place. "And become like them."

ELEVEN

October 19

Joy

YOU DON'T REALIZE HOW MANY HOURS there are in a week until you watch them pass on a baby monitor. I don't know what I'm expecting. A figure watching me, maybe, some horror-movie jump scare. Somehow the motionless grainy footage of my own locked bedroom window is worse.

No more notes have come. But if the blackmailer was finished with me, why would he have sent that last response? Just to keep me afraid? What's he waiting for?

Sometimes I wish he'd attack me in school, on my way home after school, anywhere. Then I'd have something to fight.

"If he wants to frame me for Adam's murder, he should just do it," I bite out into the phone with Preston one night.

"You're still not going to the cops, right?" Preston says.

"I'm not going to the cops."

"Good. Because if we go to the cops, and the black-mailer tells the cops you killed Adam, and they find out about the photos of Eastman, it looks really suspicious that you went ahead and did what the note said."

Sometimes I just feel like laughing.

School returns to normality as the days pass. Nobody else dies, nobody else is arrested. Ben's mom comes in with my mom and some other parents, hands out a petition for the town to pay for the quarry to be fenced off. Levi keeps helping me cheat in American History and my grade hits a C+. Cassius skips two days and when he comes back, everyone avoids him. He's made himself so small it's like he's trying to avoid himself.

Saturday morning, I weigh myself on Grace's scale and the new number alarms me. I'm forcing down half a piece of toast when a chain saw starts whirring outside. I jump up, run to the window. Dad's in goggles and he's all hooked up to the tree outside my room, cutting through the branch.

"Did you tell Dad it was rotten?" I ask Mom when she comes out of the bathroom.

"It wasn't. We checked." She knots her bathrobe around her waist, pours a cup of coffee. "But we have cottoned on to your escape route."

As long as it's gone. "Okay."

"It's dangerous. You could hurt yourself."

"Right."

"You need to eat more than that." She gestures at my mostly full plate, then looks at me. "You lost weight. You're starting to look sick."

I ignore her and get through one piece of bacon before my phone buzzes. It's probably Preston needing to analyze the notes more, talk about the blackmailer endlessly, cycle through it again and again so he doesn't have to face the fact that maybe there's nothing we can do about this, maybe it's just something that's happening to me. I push my plate back. The bacon wants out of my stomach, in there with the fear. The worst part about all this is finding out what I'm capable of getting used to.

But when I look at my phone, it's not Preston. It's Levi.

could you come to my house? really need help with something. sorry i didn't know who else to ask.

The Gordon house. Adam Gordon's house. The absolute last place I want to go.

"Who's that?" asks Mom.

Nobody, nobody. I'm not going. But if Levi's having a crisis . . .

"Could you give me a ride to the Gordon house?" I blurt. *If I'm not home, the blackmailer can't find me.*

She frowns. "You're grounded."

"Levi—that guy we gave a ride home from the funeral, remember—he's tutoring me in American History. There's a test on Monday, he says we should review."

Mom bundles me into the car so fast that I don't have time to change my mind.

Halfway up the Gordons' driveway, Mom says, "This better not be just an excuse to hang out with a boy you have a crush on."

"If there's one boy I can promise you I will never have a crush on, it's him."

"Good. That's the right kind of boy to study with." She stops the car, lets me out. "Stay away from the quarry."

I walk up to the front door and just stand there, paralyzed. This house. This place. That dark wood, all those windows. Panels of shadowed glass on the door, a crack shaped like a vein running through one of them. It wasn't there the first night we came. Grace and I went through that doorway together, and maybe the ghosts of who we used to be are still in there.

That night, Grace greeted Adam brightly, all brandnew confidence, walking in ahead of me. I'd wondered if that was what it was like to be the one trailing behind. If the only way one of us could be big was if the other one was small.

I remember thinking, drunkenly, I should check on her and Adam.

And then thinking that I didn't want to, that she could take care of herself, this once.

I dig my nails into my palms, but pain doesn't work when you're numb. I shouldn't have come here. I turn, but Mom's gone. I could walk back along the road . . .

But Levi asked for my help and he doesn't have anyone else.

I climb the steps. It's just a doorknob. How many doorknobs have I touched in my life? My reflection stares back at me, distorted.

"Joy, are you up front?" Levi's voice floats over. I grab it, breathe through it like a gas mask. "I'm down by the back porch."

I circle the house too fast, edging the slash of a shadow it throws on the ground. The porch is built into the hill that goes down toward the trees, toward the quarry. Levi's halfway up the steps, knees grass-stained, trying to haul a dead-drunk Mr. Gordon up the rest of the way.

"Thank you," he pants when he sees me.

"I haven't done anything yet."

"You came."

Mr. Gordon's evil-smelling, barely conscious. His sweatpants look like they haven't been changed in a week. We hoist him up the steps like we did at the funeral. I've got his feet. One's shoeless and rank. The shoe is on the lawn. I wonder if my shoes are still somewhere in the middle-school field, mangled by the lawn mower.

Levi wrangles open the door with his elbow. I suck in the alcohol fumes, focus on them, blot out the fact that I'm inside, *inside*, the house. It's ugly dark, the shades drawn.

I can't break. I'm carrying a man up a staircase.

If I thought being in this house would jog my memory,

I was wrong. The only memories it's bringing up are—
Don't think about it.

I'm getting good at not thinking. The key's not giving your brain any fuel or rest, and drowning it in alcohol the rest of the time. Mr. Gordon and I know that.

Adam's bedroom door—*breathe*—is blocked by a bedside table, several boxes. Was it Levi or Mr. Gordon who did that? Are they trying to keep something in or out?

We move a few more steps down the hall to the end. Mr. Gordon's room was designed to let in as much light as possible, a window covering nearly half the left wall, but it's blocked by a heavy curtain. "On three," Levi grunts. We swing Mr. Gordon onto the four-poster bed. He rolls over and starts snoring instantly, a rattily choking sound.

I am so terrifyingly dizzy for a second. *Don't pass out, don't do that to Levi, don't give him another body to deal with.*

I take a deep breath, let it out slowly. Okay. I'm okay.

Levi stares at his dad's motionless figure. Something builds in him until finally he rips a throw pillow off the edge of the bed and buries his face in it. I want to say something, but the words, the perfect words, they don't come. The fog in my head doesn't help. But he drops the pillow after a few seconds, and his expression is clean and normal.

"Screw my lack of musical talent, I'm going to write a one-hit wonder, too, and make a million dollars so I can pay you a million dollars for helping me drag my dad around," he says.

149

"I don't mind," I say. "Sometimes I lift my dad's weights."

"And sometimes you lift my dad." Levi arranges the blankets, sets out a glass of water, throws the curtain open. "Whenever you need a workout, just come over here. Dad lifting. It'll be an Olympic event."

Don't joke back. It's his tragedy to make light of, not mine.

"Sorry. You know when stuff's so real it stops feeling real? And then it gets funny?" He turns and smiles anxiously. "It was like, I got him all the way back up from the quarry and then I couldn't do the stairs and I sat down and freaked out. And I had your number."

"Should we maybe tell somebody about . . . him? This?" I say over the snoring.

"There's nobody. Adam's mom lives in Europe. He was an only child. No real extended family—just Adam. And my mom's family hates him."

We watch the rise and fall of Mr. Gordon's chest. I think we're both kind of expecting it to stop.

"I need to get out of the house," Levi says suddenly. "Sorry. I don't have my license, and Mr. Go— Dad's house is all the way up here, and you're still the only person I really know here. Sorry."

I forgot how big of a difference there is between school friends and friends you actually hang out with. "My mom gave me a ride here, but we can go for a walk."

"Down to the quarry?"

It's just an old quarry, it's not haunted, it's fine. I nod.

Downstairs, the portraits of Adam's grandpa, the framed signatures and album covers and memorabilia—they're all gone, nail holes and dustless patches left on the wall. A million empty pizza boxes are stacked in one corner, next to mountains of half-crushed beer cans.

"I didn't know where the recycling was." Levi waves hopelessly at the mess. "Nobody ever cleaned up after the birthday party."

He was here alone, piling up pizza boxes and trash with his dad passed out upstairs.

"Were you the one who cleared off the walls?" I ask.

"Yeah. The first night I was here, Dad—I'm sorry, I can't—Mr. Gordon kept apologizing to the portraits of his father. Said he was sorry he let his family die out. It was all very, *I have disappointed my ancestors.*"

Jesus. "You're still here, though."

He stops in the dining room. "The last time I saw Mr. Gordon, when I was a kid, he stuck Adam's guitar in my hands and put on a karaoke version of my grandfather's album. The minute I opened my mouth to sing, any interest he might've had in me fell off his face."

"Doesn't he like having you here, since he hasn't seen you in so long?"

"Most of the time I don't think he realizes I'm here. Pretty sure he thinks I'm some kind of hired help."

"That's awful," I stammer.

He pushes open the door, steps into the light. "It's okay. I'm dumping this on you."

"It's not okay. I'm really bad at . . . saying the right thing."

There's a burned-out circle of old firewood on the lawn. I remember there was a fire the night of Adam's birthday party. Kennedy and Sarah danced next to it. Blurry memories. Dreams maybe. I don't know.

I follow Levi down the hill, away from the house, into the trees. One step. Two steps. Walking isn't hard. Moving forward isn't hard. More memories: sticks snapping, branches cutting me. Did I go into the woods the night of his birthday party, or am I thinking of the night in July I got drunk for the first time with Grace?

"So, okay. I'm about to be Advice Levi, and I'm sorry, he's annoying." Levi picks past a cluster of bushes like the ones I peed behind while Grace stood watch. "When it comes to other people's problems, the only thing you can do is listen and be nice. Whatever advice you have, that's secondary. You can't fix anything, but being nice counts for more than people think."

"Advice Levi's not so bad," I tell him.

We step out of the trees. I haven't been to the quarry in daylight since I was young. The rock drops off sharply, the edge sanded down by years of wind and rain. It's so big. A chasm. The bottom is rough with loose boulders. It looks like a giant dragged a mace through the earth.

Levi walks to the edge and the wind lifts, like it's trying to push him over, like when Grace almost fell.

"Levi. Don't get any closer."

"No worries."

He didn't gel his hair today. The breeze swooshes it along his forehead. I stand beside him and we both look down at the same time. The craggy bottom's maybe a forty-foot drop. One of the rocks is stained rust brown. If I was responsible for that stain, there's no way I wouldn't remember, no matter how drunk I was.

Vicious things are in my head. I hope Grace's face was the last thing he thought of. I hope it hurt.

"He died there," Levi says, pointing. "Right there."

It's so weird, how differently two people can feel about the exact same thing.

"Can I tell you a stupid story?" he asks.

"Yeah." *Talk so I don't have to hear myself think.*

"The first night after the funeral, I couldn't sleep. I had this feeling like Adam was down here and wanted to tell me something." He twists his earring. "I was hoping he'd tell me at the funeral, but he looked so fake, all made up. You were the only real thing there."

"Is that a compliment?" It feels like one.

"I guess it is."

"Okay. Sorry. Keep going."

"So I got up and I came down here in the dark. But I didn't feel him here. Dunno why I thought I would."

That's because he's not haunting the quarry. He's haunting Grace's dreams and I haven't been doing anything about it. You can't kill a ghost.

"The quarry itself, though," he says. "That gave me a weird feeling."

"It's a thing about heights," I venture. "One time when we were kids, my sister and I hiked this mountain with our parents. We had this dare to see how close we could get to the edge. It was the only time she was braver than me about something."

"It's like an impulse," he agrees. "Like . . . a suicidal impulse."

"She's not *suicidal*. Jesus."

"I didn't say she was."

I catch my breath. My head pounds. "Sorry."

"No, I'm sorry. That was dark. I was, like, hmm, how could I make my relationship with this girl weirder? I know! Bring up the universal self-destructive impulses of humanity. Brilliant."

I'm so tired. I remember how Grace almost plunged into the darkness, how the fear skinned the roof of my mouth. "At night it looks so much worse. You can't see the bottom."

He shrugs. "There's nothing scarier than what you can't see."

We're silent for a few minutes while the breeze throws itself over the edge. I kick a pebble, then another. The clatter's so faint.

"I don't like living here," he says quietly.

"Stay after school," I say. "Or hang out with Pres and me. We waste tons of time at his house."

"You are the nicest person in the world," he remarks, echoing what he said when we first met.

I wince. "You can only hang out with us if you don't call me that."

"You are the meanest girl in the world. The worst."

"Levi, if you hate it here, can't you go back to your mom's?"

"Nuh-huh." The silence draws itself out. "Not yet," he adds unhelpfully. "Besides, I can't leave before I've gotten to reap the full benefits of posing as the half brother of the deceased. I can wring at least two more casseroles out of this."

"You're not posing."

He snorts. "I didn't even know Adam. I suck for showing up and acting like my sadness is special because of genetics. I don't have a right to that."

"You don't need a *right* to sadness," I tell him. "Sadness just happens."

"I never nailed down the trick of sadness. I'm the positive guy, you know? You can't help people when you're bummed out. People like Advice Levi best."

"What other Levis are there?"

"I dunno. Bad Jokes Levi. Idealizes People Levi. Fucks Up Badly When Talking to Pretty Girls Levi."

"That must be hard to write on name tags."

"Bad Jokes Joy. Nice to meet you."

I'm going to laugh and it reminds me of how much I shouldn't be here.

"What other Joys are there?" he asks.

"There used to be only one Joy." I look at the ground.

"Now I don't know what Joys there are."

"Which Joy was that?"

"Protects Sister Joy," I whisper like an idiot.

"She sounds cool. I look forward to meeting her."

"She's not around anymore."

"Something happen with you and your sister?"

I bite the inside of my cheek.

"I bet there's more to you than your sister," he says.

"It's like . . ." My head is fuzzy. "You know how you think there's one thing you're good at? Even if the rest of you sucks, it's okay, because you're good at that one thing? Until realize you aren't. You never were. And there's nothing left anymore to balance out all the bad stuff you do. There's no point to you."

"Whoa." Levi looks straight at me. "There's a point to you."

"I don't know what it is anymore." Stop *talking*.

"Man," he says. "Why does there need to be a point to anybody? People aren't parts in a robot with little functions or whatever. You're alive—who said that was contingent on being good at some big thing? Or maybe there's a lot of little reasons for you being around, like you helping me with my dad, and like watering your houseplants."

I scrape my hand across my eyes. "Advice Levi wasn't gone for long."

"That wasn't Advice Levi, that was Ramble Levi. Normally I only bring him out for final papers."

"He says some cool stuff, I guess."

"I just consulted him and he says he wants to hang out with you more. Also, he thinks you're cute."

I blanch. "I said no flirting."

"Sorry. I say this shit and I immediately get deeply embarrassed. Self-Loathing Levi is like, 'sup."

"Bad Jokes Joy thinks you're cute, too," I say accidentally. "She's the only one, though."

He grins so big. "I don't believe you. I'll have to ask the other ones myself."

I know who the other Joys are, and they're not good. But he doesn't see them.

"So, in the spirit of that," he says, "do you want to go to the movies with me sometime this week?"

I freeze.

Grace wouldn't be pissed if she knew how un-Adam he is. She probably doesn't even know Adam had a half brother who goes to our school now. And I need to keep out of the house, so the blackmailer doesn't—

I jolt. It's the first time I've thought about the blackmailer since I've been with him.

He's still waiting for my answer.

It's selfish and wrong and fucked-up, but those are the other Joys. So I say yes.

Later that night, after Mom picks me up, I sit at the dining room table with her and Dad, the three of us eating carrots and chicken and mashed potatoes like nice normal people. I mash my carrots around in one of the heavy clay bowls that Grace and I made at arts and crafts camp one summer, years ago.

"Pass the carrots, Joy," says Dad.

I pass the carrots.

"Pass the salt, Joy."

I pass the salt. "Where's Grace?"

"She's hard at work on her independent project and couldn't come down to dinner," Mom says like it's something to be proud of, that she's not eating.

"What's she working on tonight?" I ask.

They look at each other and shrug. "Research on the computer," Mom says.

"I'm sure you know more than we do," Dad says. "You girls talk about everything."

One Christmas, when we were fourteen, Aunt Theresa told Mom: "Makes your job easier, having twins. My best friend has 'em. They practically raise each other."

"Joy?" Mom says.

I jump. "What do you want? The pepper?"

"I just want to say how proud I am that you got yourself an American History tutor. I'm glad you're getting back on track."

"We always thought it'd be wonderful if you and Grace attended the same college," Dad says. "You could room together."

And get jobs at the same company, and have a joint wedding, and give birth in the same month, and live next door, and never find out who we are without each other.

Except I'm already finding out who Joy Without Grace is. And she's not good.

"I'm finished."

If I eat too much, I regain the ability to think. I get up and go upstairs.

Every time I open my bedroom door, I half expect to have to fight a nightmare figure. But when I go in, the blackmailer isn't standing there. Grace is.

"Hi," she says nervously. "Sorry."

She buffers sentences with apologies. Like Levi.

"Don't be sorry." I close the door slowly behind me. I don't want her in here, when the blackmailer knows my address and there's a knife under my pillow and notes under my mattress, but at the same time I do want her in here.

"What's up? You okay? It's been, like, a thousand years since I've seen you," I say.

I've been avoiding her, unsure if I could hide the blackmail from her. But I think I can. I think I can hide more things from her than I ever knew I could.

"Of course I'm okay." She tucks a pale blond strand of hair back. "I have to talk to you."

I'm not going to screw this up. What was it Levi said about advice?

"I found this in your backpack." She takes out one of my empty minibottles.

"Why were you in my backpack?"

"I needed a pen." She sets the bottle on my desk, looks

at me all solemn. "You're drinking these at school."

"It's just to—" Stop thinking. "I needed—" Shit. "It was before he died."

"So why's it still in your backpack?"

"I never clean it out." I pause. "And don't you have pens in your room?"

"Joy."

"I can't believe you're mothering me," I burst out. "How are you the one mothering me?"

"You can't drink these at school. Or anywhere. You shouldn't."

Why can't she be the mess for once?

"Bad things happen when you drink, Joy," she says.

I go numb. She starts to hunt through my drawers, finds another bottle, pockets it. "Any more?"

"No," I lie.

"All right. We cleared that up." The awkwardness returns. "So, um. Where'd you go today?"

"Boy from class is tutoring me in American History," I say tiredly.

"A boy? I could've tutored you in American History." She tries to push her hair behind her ear again, forgetting she already did it. "What boy?"

"Just . . . some dude from class."

"And you're alone in his house."

"His . . . his dad's there. What's with this third-degree questioning?"

"American History's not that hard. You don't need a

tutor." She scowls. "Also, stop spending all your time at Preston's house. You're always there now. Is he your boy-friend?"

"No." I blink. "Pres isn't like other guys."

"Every guy is like other guys."

"Grace, you know you can talk to me, right?" I say in a rush. "Should I ask how you feel, like, about him dying—"

"I told you, I don't feel any way about it," she snaps.

"That can't be true."

"Why are you always trying to force things out of me?" She locks her hands together behind her back. "Just let me be okay."

"I know you're okay, I just wanted you to know that you can talk—"

"There's nothing to talk about! Do you want me to be messed up? So you don't feel like you're the only one?"

I wince.

"I'm sorry," she says, squeezing her eyes shut. "I shouldn't have said that."

"No," I say hopelessly. "You're right. That's exactly what I'm doing. Trying to get you to be the fucked-up one so I can be the one who's not. I'm garbage."

"No, no, Joy." She does a motion like she's gonna hug me, then lets her arms fall back. "You think you're capable of all these bad things, but you're not."

"You're not the one supposed to be comforting me."

She sighs, exasperated. "We can't both need comfort-ing."

"You're the one who has a right to. And I'm taking it away. I wish I was like you."

"Someone has to be me and someone has to be you," she says strangely. Then she shakes her head. "You're acting like it's my crisis and it's not. It's yours."

"Girls?"

We stiffen. Mom's knocking.

"I just checked the mailbox and there was a letter for you, Joy," she says excitedly through the door. "I think it's a college recruitment newsletter."

What would happen if Mom and Dad listened harder, walked in at the wrong moment, reached into the wrong pocket of my backpack? There's a whole world they miss by inches every day.

A thick manila envelope zooms under my door. Grace has been getting them for months. It's my first. They must collect student names by GPA.

"What are you talking about in here? Boys?" Mom only gets this girlish teasing voice when she finds Grace and me alone together. "Can I come in? I have a thing or two to say about boys."

"Homework," I manage.

"All righty then." She's not hurt. She's always assumed that our world was whole and safe and she didn't need to be a part of it. "Don't stay up too late."

Her footsteps disappear.

"College, huh," Grace mumbles.

Safe topic. "You still getting all those emails from Brown?"

"I don't think I'm going to go."

"To Brown?"

"To college."

I stop in the middle of opening my envelope. "Oh thank God, that's the first joke you've made in ages."

She shrugs. "Who's joking?"

"College has been your main hobby since we were, like, five." When I was thirteen, I had posters of boy bands. She had posters of Dartmouth.

"What's in college? Guys? Parties? I don't care about that stuff. I can learn on my own. I'm proving that now. And no college is going to want someone who took her junior year off."

A new panic rises in me. "You can go back to school next semester."

"There are still guys there. And all guys are like him."

"No, Grace. You can't throw away college—"

"You never cared about college, either."

"So what? That's me!"

"And it's fine if you don't have a future as long as I have one?"

Yes.

"Maybe this is your turn to be the good-grades twin. Is that why you got a tutor?" She chuckles. "Maybe I'll turn my room into a mess so you'll clean yours for once."

"Nothing bothers you anymore," I say.

"You get bothered for me." She touches my nose, like I used to do to her when we were little. *When we were little.*

I never knew a phrase could make me long for something so much.

"I was just worried about you drinking in school," she says by the door, like the rest of our conversation didn't happen. "Don't do it again."

And then she leaves.

I cry for a few minutes, mostly to get it out of the way. I used to cry loud, so Grace would come. Now I don't want her to know I'm still stealing the sadness that should belong to her. I'm sucking the heart out of her and I don't know how to stop.

I go to throw away the stupid college envelope, but then I notice there's no return address. What college is it even from? Mom probably glanced at it, saw it was for me, and hoped. I dump the contents onto my desk.

A DVD, and a note.

Joy Morris—

I slam my hands over the note, covering the words. I need to focus on my sister, I can't do this, I can't—

I tear through the bottom drawer of my desk, find a full minibottle of Schnapps. I'm sorry, Grace. Levi's dad flashes into my head, but I force him out and I down the bottle, swallow, swallow, good.

Then I call Preston.

"I can't do this anymore."

"What's wrong? Did you get another note?"

"I give up." My voice is strangled, wet. "I'm making

things worse for you and Grace and I need to take myself away so you guys are safe from me, but I'm too scared to be alone. It's the worst thing to hate how you are but not know how to *change*."

"Joy—"

"I deserve all this, you know? I deserve all of this."

"Shut up."

I shut up because I don't think he's ever said that to someone before in his life.

"Shut up and stop being a jerk to yourself," he says, all wavery. "I'm standing up for you."

"I'm not a bully."

"Right now you are." He breathes out. "Read me what the note says, and I will help you figure it out."

"I don't want anyone to have to help me anymore—"

"Too bad! That's life. People help people. Now tell me what it says."

Grace doesn't need help.

But instead of saying that, I smooth out the note, blink until my eyes are clear, and start to read.

TWELVE

July 29

Grace

THE RAZOR CLATTERS TO THE BATHROOM
floor. Blood wells on Joy's knee. She groans, balanced on
the edge of the tub. "I never shave my knees. But apparently you have to be all slippery smooth like a dolphin
if there's even a chance of a chance that a boy might see
you naked."

There's less of a chance than that. But Joy and I have
spent the last two hours in the bathroom anyway, prepar-
ing to go to Adam's house. I feel sanded down, purified. We
change into the outfits we bought for this night: Leggings
and a loose, sheer shirt for me. A summer dress for Joy.

In her room, she throws herself on her bed, opens her
laptop. "I was doing research. Listen to this. 'Here's how

to ask for what you want in bed without bruising his ego . . . or anything else.' That's ominous."

I crowd in beside her. "'Top ten shortcuts to orgasm.' Like keyboard shortcuts?"

"Command D."

And then we're both snorting. She collapses against her pillow, chest bouncing. I collapse with her. We're sisters again. Better: friends.

"We're not really going to have sex," she admits.

"Obviously." But I have this tiny thought: What if I do and she doesn't? What if I finally pull ahead of her? I haven't told her about the nude modeling.

If I can tap my heel against her bed thirteen times before she gets up, it's my turn to lead her by the hand to wilder places.

She stares up at the smiley-face stickers she plastered all over her ceiling in third grade. It would never occur to her to scrape them off. "I've talked to Cassius, like, a grand total of never."

He hasn't shown me the painting yet—he says it's not done. I'll tell her when it's done.

"I look at Cassius, and he's wearing clothes, and then in my head, he stops wearing clothes. I thought it was a guy thing, thinking about naked people all the time." She presses her palms to her eyelids, messing up the mascara I did for her.

"I mostly just think about me and Adam . . . talking." I sink into the mattress.

She toys with her hair for a silent minute. "Are you in love with him?"

"No!" And yet. "I just . . . I want to, like, ask him if . . . It's hard to explain."

If I could take a damaged person and love him better, wouldn't that fix me, too?

"Is it bad to want to have sex with someone and not be in love with him?" Joy asks the ceiling after a minute.

"It's just sex." It's so easy to sound like I know what I'm talking about.

"Are you too young for this?"

"For what?"

"I don't know. This. Alcohol. Boys. The sentence 'It's just sex.'"

"Joy. We're the same age."

"I'm eighteen minutes older," she says, but she's younger than me. She always has been. Just like she's taller than me, even though we're the same height.

"Nothing's really going to happen," I tell her. Am I lying? I can make things happen, I've discovered. I could make this happen. A boy has already seen me naked. Now I could try it with the right boy.

Her breathing quiets. "I'm glad we're talking like this again. Like we used to."

My heart melts. "I'm sorry I've been so busy with school."

"I'm sorry I've been with Nov so much. You should hang out with her alone sometime. You need more friends beside me. So you don't get lonely."

In grocery stores, in the doctor's office, everyone used to say to us when we were kids: "Well, they'll never be lonely!"

But maybe being lonely just means that you get to fall in love with other lonely people.

Joy's watching me. I smile. "How could I be lonely when I have you?"

"I know I'm not always a good listener. And I do things without thinking."

"I'm not always a good talker," I reassure her. "And it's because of you that Adam paid any attention to me. So don't feel bad."

She grins proudly. Then it falters. "You're sure Cassius is going to be there tonight?"

"Pretty sure. Cassius is always there. They're best friends."

"Do you know how many people are going?"

"No. But I mean, even if it's not that many, he said he was having a big party for his birthday after school starts. I'm going. You can come."

There's such a difference between *We should go* and *I'm going, you can come.*

"Sounds like Adam Gordon wants you at all his events." She leaps up. Punches the air a few times. "Let's take you to the lovebird."

I stand up. She opens the window. Glances at me uncertainly. I haven't touched that tree since I fell when I was little. She climbs out first, her dress bunched high on her hips. Then she's sitting on the branch, twigs in her hair.

She's still a kid, gangly. In my makeup. Sometimes I forget we are the same age.

"I'll catch you if you fall," she says uncertainly.

I edge out onto the tree, bark scraping my arms. My heart shivers in my throat. All the nothingness beneath me. She reaches for me, but I don't take her hand. I don't need her. I'm going to stop myself from falling on my own.

Adam's house is a shrine to his grandfather.

Memorabilia everywhere. Vintage guitars. Empty liquor bottles, too, half hidden in cabinets. A classic rock museum turned midlife crisis hovel. Not a single photo of Adam. It's cold, too big, empty, even with the clutter. I don't like to think of him growing up here.

He hugs me at the door. "Grace!" Barely acknowledges Joy. She shifts. She's not used to disappearing. It's my turn to have solid outlines.

"We left our bikes on the lawn," I say.

"Ben'll give you a ride home later." The word *later* has a special tilt to it that I don't understand.

We walk down to the basement. There's a foosball table, old Godzilla movie posters, an abused leather couch. Cassius is on the floor with his knees to his broad chest, intently watching an animal documentary that no one else is paying attention to. The shapes on the skin of his neck disappear into his sweatshirt. Kennedy-Ben-Sarah are playing Cards Against Humanity. Two random seniors bend over a coffee table, rolling weed into cigarette paper.

Three others shout over a video game on a second TV.

Joy sticks close behind me. Hoping I'll keep her visible, maybe. She shrugs at me. I shrug back. I don't know what I was hoping for.

Adam mixes Coke and something else in a tall glass that says *Guinness*. He hands it to me. I hand it to Joy. He frowns and makes me a new one. I want to brush his hair out of his eyes.

Joy makes silly faces at me when he's not looking. We squish together on the carpet while the seniors ignore us. We're overdressed. Adam plucks softly at his guitar strings, in the middle of everything. We finish our drinks.

"I'm getting more, I don't care. I can't be sober right now," Joy whispers, like she's an expert at not being sober. She retrieves the bottle from beside the foosball table.

Cassius finally looks away from the nature documentary with a daydreamy smile. I swallow, but he's not looking at me in the way that boys look at you when they're picturing you naked.

"How long have you been here?" he says.

I shrug as Adam's guitar music floats between us. "A bit."

"I'm sorry." He waves at the TV. "Antelopes. Totally captivating."

I laugh. The alcohol starts taking hold. I reach up, catch his wrist. I have no idea why I do it. "This spot on the back of your hand, it looks like a flower."

"You think?" He examines the lighter skin.

"And this one here, it's a comet."

"I have another one like that on my leg, too," he murmurs. "I was born under a comet."

Kennedy-Ben-Sarah laugh hysterically, and Ben throws his cards at them. A couple hit my foot. I flick them across the floor. All our preparation for this seems so silly.

"Maybe that's why you look so special." I say.

"Why are you so nice to me?" he asks simply. No accusation. He's just curious.

Because I know how much it sucks to hate the way you look. Maybe that's how people become kind, by not wanting others to feel the things they felt.

"What's up, Cassius?" Joy's back, blasting through everything, handing me a big glass. It tastes like nail polish, maybe two drops of Coke.

"Not much." He shies back. She has no idea how to talk to people who need quiet voices.

"Mmm." She gulps, grimaces

This is terrible.

The two seniors with the weed disappear and never come back. The video game guys argue loudly over a controller. Ben rolls under the foosball table and falls asleep. Kennedy and Sarah are in a corner, tangled up in each other. Poking each other's stomachs. Laughing with their foreheads together. Cassius goes mute, the glow of the TV on his forehead. Taking himself someplace else. Adam plays his guitar and sings to himself, but every so often he glances at us to see if we're listening.

"When can we leeeave," Joy whines in my ear. "This is really boring."

We've only been here an hour and a half. "Ten minutes," I say. I want to listen to Adam sing. I drink all the nail polish. It's bad enough to distract me from how awkward this is.

And then.

Suddenly.

I am very.

Very.

Drunk.

"Joy?"

"Mmmyessss?" She drapes her arm around me. She drank hers, too.

"This is a shitty party," I whisper.

And suddenly both of us are laughing so hard we're not making a sound. Mouths open. Tears. Nothing has ever been this hilarious.

"I shaved my knees for this," she gasps.

Kennedy-Sarah have vanished. Ben is still passed out. Everyone else? When did they leave? Time's choppy, minutes disconnected from each other instead of moving along in a chain like normal. The ceiling spins. Cassius says something I don't catch. He sounds worried.

Suddenly: a man! In the basement. Wobbling. Wearing sweatpants. Shirtless. Do all middle-aged men look like that?

"Adam?" he says.

Joy and I are frozen. Shoulders pressed together. Will he call the cops? Do we run? I'm still giggling.

Adam throws down his guitar. Snarls, "What do you want?"

"You got my rum?" he slurs.

Adam shoves a mostly empty bottle toward him. "Jesus, Dad, get the fuck out."

His father sways. Looks at us. "Nice," he hiccups before stumbling upstairs.

Joy keels over with a noise like air escaping a tire. We're bent double. Dying.

Adam, glaring at us. Especially me. I stop laughing, which sucks because I notice how nauseous I am.

Then, Adam and Cassius: in the corner. Talking. Adam gestures at Joy. Cassius shakes his head. Then, then, then, both of them: taking shot after shot from a new bottle. Weird that they're best friends. They're so different. Do they tell each other their secrets? What are boy friend-ships like? Do I even know what girl friendships are like?

Joy's standing up. Swaying. "I have a speshul announcement to make. Speshul Joy announcement, everyone. Listen up. You!" She's pointing at Cassius, who puts his empty shot glass on the foosball table. He looks at the carpet. Joy doesn't lower her finger. "You. Are fucking. Attractive."

"There it is!" Adam hoots. "Yes! Cassius, my man." Cassius forces a smile, steals a glance at me. Holds it a little too long. Adam moves next to me. Tucking me under his arm, just like the night on the middle school field. My face hurts. I'm grinning too hard.

"You," he says in a low voice only I can hear, "are fuck-ing attractive."

"You," I whisper, terrified, "are fucking attractive."

"Is that a suggestion?" he says, confusingly. Then: two more glasses in his hands. Full. One for me.

Cassius hunches on the carpet near us. I want to break him open. Like I broke open. Show him it's possible to be more. It's so much better this way. Everyone's playing the game except him.

"Drink!" Joy shouts.

"My sister really likes you," I tell Cassius, the stupid words spilling out of me. "Give her a chance. She's really, really great. She's really, really, really great."

Things fade out. Back in.

I'm tired of being this drunk.

"Really, really, really, really great," Adam mimics.

The walls blur and Joy is whispering in Cassius's ear and his brows are knitting together, he's determinedly talking back, determinedly smiling back. Her hair's loose, a huge shape. Adam turns the TV off.

Joy's crawling over Cassius hungrily. He's taking off her shirt. Kissing her neck. She runs her hands all over his back. He's looking at me over her shoulder, his eyes a mixture of confusion, desire, and resentment. I don't know if those things are for her or me. For a second, I think he's going to call out to me, but then Joy swings in front of him, her hair a pendulum, and says something that dissolves into laughter. She's so happy. I want Cassius to make her happy. But not so happy she leaves me behind.

Adam's warm breath in my ear: "Let's give them some privacy."

I start to say "Joy—" but Adam guides me to the stairs. I can't do stairs, so he carries me up them.

His bedroom's full of musician stuff. Posters: Bob Dylan. Jim Morrison. Guitars, sound equipment. One window, facing away from the trees, away from the quarry.

He puts on some music.

Time rolls in and out, like the tide. I'm on his bed. His face is close. No one has ever been this close to me. His chin's stubbly. He didn't shave for tonight.

"Are you okay?" I say it so badly. I ruin it.

"Of course I'm okay." He's kissing me. It's wet, slimy, I can't catch up with what's happening. This is supposed to feel different. Anxiety crawls all over my body.

I push him away. "I just mean . . . you seem sad, some-times."

"I think about a lot of things." He trails his fingers down the side of my neck.

"You can talk to me about the things." My voice shiv-ers in the dark. "I think about things, too."

"You see, Grace? You understand me." He slides his hands under the hem of my shirt. No. He'll feel how fat I am. "That's why I like you. Because you're smart. Not like other girls. Not like your sister."

My shirt's off. I hold it to my body.

"Why not? You're so pretty."

"No." I can't arrange myself the way I did for Cassius. He's not giving me the chance.

"Yes. You are." He peels my shirt away. Peels my hands

away. "You're way hotter than your sister. You're so beautiful."

He says it like the end of a story. I want him to feel like he makes me feel beautiful.

"You inspire me. I'm going to write a song about you," he says. "Just relax. Your sister's relaxed."

I just have to enjoy it.

A normal girl would enjoy it.

"You said I was 'fucking attractive,' remember?"

I don't feel right. This is a mistake.

"I really need this, Grace. Come on. Just do what your sister's doing downstairs."

I'm not her. I'm me. I'm trapped in being me.

"You're not gonna get this chance again."

Come upstairs, Joy. Look at me, please, look over here. See me for once. You never see me. You never look past what's in front of you.

He turns up the music.

I don't want to be in this skin anymore, I don't want to be anywhere anymore. I am disappearing. Everything is slapping together in waves. I can't breathe. Where's my sister?

Him: holding me down.

He keeps talking, saying it: "This isn't so bad, is it? I knew you'd like it. I knew you needed this, too."

THIRTEEN

October 20

Joy

ALL I CAN DO IS SIT ON THE EDGE OF PRESTON's bed while he puts the DVD in his computer. My muscles feel atrophied, like I'll never be able to lift anything heavier than a paper clip.

"Did you watch it last night after we got off the phone?" he asks.

I shake my head. "My laptop doesn't have a DVD drive."

A grainy black-and-white video starts, text in the corner dating it years ago. It looks like it's from a security camera. At first, the street it shows is empty. Then a police car pulls a Toyota over to the curb. A man gets out.

"That's Officer Roseby," says Preston, startled.

A woman gets out of the Toyota. They argue briefly. I can't hear what they're saying.

Then Roseby slaps her to the ground, pulls her back to his car by her hair. He shoves her in the back and the video ends. My mouth goes dry.

"Jesus Christ." Pres leans away from the computer, as far back as he can. "How does he still have a job?"

I bend my pinkie the wrong direction until the pain clears my head. It's funny, all the little ways you can hurt yourself without anybody noticing.

"Maybe they just gave him a citation. I don't recognize the street. Maybe it was before he moved here." Preston's muttering to himself. "Or maybe nobody ever saw this. In which case, how'd the blackmailer get ahold of it?"

I move my numb tongue. "We don't know how he got the photos of Principal Eastman, either."

He flinches the way he always does when the photos come up. I overheard him in the hall today, asking if anyone knew how Savannah Somerset was doing. I think he does it for the same reason I bend my pinkie back and dig my thumbnail into my wrist.

"Let me see the note again," he says.

I pass it to him. I don't look at it. I read it last night over and over again. At this point I don't even understand it—it's all gibberish.

Joy Morris—

We've shown everyone the truth about one man at your school already. It's time to do it again.

This week, Officer Roseby will be giving a lecture in the auditorium at your school. Enclosed please find a DVD. Your job is to replace the DVD that he will be using in his presentation with this one.

If you don't do this, or if you tell anyone, I will go to the police and tell them that you killed Adam Gordon.

"It's definitely someone who goes to our school." Preston says. "Otherwise why would they know or care about the people who work there?"

"Maybe it's a staff member." I say it so he thinks I'm trying.

"That doesn't fit with everything else. It's got to be somebody who went to the party, somebody who doesn't like you and knew you hated Adam—remember how we figured all this out?"

I raise my shoulders and lower them.

"Joy?"

"I just keep thinking . . . What's the point? It's never going to be over." I wrap the tail of my backpack strap around my forefinger until it turns purple. "I keep thinking—everybody has secrets. And the blackmailer apparently knows all of them, and he's not going to stop until I make sure everybody else knows them, too."

"Maybe this is the last time," he says unconvincingly.

"How did this happen to me, Pres?"

"You're going through a lot of stress. But I'm here for you," he says like a therapist. He pops the DVD out. The video player window closes, and in the second before he shuts the screen, I notice the title of the article he had up. "How to Help a Friend Going Through a Difficult Time."

Oh, Preston.

I am going to pull myself together.

"This one won't be too hard," he says. "Remember when my mom gave that mental health presentation in the auditorium? She showed a video, too. They have the tech person set up the DVD player and the projector, then they store it in the downstairs supply closet near the auditorium. The presentations are always right after lunch, so they'll set up the stuff beforehand. We can swap the DVDs during lunch."

"I don't know . . ." Pulling. Myself. Together.

"I understand why you didn't want to put the photos up," he says. "But don't you think people deserve to know about this? He shouldn't be hanging around a school."

"Yeah, but . . ." I ball the note in my fist. "It's November's dad."

"Doesn't she hate him?"

"I don't want her to have to watch this."

He looks at me for a long minute. "You should tell her, Joy."

"I can't. I don't want her to think—to know—" I bite my lip. "I can't."

"You told *me* about it."

"Because you always like me, no matter what I do. I need Nov to think I'm . . ."

"If you don't do it, you're in danger," he says. "They could find you, hurt you. Or they could frame you. November would agree with me. Until we figure out who it is, we need to go along with this. If you won't tell her, we'll just find a way to keep her out of the auditorium."

"You're really good at handling all this, Pres."

"It's like, when you're panicking, I feel less scared. It's nice to be the one helping you for once." He fiddles with the hem of his shirt. "You still haven't told Grace what's going on either?"

"She doesn't need another reason to worry about me."

"You ever think maybe she worries about you anyway?"

"I don't know anything that goes on in her head anymore," I say.

Everything at school the next day is bright. Yellow light and noise and plastic food smells. I smile and nod when November stops me by my locker after first period and asks if I'm okay. I don't trust myself to open my mouth.

I don't go straight to the supply closet at lunch. There's somebody I have to find first. But he's not in the cafeteria or any of the upstairs classrooms. When I finally track Cassius down, he's alone in the art room, tearing down his paintings in jagged strokes. Tacks fly off the wall, pinging off the paint-stained sink. The paintings drift to the floor, edges ripped. I've only ever seen him touch things like they were made of feathers. The same way he touched me that night.

"Can we talk?" I say.

He freezes when he sees me. "Why?" His voice sounds so fragile. I can't believe I ever thought he was the blackmailer. "I mean, about what?"

Being near him used to be enough to make my heart pound. Now it makes my skin crawl. No wonder he acts so scared around me. I must make him feel the same way.

"I was hoping you could do me a favor." I try not to imply that he owes me one. "I need you to keep Nov out of the auditorium during her dad's presentation today."

He lets this thaw between us for a few minutes. "How come?"

I might as well tell him. He'll figure it out no matter what.

"I'm going to publicly shame Officer Roseby." It sounds almost badass. Maybe this will make up for everything between Cassius and me. "I have a video of him. Police brutality. I'm gonna show it to everyone. He deserves it, after how he's been treating you."

He stares at me. "Am I supposed to say thank you?" There's a little lightning in his dreamy voice. "Like you're saving me from him or something?"

"No! No, not like that."

He looks down again. I can't understand how I saw him as a sex object. He holds himself like Grace.

"I'm sorry about this summer," I explode. "I'm sorry I never called you afterward."

"I didn't call you, either," he says quickly. I hadn't even noticed.

"Right, but I was the one who climbed all over you, and kissed you first, and just generally instigated things, so it was my responsibility to call. And I probably justified it by being, like, well, the guy is supposed to call, but it was on me."

A fraction of the tension dribbles out of him. "It's okay."

"No, it sucked. I was using you, and that was gross." I twist my hands together. God, this is hard. "You didn't deserve that."

"It was a messed-up night," he says. "I think we were both kind of using each other."

Which hurts some past version of me that I guess I'm still carrying around, but I let it go. His eyes are on the door. We're not having the heart-to-heart I thought we'd have. What if all his avoidance is more than just awkwardness? What if he *is* scared of being near me? A possibility crashes into me.

"Cassius . . ." Real fear isn't hot or electric. It's deep, outer-space, never-ending cold. "That night . . . I didn't . . . You were okay with what was happening, right?"

His eyes widen. "That's not why it was a messed-up night. I definitely consented."

"Okay. Okay. Just making sure."

"Right." His gaze softens a bit. "Don't worry about that."

One of the paintings on the floor is of the quarry. There's a shadow splashed across the center of the page, a flare going up in the middle, a pillar of yellow.

"I'm leaving," he says suddenly.

"Oh. Bye . . ."

"No, I mean I'm leaving this school," he says. "Savannah and I, and Mom. We're moving back to the city with our aunt. Savannah doesn't want to come back here, and people think . . . people think some things about me now."

"They'll get over that," I say because I'm supposed to. It sounds weak.

He shakes his head. "Everyone here's already decided what they're going to see when they look at me. They decided it a long time ago, and they were just waiting for something they could call proof. Same for Savannah."

"Is she doing okay?" The question cracks between my teeth.

"She says Principal Eastman told her she was modeling for a private art project, that she inspired him. She'll be happy once she's somewhere nobody knows what happened."

I'm the reason everybody knows what happened.

"Anyway, sure, I'll keep November out of the auditorium today. She was there for me when no one else was." He turns like he's about to leave, then adds, stiffly: "How's *your* sister doing?"

"She's fine." My chest pops, but his face doesn't change. He doesn't know. He's just being polite.

He nods, and then he's gone, abandoning his paintings on the floor. We're never going to be friends, he and I. But that's okay. Maybe sometimes it's all right to let someone quietly out of your life.

The supply closet door is locked.

I twist the knob for a fourth time. There's no way I could swap out the DVDs after they roll the projector to the auditorium. But there's no way I'm getting through this door. Pres must not have known it'd be locked. I can't call him—he has a meeting with a teacher today that I told him not to skip. I slump against the door.

"Most people want to come out of the closet, not get into one."

Levi's walking toward me down the hall. He always finds me at these moments.

"Sorry," he says. "That was a terrible joke. Wow."

"It's almost like you make bad jokes when you're nervous or something," I say to distract him from my shaking hands.

"I was looking for you in the cafeteria. It's awful, looking for people in the cafeteria. It's like there's a timer winding down before everybody notices you have nobody to sit with." He's close now. Too close. He reaches past me, tries the door handle. "You need to get in here? I'm good at picking locks. My mom's always forgetting her keys inside the house."

"You'd pick a lock for me and not ask why?"

"If I ask, you might not tell me, and then you might not let me help. And I owe you for the other day." He leans into the door with his sharp shoulder. "Plus sometimes I just want to get into a place where I'm not supposed to be."

There's nobody else in the hall.

"If you think you can do it," I say.

"Easy." Levi pulls a pin from his pocket, inserts it into the keyhole. He crouches over a series of clicks, swearing under his breath.

I'm sweating. "Not easy."

"Still easy." He twists the pin.

"If you can't do it—"

"Let me impress you with my mad lock-picking skills, if not my jokes." He fights with the lock for a few more minutes until the knob twists, the door springing open. He grins and holds the door wide, bowing low. "After you, sweet madam."

"I've never been called sweet before," I say, stupidly relieved.

Then, behind us: footsteps, laugher. His grin vanishes. I seize his shoulders and steer him into the closet, shutting the door after us just as a few girls walk by. The closet's dark, too small for both of us. Our shoulders press together. His breath in my ear reminds me of Cassius.

"Now I *am* going to ask what you're up to," he whispers.

At that moment, I want to tell him everything. I have to physically clamp my mouth shut. The truth is so close to the surface that it scares me. What would he say if he knew what I was getting blackmailed for?

The girls argue in the hall. If they see me here, they might tell somebody.

"I found this video . . . online," I start quietly. "It's of Officer Roseby assaulting somebody. I want to have it play during the presentation, so everyone knows what kind of person they're letting patrol our school."

"That's really . . ." He hesitates. It's too dark to see his face. "Brave," he finishes finally. "Intense. I'd never . . . Wow."

For a second, I'm warm, like I'm doing something to be proud of. But it's the blackmailer, not me. I'm not doing this for righteous reasons. I'm doing this so I don't go to jail for a murder I may or may not have committed. I'm doing this so Grace's secret stays a secret.

I worm around, find the DVD player in the light from the door slats, pop out the disk, and swap it. It barely takes fifteen seconds.

"When do I get my official sidekick outfit?" he asks. "Can we color coordinate? Blue's my color. It'll match your eyes."

Unbelievable.

He squints at me and brushes the corner of my mouth with his pinkie, just the top layer of my skin molecules. "I don't think I've seen you smile before."

The girls in the hallway are gone, but I'd've tumbled out even if they weren't. Levi's framed in the shadows,

188

one foot in a bucket, a guilty look on his face.

"Let's just go to the auditorium," I say, panting, trying to kill the feeling in my stomach.

"I'm just going to run to the bathroom real quick and make sure my face isn't as red as I think it is," he says before bolting toward the opposite end of the hallway.

It's dangerous, the way he makes me smile when I have nothing to smile about.

The auditorium's always felt safe to me. It's dark, cozy, rustling all around you while you sit safe between your people. I used to sit with Grace, the two of us tucked into each other, or between Preston and November. But Nov's not here. I crane my neck to look behind me, accidentally hitting Preston with my elbow.

"I can't see Cassius. He did find a way to stop Nov from coming," I tell him.

He nods once.

"How are you doing?"

He just nods again, his jaw set.

The stage is empty, but the projector's set up and waiting with the blackmailer's DVD hidden inside like a bomb. Usually Officer Roseby's auditorium presentations are a lot of bullshit about sex or drugs, because clearly the only useful information about either of those things is *Don't do them*. Even Grace, who used to be the queen of *Don't do them*, would roll her eyes.

"He'll be fired after this," I say even though I have no

idea what's going to happen after that DVD plays.

Another jerky nod from Preston. I want to swamp him in a huge hug that both of us would hate.

Someone slides into the empty seat beside me. Levi's back from the bathroom. His wrist brushes mine and my arm tingles all the way to my fingertips. He leans in, but before he can say anything, the lights dim, the shadows swallow his face, and Officer Roseby swaggers onstage. Anger leaps up in me like a stove flame, higher and higher, canceling out some of the fear. I know Preston feels it, too.

"I know many of you are still shocked by the recent tragedy." Officer Roseby glances smugly out at the school. He thinks his uniform means he's a good person. "But that's not what I'll be speaking about today. Today we are going to talk about the women and girls at this school."

It's a lecture on women's safety. Incredible.

"Many of you are likely still concerned about the incident with Principal Eastman. So I organized this presentation to discuss appropriate conduct between members of the opposite sex at this school. It should go without saying that no girl at this school, or any school, should distribute nude photos of herself to anyone."

"She didn't send them." Levi simmers with outrage. "The principal took them. He was *in* them. And why is this directed only at girls?"

"With that obvious thing out of the way," Officer Roseby says, hammering in the final nail of Savannah's coffin, "I'd like to show a video with some samples of appropriate and inappropriate behavior."

He starts fiddling with the projector. Everything inside me contracts. This is happening because of me. Whatever happens next is my responsibility.

"Where are you going?" Levi whispers as I stand. "Is everything okay?"

"Everything's fine. Stay with Preston."

I edge past him, past the rows of people, and as I slip away into the hallway, I hear the video start.

FOURTEEN

August 7

Grace

JOY STARTS GETTING UP AT NOON. THEN
two. Then three. She eats only Saltines. She lifts weights
in the exercise room until four a.m., straining every
muscle in her body. Her room turns into a garbage can.
She leaves the house only once to buy us both Plan B.

Mom and Dad have always whispered about her. Now
they whisper more. *She's going through a phase.* They dissolve
their own worry for their own sakes. Nobody whispers
about me. Which is good, because I don't need to be whispered about.

One day Joy walks back from Preston's house in the
rain. Her orange shirt's dark with water, a rust color, like
dried blood. Her socks are sponges on my floor. Her hair
tangling around her neck in wet ropes, like a noose, she
asks: "Are you mad at me?"

I put my arms around her. I feel like a machine.

She wants to go to the police. She wants to go back to his house and kill him.

"I know you're mad at me," she repeats. "I can tell you're mad at me."

I'd never be mad at her. I'm not avoiding her because I'm mad at her. She just makes me tired.

She pulls me into the bathroom while Mom and Dad talk about colleges downstairs. She's full of thunder. "We need to tell somebody. I can't do this silence. You can't."

Why do I have to be the one to make her feel better? Nothing even happened to her.

Did anything even happen to me?

Five hours of sleep. Four hours of studying. Two hours of exercise. Three hours of self-improvement reading. If I don't go over six hundred calories a day, I won't have bad dreams. If I can do my makeup in under two hours, she'll stop asking if I'm mad at her.

I build little pyres out of my emotions and burn them. I am clean.

She comes to my room at night and whispers, even though I pretend I'm asleep: "Just let me do something. Let me go to his house. I'll . . . I'll . . . You're not being normal about this."

I'm not normal. I'm stronger than normal people. It's my head. I'm in control of it.

She's not in control of anything. Why did I ever want to be like her?

She comes to me outside, when I'm sitting on the porch,

tying and untying one shoe.

"Are you sure you're not mad at me?"

"Yes," I tell her. But my voice is different now. I can't tell if she's not listening or if I didn't speak.

Time slips in and out, like it did when I was drunk, but I'm not drunk now. Whole days pass without me noticing. Everything is dry and clear and flat. And far away. Joy feels very far away.

She comes to me in the exercise room when I'm sweating off breakfast. "We can't just pretend like it didn't happen."

"Yes we can." If I don't call it anything, it isn't anything. "Nothing even happened."

"That's not what you said the night it—"

"I don't know what I said. Leave it alone, Joy."

She whispers to me in the bathroom, when I'm flossing too hard, cutting my gums. "Mom and Dad ask me to do the dishes and I'm screaming the truth at them in my head. We need to tell."

"Please don't tell," I say, my mouth full of blood. "Promise me you won't tell. If you tell, I'll hate you forever."

After that, she stops asking if I'm mad at her.

That night, I dream I'm in a crowd and everyone's wearing Adam's face. I'm called into Principal Eastman's office, and Eastman is wearing Adam's face. I walk into Joy's room in the middle of the night and she's wearing his face.

He's astral projecting into my head. This dark-haired,

guitar-playing person . . .

All my old fantasies transform. It's me who finds his body at the bottom of the quarry. He comes to me with his problems and I bash his brains in with a rock. I'm in a crowd of people wearing his face, and I set off a bomb, blowing them all apart.

Dream: I stick a knife between his ribs. I feel it go in.

I don't want to be someone who dreams about this.

It's fine. It will go away. I'm stronger than this. I'm better than normal people.

FIFTEEN

October 23

Joy

AS KIDS, GRACE AND I SPENT A LOT OF TIME at the elementary school playground, on the wooden ship with the fake wheel. I'd steer us over oceans, away from pirates. I'd climb to the top of the jungle gym and she'd wait below me, face screwed up in fear, arms out to catch me if I fell, even though she wasn't big enough. Even though she knew I'd bring her down with me.

"Sorry I didn't reply to your texts." November's sitting on the swing next to me. School's been out for an hour now. The sky's cloudy, rain threatening. The wind scatters dead leaves underneath the jungle gym.

I'm the one to say it for once: "Are you okay?"

"I hate him, I hate him, I hate him." She says it like she's tearing off chunks of something inside her chest and throwing them into a fire. "The department's put him on unpaid leave. He was already in trouble, the way he went around asking unauthorized questions about Adam dying. He punched a hole in the basement wall."

"Are you okay, though?"

"That woman in the video sued my dad, back in NYC. But the security video from the street camera disappeared. That's why the chief suggested he apply for jobs in upstate New York instead of straight-out firing him." The swing chain's pinching her fingers. "I just don't understand who found it."

I twist my swing and then I let go, spinning. The playground blurs. "Are people giving you shit at school?"

"Most of the time, people forget he's my dad. We're not exactly color matched," she says sarcastically. "Besides, I am known for not caring and that means people tend to return the favor."

"But you're okay?"

"Whoever it was who did it, however they found the recording, I'm grateful to them. My dad's a bad person."

I'm quiet.

"Next month I'm eighteen, then I'll be in full control of my inheritance from my mom. Gonna sublet an apartment, graduate at Stanwick. I applied to NYU. So did Cassius, I guess."

"He moved out yesterday," I say. "I watched the U-Haul pull down the end of our street. Will you miss him?"

"We were temporary friends. Sometimes you gotta be

friends with somebody because they need someone, not because the two of you have anything in common."

My head hurts. "I'm here if you ever need someone."

"You don't wanna hear my garbage. I want you to keep looking up to me." She grins briefly.

There's something special about being liked by someone who hates almost everyone else.

"It's easier than you think, not looking up to someone anymore. All it takes is you seeing their cracks. I used to look up to my dad." She pushes off the ground, swings high. Her voice whooshes past me. "My mom was smart, rich, pretty. I know my grandpa's mind was blown when she picked him. All the people in the world, and she goes for a white cop? Jesus."

"Jesus," I echo, thinking about people we're not supposed to like, thinking of Levi.

"Mom saw the best in everybody. She looked at people like they were better versions of themselves, and it made them want to be better. She was like you." She smiles at me for a second. "Maybe he used to be different. You get trained to see other people as screwups, rule breakers, and you forget how to treat them like they're human. Sometimes I'm glad my mom died before she could see what he turned into."

I shut my eyes. "I'm so sorry, Nov."

"It's one thing to *say* you hate your dad. Everyone's dad is an asshole sometimes. But it's different to realize you're never going to wake up one morning and have a dad who isn't an asshole, and that you're going to be one of those people who never talks to their dad as an adult, and when he dies someday, you'll only find out because the hospital digs up your name in some phone book. . . ."

I jump off my swing, hug her. She's got bird bones. The feel of human skin on mine starts to bring back far-off fireworks of that night with Cassius. My nerve endings reroute straight to it now.

"I'm sorry," November says. Her forehead's on my collarbone. "I don't want to be this way to you."

"You're not any bad thing to me," I say, but she's already gathering the calm back on her face like she's tying up her hair.

"When you're a kid, the people you're stuck living with, it's a lottery. If they're assholes, too bad. There's nothing you can do until you turn eighteen."

"Parenthood is weird," I agree. "It's like, here, have this small person, do whatever you want to it until it's a bigger person, we don't care."

"I think that's why we end up being each other's parents. We're the only ones who know what it's like." She hops off the swing, lightly punches my shoulder. "That's why it's my job to look after you."

I have to tell her about the blackmail. I can't spend my life not telling people things because I'm afraid they'll stop liking me.

But my phone buzzes first. It's Levi.

  there is an absolutely terrible zombie movie playing

tonight. sounds like a great excuse to sit awkwardly
next to each other for a couple hours and get blushy
every time our arms touch. you in?

I completely forgot that we were going to see a movie.

But I can't go when all of this is happening. That would
be insane.

November grabs my phone.

"Hey!"

"I reserve the right to know who's texting my friend
and making her turn that shade of red." She skims it.
Her eyebrows fly up. "Levi? As in the new kid Levi? As in
Adam Gordon's half brother?"

"He's tutoring me in American History. It's nothing."

"Yeah, I'm sure your American History homework was
to go watch a shitty movie and 'get blushy.'" Her knuckles
tighten on the phone. "What's he want with you?"

"He's nothing like Adam. At all. He didn't even know
Adam." I'm babbling. "He's just new. We're temporary
friends, like you and Cassius. He'll make better friends
soon."

"Better friends?" November repeats, and starts laughing so hard she doubles over.

"What?"

"You're not good at much, you know that?" she splut-
ters. "You're shit at grades, you're way too aggressive at
sports—remember when you tried to join the soccer team
and kicked the goalie in the face? You suck at art, your
fashion sense blows. . . ."

"That's what I meant." I stick out my tongue at her. "He'll find better friends."

"That's why I'm *laughing*." She flicks my hair affectionately. "You *are* the best friend. That's the one thing you're good at. I've never met anybody who obsesses over doing right by her friends as much as you."

I tense. "Don't say that."

"Why not?"

"Because I'm actually a selfish bitch," I say lightly.

She bursts out laughing again. "You're cheering me up."

I smile, but my heart is pounding. "Everything I do is selfish. I do nice things just to feel better about myself. I'd probably throw somebody in a shark tank so I could be the one to pull them out. Best friend ever."

"I know you're kidding. But there's a good and a selfish reason for everything, and the fact that the selfish reason exists doesn't cancel out the good reason." She rolls her eyes. "Senior wisdom from November Roseby. So are you gonna go hang with the new kid at the movie theater or what?"

"You'd let me?"

"What do you mean *let* you? I'm not your babysitter." She snorts. "If I am, I'm a cool babysitter with a radical taste in music."

"I just meant . . . you didn't like Adam."

"I of all people understand that people aren't clones of their family members. In fact, I think people tend to swing the complete opposite way. So by that logic, Levi's a saint."

"I won't hang out with him if it makes you uncomfortable."

"You're ridiculous. I am not an asshole." She hands my phone back. "Plus, you've been stressed, even if you won't talk to me about it. It's okay to take a break to do something that makes you happy."

"I don't want to go off and see a movie when you're bummed."

"I'll get over it. You can be happy. It's not cheating. Go to the movies or I'm going to be pissed at you."

"But—"

"*Go.* Leave. I'm not saying another word to you."

I open my mouth again, but she mimes zipping hers shut.

So I go. Just this once. Just so Levi has an excuse to get out of the house.

As I walk across the playground, I hear her mutter to herself, "*Better friends.*"

And she starts laughing all over again.

The movie's long, boring, a chance for me to doze off, shut down, not think. It's like being in the auditorium—a cool dark place with Levi next to me. It's probably why people go to the movies so much, even though they're expensive and you can watch them all online. It's an excuse to sit in the dark next to somebody nice without worrying about messing it up with words.

When Levi and I walk out, it's dark. He buys us two sodas

and we sit by the fountain outside the shopping center.

"I don't remember anything from that movie," I confess.

"Guts everywhere and explosions. That's what I remember about Adam when he was nine, how he loved that shit, how our dad loved that he loved it. Like he was doing manhood right. I cried through those movies." He laughs. "This is how I make girls like me. I tell them about all the times I cried."

"That's the only time you told me about when you cried," I point out.

"Are you asking about other times?"

I shrug, but I am.

"I'll tell you, because I want to pretend you're interested. Let's see. The last Harry Potter book, obviously."

"There's got to be more than that."

"You are interested." He smirks. "I can't think of any. I told you about the movie thing—now you think I'm a crier. But I don't cry. I'm very manly."

Talking to him is so easy. He doesn't expect anything back.

"People never think Asian guys are manly," he says. "Obviously gender stereotyping is bullshit, and so is the gender binary, et cetera. But I'm manly as fuck. I've gotten into so many manly fights."

"You get along with everybody." Except Ben.

"I don't get along with people who say shit about my mom. And people at my old school liked to say shit about my mom." He rubs his sneaker through a glob of melted ice cream. "Man. Now I brought that up, and you're going to ask. But I don't really want to talk about it. Perils of being somebody who never thinks before he speaks."

I desperately want to know about his mom, why he hasn't gone back to Indiana yet. "I won't ask," I say anyway.

"Cool. I'll change the subject back to crying, then. You know I haven't cried about Adam yet? I thought I was going to at the funeral. I was like, shit yeah, Levi, you're almost there, but then this other girl started bawling and I went into Advice Levi mode."

He digs a coin out of his pocket and flips it into the fountain.

"It's so cliché, isn't it? Me not crying shows how I haven't processed my feelings about Adam. Eventually I'll have a big cry fest and grow as a person, probably in the rain, et cetera."

"It might rain. It's cloudy."

"It's been like this all day. The sky and I are doing an excellent job of repressing our tears." He grins.

I smile back, letting this happen. *Don't think about Grace, don't think about the blackmailer, don't think.*

How long am I allowed to do this? November said it wasn't cheating.

It feels like cheating.

"That police officer, did you hear if he got fired or not?" he asks. "Where'd you find that video again? Online?"

I stop smiling. "Can we not talk about that?"

"Sorry. Anything you don't want to talk about, I am militantly against talking about."

There's a brief silence.

"There," I say.

"There what?"

"An awkward silence. I was wondering if you'd let one happen."

"Normally I never let one of the bastards slip by me," he says. "People are like, learn to be comfortable with silence. But fuck that. Silence is awful. Silence was all I got from Adam for years."

"Do you ever think maybe he's not worth all this?"

"Worth has nothing to do with it. Maybe he was an asshole. But he was family, you know?"

I nod. I do know.

"I wanted to find out the stupid things. Like which of us would've been the smart one and the dumb one, or the cool one and the awkward one, or the talkative one and the quiet one. I think I would've been the talkative one, but maybe I'd've switched if he wanted to be. Like, who would I have been in the context of Adam?"

My throat's dry. "I like who you are in the context of you."

"I wonder who I am in the context of you," he says.

"Let's go back to talking about the weather."

"That was too flirty," he admits. "Tell me more about your sister. I like hearing you talk about your sister."

"She's awesome." My chest aches. "She's, like, a genius.

She's always on top of everything and nothing can touch her. She's perfect."

"All right, I lied. I'm not that interested in your sister. I just like seeing you smile."

I look away. "I can't tell if you're serious."

"I like to leave open the possibility of it being a joke. That way I don't have to take responsibility for it."

The old Joy would have loved him. Would the old Grace have loved him?

"Joy's Grace sounds pretty cool," he says. "I hope I get to find out what Grace's Grace is like sometime."

He'll never meet her. "Joy's Grace?"

"You know. Grace in the context of Joy."

"Grace is just Grace. There's no secret version."

"Maybe it's different with twins."

"What do you mean?"

"Maybe you're too used to being in the context of each other," he says. "Most people get the chance to try out lots of different versions of themselves, depending on who they're with, then settle on the version they like best. That's probably why people get married and shit. So they can go on being in the context of that person forever."

"But then that's a lie, isn't it?" I say quietly. "Believing in the way somebody else sees you instead of the way you actually are."

"I don't think there's one real version of a person and everything else is fake," he says. "People have lots of parts."

"I think I just met Philosophical Levi. He was unexpected."

"Not as unexpected as Exposer of Evildoers Joy, let me tell you."

I flinch.

"It's okay. That police officer was a dick. People deserved to know." He gently nudges my shoulder. "Sorry. Not talking about it."

But it's too late. The blackmailer's back in my head. I've stolen too much time here. "I . . . told my sister I'd help her with her project tonight."

"You're gonna go have giggly sister talk about the date you had with this cute dude. Don't try to hide it."

I smile painfully.

"Do me a favor, would you? Just, like . . . enjoy hanging out with her tonight. It's special, getting to have time with your family. I always thought I'd have time with Adam someday." He shrugs so casually it hurts.

But he's wrong. I'll always be with Grace. It's him I won't have much time with. He's going to go back to Indiana and forget about his temporary Stanwick friend, and I'll never have to tell Grace that I spent any time with Adam's half brother.

I figured out how to keep her secrets. Now I'm learning how to keep mine.

When I get home, Mom and Dad are in the living room, watching TV. I wait, but neither of them says anything about the fact that I'm home so late. Either they've forgotten to be suspicious of me or they've given up completely.

"Did any mail come for me today?" I ask.

"None." Mom doesn't look away from the TV. "Leftovers in the kitchen for you."

I ignore the plastic-wrapped spaghetti on the counter and go straight to Grace's door.

Come on, Grace. Open your door so I won't have to. Sense me standing here. I reach for the knob, and an invisible monster folds each of my fingers back until the snapping is deafening. But I twist it with my mangled hand.

Grace would never lie in bed with her laptop like I do, marinating in crumbs. She's sitting at her desk. She's organized all her books by color since the last time I was in here. It's hermetically clean, vacuum sealed.

"Are you busy?" I ask.

The profile of her face is lit up blue by the computer screen. "I have a lot of work to do."

Does she even realize how much she sounds like Mom?

I sit on the edge of her quilt, the blue-and-green-patterned one she's had forever. It's the only thing in her room left from our childhood, since the lamp broke. She put everything else in boxes or threw them away.

"I don't want to keep secrets from you," I say.

She closes her laptop. "You've never kept a secret from me in your life. You can't even stop yourself from telling me what you got me for Christmas."

"Would you be mad if I was keeping one?"

"I would never be mad at you about anything."

"You're allowed to be mad at me, Grace."

She bends her legs underneath her, balancing on top of her desk chair in a position that looks uncomfortable. "Where are you going with this?"

I have to tell her about the blackmail. She's my sister and she deserves to know. She's my sister and she would never stop loving me.

I don't want to do this without her anymore.

"This is going to sound ridiculous," I manage, and then I steel myself and let it all spill out. The notes, the photos of Principal Eastman, the security video of Officer Roseby . . .

It does sound ridiculous. It's so ridiculous I'm not even afraid.

"And I should have told you sooner," I finish. "I should have told you the second it started. I was scared you'd think . . ."

She's so quiet.

"That the blackmailer is telling the truth," I stammer. "That I really did . . . kill him, and I just don't remember. Even if Preston says I left the party before then. What if I came back?"

"Do you think you did it?" she asks.

I have no idea what her thoughts are, behind that face that looks just like mine. "I've been trying not to ask myself that. If I'm capable of it, I don't want to know. But what if I am, Grace? I wanted to."

It burns a hole in my chest.

"How do you do something like that and live with yourself?" I whisper. "The worst possible thing."

"Him dying was not the worst possible thing."

"That wasn't . . ." I flush.

"I'm sorry." She pulls her hair over her face. "This is so crazy. I can't believe you didn't tell me."

"I didn't want to make you worry."

"You should have come to me." She softens. "You should always come to me. There's no way you killed him. Just because you said you wished he was dead. People say things they don't mean. Okay?"

She smiles at me anxiously.

I breathe.

"You wouldn't do that," she repeats. "You're not capable of that. I don't care if you don't know. *I* know. I know you better than anybody. I know you better than you do."

The last piece of doubt lodged in my heart starts to dissolve. Maybe Levi's right, and Grace's version of Joy isn't a complete imposter. Maybe I could be her again. It'd be so much easier than finding out who my own version of myself is, and not liking her.

"I can't stand that you've been dealing with all this on your own." She peers at me, eyebrows knotted. "Are you okay?"

"I told Preston."

"You told Preston and not me?"

"Like I said, I was scared you'd be mad—"

"I'm never going to get mad at you, okay? You could stab me and I wouldn't get mad at you. You're my twin." She sits back down. "Does Preston have any ideas about who the blackmailer might be?"

There's a jealous tilt to the way she says *Preston*.

"He doesn't think Adam's death was an accident. He thinks the blackmailer is the real murderer. And he thinks it must be someone at our school, somebody who was at the birthday party and someone who knows what—"

I stop.

"What he did," she finishes for me, eyes fixed on the carpet.

"Nobody knows about that, though." It's amazing, all the ways you can talk about something without naming it.

Then she says something weird.

"How much would you say you know about November?"

I blink. "A lot."

"But how much do you know about her past?"

I don't understand where this is going, but this is the most Grace has talked to me in ages. I run through a checklist of all the things I know about Nov. "Her mom died before she and her dad moved here from the city."

"But what about after that? Do you know why she was out of school her sophomore year?"

"That was before I met her." When she was Annabella.

Grace taps the side of her knee in a steady rhythm.

"Did she go to Adam's birthday party?"

"Well . . . yeah. But she didn't stay."

"She's always hated Principal Eastman," she murmurs. "And her dad."

"Grace." I hold up my hands. "Stop. I get that you're trying to help. But Nov isn't *blackmailing* me."

A long silence.

"You idealize people, did you know that?" she says.

I don't say anything.

"You put them on these pedestals, so high up you can't see any of their flaws. But I can see them. November's always given me a weird vibe."

A snake rears its head in me and says *you're jealous*. But I cut off its head before it slithers out of my mouth.

"The way November acts around you, that's not who she really is," she says. "She puts on this act around you—"

"Besides the other one billion reasons you're wrong, Nov would never *murder* someone."

"Do you really know what she's capable of?" Her eyes are faraway. I always forget how analytical she is. "What the blackmailer is doing, it's just like November. She likes to shame people. Put up signs, call people out, make a scene. Remember how she put up all those posters about Principal Eastman's dress code being sexist?"

"That's different," I say desperately. "How would she have even found those photos of Eastman?"

"She's the head of the school newspaper. She's always digging around, looking for things to publish. Maybe she searched his desk. I don't know."

It does sound like something she would do. I shake my head, feeling sick. "The video of her dad, though. There's no way."

"You know how much she hates her dad. You really don't think this is something she'd do to get revenge on him?" she says. "Like, how would anyone besides her even get ahold of that video?"

Today she told me she was grateful to the person who showed the video.

What if that was her way of thanking me?

All it takes is you seeing their cracks.

Before I got the first note I'd told her I couldn't remember anything from Adam's birthday party—

What the fuck am I thinking?

"November's not the blackmailer," I say, hard. "If she wanted help exposing the principal and her dad, she would have *asked* me, not *threatened* me."

"Maybe you were the only person she trusted to help her, but she didn't want you to know that it was her doing it." Grace is lost in thought. "What if she tries to hide that she's unstable by acting like nothing gets to her, but in reality, she's losing it—"

"Shut up!"

She flinches.

"I'm sorry. I'm sorry." I want to drown myself. "It's just that this is screwed up. There's nothing wrong with Nov."

Her eyes are big and sad. "Joy, November was out of school her sophomore year because she was in a mental health facility."

I shake my head. "She would have told me."

"I'm not lying."

"How do you know that and I don't?"

"I've been keeping stuff from you, too." A spot of blood appears at the edge of her thumb where she's been picking it. "I wanted to put everything about this summer behind me. That's why I never told you . . . that November knows about what happened to me. She's known for ages. I told her."

"You told her about Adam? Why?" I whisper. "You don't even *like* her."

"Because—" She hides her bloody thumb in her fist. "Adam raped her, too."

SIXTEEN

August 18

Grace

SUMMER'S NEVER FELT LIKE THIS BEFORE. The sun's too bright. My skin's thinner than normal—I can see all my veins when I go outside. I hate looking at them. Joy keeps asking why I'm wearing long sleeves. She asks a lot of things.

One day, she's sleeping late when the bell rings. Mom and Dad aren't home. When I open the door, November's standing there, her hair swept back, her forehead creased.

I'd forgotten she existed.

"Is Joy home?" she asks.

"She's sleeping." I keep the door half closed between us, but my eyes burn from the light anyway.

"She hasn't answered my texts in ages."

Her forehead creases more.

"Sorry." I don't have the energy to fight her for my sister.

"I heard you guys hung out at Adam Gordon's house," she says fake-casually.

My skin feels like it's being stretched out.

"I told her not to go anywhere with him." Not so casually. "You don't know if . . . she went off anywhere with him . . . did she?"

Her voice shivers apart.

I want her to go away. I *hate* her. We were fine before she came along. Before her, Joy didn't need to prove anything to anyone.

"I just need to know what happened." All her cool sunglassy calm is gone. She's fragile, cringing.

Go away.

"Like I wouldn't be able to live with myself if anything did," she explains, her calm returning in a strange way.

It's hard to think with the sun in my eyes, but slowly I begin to understand why she hates him so much.

It should feel different, this realization. I should feel sad, angry, something. All I am is cold, cold, cold.

"He did it to you, too," I say numbly.

Her face doesn't change, but it's like something happens to the air. It gets harder to breathe. She wraps her arms around herself.

I need to do something to help her. What's wrong with me?

"So . . . you're saying . . ." Her voice is hoarse and low. "Joy won't text me because . . ."

She thinks it happened to Joy. It never would have happened to Joy. Joy would have fought him off, like I should have.

I hadn't turned into her after all.

I was always me.

I point to myself. Pick the victim out of a lineup. If I press my finger against my collarbone I can feel how thin my skin is.

She recoils. There are tears in her eyes.

"I'm sorry I didn't say . . . I didn't want Joy to think . . ." Her words are tangled. She's so affected by this. Everyone else is so affected. "I am so, so . . . What can I do? Tell me how I can help."

Everyone else feels it so much more than me.

"It's okay. I'm fine. Just don't tell."

"I should've told. Then this wouldn't have happened."

Why is everyone else allowed to make their sadness so big?

Does November think she and I are the same now?

We're not.

"I thought no one would believe me." She's stammering now. There's sweat on her narrow shoulders. "My dad didn't know what was wrong with me. He sent me to a mental health facility for a year."

"I have to go," I say mechanically.

"Please don't tell Joy."

Joy was the one who wanted a special bond with November. Now I'm the one with it.

I wish she'd never moved here.

"I'm . . ." She's shaking. "I'm going to kill him. I'm really going to . . ."

"What are you talking about?"

"Fuck him, *fuck* him. I'm going to do something to him. I'm going to hurt him." She spits the words like weapons.

Joy said that, too. But neither of them are actually going to do it. They talk like their rage can change things, but tonight he's going to eat dinner, go to sleep, and he won't feel a breath of this.

"If you were going to do something, you would have done it before now." I say it with only the top layer of oxygen in my lungs. Barely aware that I'm saying it.

"You're right. I should have, ages ago." She forces her arms down by her sides. "If I had . . ."

If she had.

But that's the thing. People don't. They let things go, and nothing changes.

Nobody changes. Ever.

"Tonight," she says huskily. "I'll do something tonight. I'll make him pay. We'll make him pay. Come with me."

"What are you planning?"

"Don't tell Joy," she says. "We're going to break into his house."

When you're nothing, when you're emptied out, you can do anything. There's nothing inside you that tells you to stop. The jungle inside me has been cleared away. There's a kind of power in saying yes just because it doesn't matter.

I wait until everybody else is asleep before I leave my

house. November picks me up at the end of the street. We don't talk on the way there. Sometimes I glance at her profile, sharp and thin. Cassius would have a hard time painting her.

Thinking about Cassius stings.

"Adam won't be here tonight," November says, clutching the wheel. "He's going to a party. I saw on Facebook. We'll hit up his room, find something he's hiding, something to blackmail him with. Some way to run him out of town. There's got to be something. You can't be that fucked up and not have something to hide."

I just nod. We park halfway down the road and wait in the trees until Mr. Gordon stumbles out of the house. The nearest liquor store is on the other side of town. He doesn't bother locking the door behind him.

"He'll be gone for a while," November whispers. "We're safe."

Safe.

His house doesn't look solid. It's a shape on a hill. A slice of the night. No lights in any of the windows. November creeps ahead of me, her shoulder blades protruding under her tank top.

Inside: moonlight on the floor, on the dusty portraits of Adam's grandfather, haunting us. In the kitchen, report card on the fridge—mediocre grades. He's nearly failing math. So much for his brilliance.

There are pictures of him above the dining table. An eight-year-old at Christmas. I shut off everything in my head.

"What are we really doing here?" I ask in the dark.

"We're finding some way to get back at him, I told you." She's furious, quaking, frantic.

I don't think I'll ever feel real again, I realize evenly. Which is good. I don't want to know what real feels like.

We find the bathroom, open the medicine cabinet. Antidepressants prescribed to Mr. Gordon. Caffeine pills, ibuprofen. Some hot-cold packs.

"Can you handle going in his room?" she asks me in the hallway.

"I'm honestly not, like, traumatized." It's a funny feeling, listening to your own voice like it's detached from you. Have I always sounded like this?

She gives me a painful look before we go upstairs.

His room . . .

I stand in the doorway while she sifts through shadows, purposeful now. She tosses aside rumpled Jimi Hendrix T-shirts, empty ramen packets, a crushed box of Marlboro Lights. She yanks open a dresser drawer full of beer cans and slams it shut again. A hidden shoebox looks promising, but it holds only two withered flowers, a colorful glass pipe, and a packet of weed.

I don't look at his bed.

Shadows in the dark, that's all this is. Blurry shapes. No detail.

I don't know why I was ever afraid of the dark. The dark is keeping me safe.

I hover over November's shoulder while she opens his laptop, clicking through old school assignments, *FUCKmrtilandre.docx* and *stupidshiteuropething.docx*. On his desktop, there's a picture of the Beatles.

"There's nothing personal here," she says, her voice wound tight. "No diary, nothing . . ."

No secret confessions or apologies, no private unsent letters.

No songs about me.

She finds a folder labeled PRIVATE. It's full of porn. My stomach revolts. She deletes it, empties the trash, and opens Facebook. Reads chatlogs with girls whose names I don't know. November writes them down. There's a message, also unanswered, from someone named Levi Pham:

> hey man. you might not remember i exist, but we're
> related or something like that so i thought i'd say
> whatsup. hope this doesn't sound dumb.

"We could change his Facebook status to a confession," November mutters. "But people would think it was a prank."

She checks his email: 873 unread messages, mostly spam. One from me, from a week after that night in the middle school field. I got his email address from the school directory.

> Adam! Hi. Just wanted to let you know that
> everything worked out okay. Officer Roseby let us
> go. I'd text but I don't have your number. And I don't
> think we're friends on Facebook. Anyway I'd love to
> come to your house next week! It was really sweet
> of you to ask. Is it okay if I bring my sister? See you
> then xxxGrace

A different girl agonized over those *x*'s. Deleting one. Putting it back.

We weren't even friends on Facebook.

"He didn't deserve a second of your time, Grace." November's voice is wet with pity. None of it affects me. I reach over her shoulder and delete the email.

She stares at the screen. "I thought there'd be something here that'd prove what a sick freak he is. Something we could use to show everybody what he's really like."

I wonder if Joy's asleep.

"It's just ordinary-guy shit here, but he's not an ordinary guy." November shuts off the computer. "I have to believe that."

Suddenly, light pours in from the window, blinding me. Headlights, lightning on the wall. Illuminating the details on the bed. The creases in the blanket. The blotchy stain on the moss-green pillow.

The door downstairs clicks open.

My veins ice over.

"It's his dad, not him," November says, fast and calm. "He'll go to his room in a second, pass out, and we'll sneak away."

Giggling. A girl, not a man. The stumble-crash of someone knocking over a chair in the dark. And: "Let's go upstairs, my dad's not home. I'll show you my bed. Tempur-Pedic."

Footsteps on the stairs—where do I hide—there's nowhere—

November leaps for the closet, and I dive under the bed just as the door opens.

"Adam, your room is so gross." A girl, laughing.

I'm in a world of trash and dust and dirty clothes. I worm backward into the shadows as shoes take up my vision. Oxfords and sequined flats. The flats come off and a girl's bare feet knock aside a pair of jeans.

"Come check out the bed." His voice. "It's so comfortable."

I orchestrate my movements. *Put my arm under my chest so it doesn't stick out. Fold my knees against each other. Take up as little space as possible. Disappear.*

"Is it?" the girl says teasingly. A tank top floats to the ground by her bare feet, tiny lace flowers around the neckline.

I could burst out and race down the stairs. I could grab their ankles, trip them, jump over their bodies, leave November in the closet. I could close my eyes and never open them again. Force my own heart to stop beating.

My body is keeping me here. If I wasn't attached to it, I could slip away. Be part of the dark. Be a shape that doesn't mean anything until the lights turn on.

They crash onto the bed so heavily. The bottom sags until it almost touches my nose, fabric poking through wooden slats. A spider's body is caught in a loose thread. There's a whorl in one of the boards shaped like the flower on Cassius's wrist.

If she starts saying no—if she starts trying to escape—I'll roll out, I'll grab something, a lamp . . .

"You're so beautiful." His low voice. "I'm going to write a song about you."

I'm alive. My heart is beating. I'm breathing. But the air around me stops moving. Something crucial in the atmosphere is dying. The heat is unbearable. I cover my ears but I can still hear them.

The bed creaks up and down for a long time. Heavy breathing. The spider's body dislodges and drifts to the floor next to my face. Its legs are curled up, like it was trying to hide from whatever killed it. But it still took up too much space.

"You should really clean this place." The girl is getting up, gathering her clothes.

"It's not that messy." He sounds lazy. Satisfied. Something vicious happens to my stomach. I bite the edge of my tongue until it bleeds. I list all the terrible ways I'll punish myself if I vomit.

"Let's have a beer," he says.

"I gotta drive home." She opens the door. "Sleep tight."

I'm soaked with sweat. My arm is asleep, my chest burning, my legs knotted. He doesn't get up. I hear him roll over. Then he goes still.

All I have to do is sneak out while he's sleeping.

I start to edge out a couple times and lose it. If he sees me . . . if he sees me. The third time, I almost make it before he shifts. I freeze, not breathing, but he stays asleep.

I don't move again until I see the closet door crack open. Then I inch out from under the bed. My heel crinkles a candy wrapper, but he doesn't wake up. Slowly, I rise. November emerges, too, a quiet silhouette.

She's holding a pair of scissors. Where did she find them?

Our eyes meet.

She stands over him. The moonlight from the window falls on the ugly ridge of his nose, the zit tucked beneath his lower lip, the stray hairs under his chin. I stare until my eyes water. The movement of his chest up and down seems so flimsy. Like I could press my finger there with the barest pressure and stop it from ever lifting again.

Do it, I say without speaking. The scissor blades are bright.

November's small and shivering. She lifts the scissors. Her arm lowers. She shakes her head, again and again, moves next to me.

Presses them into my hand.

I'm nothing, so I can do anything. I could stop him.

He twitches in bed. I don't blink, letting my eyes blur so I don't have to look at the details of his face. This is it. The moment before and after.

If I were Joy, I could do it.

My hand trembles.

But I'm not Joy. And I'm not nothing.

I'm me. Forever. The worst possible thing I could ever be.

I bolt, fast and quiet, out his bedroom door, down the

stairs, and across the lawn. November's coming after me, but I'm too quick for her. I half run, half stagger into the woods. I lose myself in the trees, wrenching through bushes, kicking branches, kicking everything, breaking things in the night.

I don't know how long it takes November to find me. When she steps out from between the trees, she takes me by the arm, tries to lead me back toward the road. I shove her away.

"Grace," she pleads.

I hate my name so much. I'm not graceful at all.

"There was nothing about me in there." My voice flames in the rustling quiet. "I thought if he could do that to me, he at least loved—" I bite off the word with my teeth, shatter it.

"There was no song," I whisper. "I was just another girl."

"That's how he gets us." November's still holding my arm. Her words break. "It's so nice, having somebody think you're special. That you're worth making art about."

Like Cassius did. But Cassius must have been lying, too.

"You told Joy what he did to you, right?" November asks. "You told."

"Obviously," I rasp. "She's my sister."

"Is she . . . okay?"

"Of course she's *okay*." I kick at a fallen branch. "Why wouldn't she be okay?"

"She cares about you a lot."

"I *know*," I yell.

"I just thought she might feel . . ." Her voice trails off. "Guilty."

"Why the hell would she feel guilty? It's not her fault. She didn't do anything. That's ridiculous." I can't breathe. "Does she think I'm the kind of person who'd blame her? Is that what you think of me?"

"Grace," she says softly.

"Because that's not how I feel," I snarl. "I love my sister and everything is fine so just *leave. Us. Alone.*"

I turn sharply and start walking toward the road. I can see it through the trees. I don't need her to drive me back. I don't need anyone to do anything for me ever again.

SEVENTEEN

October 24

Joy

"GRACE'S RIGHT. SHE HAS TO BE." PRESTON stares unseeingly at his bedroom walls. "November knew about Grace, she was at the party, she knew you didn't remember anything . . . it all fits."

I'm flat on my back on his bed, gazing up at the faded glow-in-the-dark star stickers on his ceiling.

"When I woke up this morning, there was this second between me opening my eyes and me remembering everything, and I felt fine," I say. "Normal. As if none of this ever happened."

"You slept last night? That's good!"

I shrug.

"What are you going to do?" he asks quietly.

I curl up, pressing my knees into my eyelids so hard

that my head throbs. It's nothing compared to the pain November must've felt, every single time we passed Adam in the halls and all she did was sneer.

"Are you going to confront her?" Preston asks.

I flatten out again, the pulse behind my eyelids fading. "Why didn't she tell me? I would have hated him right with her. I would've—dome something . . ."

"If she'd told, nothing would have happened to Grace."

I jolt upright.

"No. Don't blame her for that. That was my fault. Nobody else's.

"The thing about guilt is that it stops you from fixing anything. It makes you avoid the person you hurt because you can't face them, and then you hate yourself because you need to face them."

I know you love her, Grace whispered to me last night before I left her room. *But you have to stop believing the best of everybody.*

"We don't know that it's her yet, for sure," I manage. "And even if it is, I don't care. She's my best friend, other than you. If she's mad at me, I want her to be able to tell me. If I did something wrong, I wanna fix it. I'll talk to her after school tomorrow."

"Joy—if she's been blackmailing you—"

He's looking at me in a way I don't like at all, like I'm about to break. "What if she's dangerous? What if she *is* the one who killed Adam?"

"She's not dangerous to us. He deserved it."

"That's an intense thing to say," he says slowly.

Preston will never understand in the same way we do.

"He fucked up everything. I'm never going to be sad that he's gone."

I yank his sheets over my face until I stop crying.

"I don't know how to stop bad things from happening to people I love," I grit out to the rough fabric.

He grunts deep in his throat, and lies down beside me, gathering me into his arms. All my muscles ball up but I let it happen.

"I don't want bad things to happen to you either," he says, his heartbeat drumming into my back.

"Nothing bad's happened to me. It's Grace and November."

"I don't know if you've noticed," he says, stiffly. "But you've been through hell, too."

"It's not about me."

"You're allowed to be affected by this."

He's wrong but I don't say it. "I would be so fucked without you."

"I would be ten times more fucked without you."

He presses his forehead into my hair, and we stay like that in silence for a few minutes. Then my phone buzzes, hard and loud. I draw back, slip it from my pocket.

A long text from Levi.

so i've been shanghaied into gathering signatures downtown for the quarry fence petition. apparently i'm usefully pitiful as adam's half bro or something. but i'm

sure i'd get way more signatures if there was a cute
girl next to me. god that was stupid. anyway wanna
meet me at the end of barlett street in an hour?

"Who's that?" Preston's sitting up.

"It's nothing." I try to hide my phone under the sheet,
but he steals it from me. He reads the text and his eyes
widen. "Does Grace know you're hanging out with Adam's
half brother?"

"He's leaving for Indiana eventually anyway. She doesn't
need to know." My stomach twists with guilt. "He helps
me not think. He drowns stuff out."

Preston is silent for a minute.

"He's not part of it," I try to explain. "When I'm with
him, I can pretend it's not happening."

"Joy, tomorrow you have to ask one of your best friends
if she's been blackmailing you."

I dig my fingernails into my wrist. It's not working as
much it used to.

"So maybe you deserve to do something that takes your
mind off it for now." He meets my eyes. "It's not wrong of
you to feel okay for five minutes."

It's almost the same thing November said. That must
mean some part of her still cares about me.

"Preston?" I say.

"Yeah?"

I don't know the right words. There's something so special and strange about being loved by somebody who isn't
related to you, someone who has no obligation.

But the right words don't exist, so I just rest my forehead against his.

And then I leave, because everybody has something they use to cope.

The clouds are back by the time I meet Levi on Bartlett Street. They're darker than they were the day we went to the movies, more threatening. This time it's really going to rain.

"I already have fourteen signatures," he says excitedly when I walk up to him.

"Couldn't your dad have the quarry fenced off?" I say it in my most normal voice.

"The quarry's not actually on his property. It belongs to the town," he says. "He's the one who asked me to get signatures. And he was sober when he asked."

We walk together down the sidewalk. I breathe in his presence, use it to block out my thoughts.

"It feels like something I can do for Adam," he admits.

I wait by mailboxes while he rings doorbells. Some people aren't home, and some people pretend not to be. But some nod while Levi talks, and then they sign his sheet of paper.

We turn down another street. "It's gonna rain," I say, to try to get my mind off November.

"That's what the weatherman wants you to think. But I'm an optimist."

"The sky's crazy dark."

"Very," he corrects. "The sky's very dark. Or super dark. Or extremely dark."

I'm still thinking about November. "What?"

"I just don't like that word," he says tensely.

I blink. I guess it's not impossible to annoy him.

"Sorry." He shifts his clipboard to his other arm. "I still haven't told you why I haven't gone back to Indiana yet, have I?"

"You don't have to," I blurt.

"I want you to know things about me." His voice thins. He sucks in a sharp, fast breath and spits out, "It's just not super easy to tell someone your mom's in a mental hospital."

A mental hospital. Like November.

"The shitty thing about schizophrenia," he continues, even faster, "is that it's manageable with medication, but the illness itself convinces you you don't need it. So I should have made sure she was taking it."

I locate my voice. "You're not responsible for that."

"Yeah." But I can tell he doesn't believe me. "She's doing really well, though. I call her every Friday."

"That's great!" I sound so fake. I crush a dead leaf beneath my foot.

We've walked by two houses without knocking on any doors. He's clutching his clipboard tight against his chest like a shield.

"It's just that if you tell someone that the police found your mom naked under an overpass because she thought somebody was poisoning her laundry detergent, that'll always be the only thing they think of when it comes to her."

"My friend went to a mental hospital for a while. But she never told me. I found out through someone else. Maybe she thought I'd look down on her."

He nods rigidly.

"But I would never do that." I stop at the end of the sidewalk. "It's nothing to be ashamed of. And if my friend has some sort of mental problem, that doesn't change the fact that I know she's a good person. I'm sure your mom is a good person, too."

Just then the sky splits open. Rain drenches us instantly, soaking the pavement. Levi yelps and drags me forward. We take refuge under somebody's gazebo, the rain pounding over the edge of the wooden roof. Levi pants, wipes his forehead, looks at me.

"Everything good that's happened since I've come here has been because of you, you know that?"

A shiver runs through me that has nothing to do with the rain.

"When I got here, I was pissed. Pissed at Adam for dying, pissed at my mom. Do you know what it's like to be pissed at people you love for things they can't help?"

Am I pissed at November?

If she did it, there had to be a reason. Something I did to deserve it.

Maybe she blames me for what happened to Grace, too.

"But with you, I get to feel like—this charming guy, this funny guy . . ." He stares at the blurry silhouettes of the rain-drenched houses across the street. "I like who I am in the context of you."

That's not something you say to a convenience friend. There's way too much warmth in his eyes.

He moves closer. "Sorry I'm so awkward. I bet I'd top the list of awkward people you know."

Numbly I say, "No. Preston's at the top."

"Second place isn't so bad." His face gets nearer by degrees. I can see the curve of his lips and his cheekbones and his dark eyes.

He looks nothing like his half brother. Whose murder I'm being blackmailed for.

I've been lying to him about every single thing from day one. Using him as a replacement for booze and not sleeping or eating. I told myself he wasn't a part of this, but he is.

What am I *doing*?

I yank back, my legs bumping into the wet side of the gazebo. Rain soaks the back of my head. "I can't do this."

Shame sprouts all over his face. "Oh God, I'm sorry. I just came at you out of nowhere."

Guilt strangles me. I've been using him.

"I didn't think you were serious . . . about all the flirting."

I'll never be able to tell Levi what his half brother did to my sister.

"I wasn't. Mostly. Kind of." He groans. "Can I fix this?"

"We're temporary, right? Convenience friends," I stammer. "You're supposed to go back to Indiana and then we never talk again."

"You weren't ever going to talk to me again?" He looks so sad.

I should have stayed away from him.

"You weren't supposed to be part of my real life," I try to explain. "Like a—a distraction."

"A distraction?" He steps back. Water from his hair runs into his eyes.

I'm making it worse. "I have to go."

"Don't. You'll get soaked."

He reaches out, but I'm already slipping away into the rain.

People shouldn't have to go to school when every particle of them is made of anxiety, when they haven't slept and the halls are a minefield of people they can't face. But if I said that to my parents, they'd tell me to stop being dramatic.

I'm just not going to think about him ever again. Easy.

Back to the avoiding game. The next day, I avoid Levi by skipping American History. I avoid November by eating lunch in the bathroom. Time passes fast when you're running from everyone.

But time stops to a dead halt after the final bell. When I'm gearing up to go find November and tell her everything, I open my locker and a note falls out to the floor.

Joy Morris—

Four years ago, Adam Gordon sexually assaulted
November Roseby. I want you to tell the whole
school.

Some may not believe you, but enough will. Don't
you think everyone deserves to know what he was
capable of?

I grip the note until the edges tear. Then I let out a
choked laugh, so loud that Mr. Fennis sticks his head into
the hallway and shushes me. I ignore him, balling the note
in my fist.

Grace was wrong. November isn't the blackmailer.

My laugh turns to a shuddering exhale. I lean hard
against my locker.

The blackmailer isn't somebody I love. I don't have to
believe that somebody I love could do this to me.

I don't care if this goes on forever. I deserve that. But
November's not mad at me and that's all that matters.

I find her alone in the empty computer lab, earbuds
slung around her neck, editing the layout of next week's
newspaper. It takes her a second to notice me. She turns,
but I'm talking even before I reach her.

"I've been a shitty friend, Nov," I blurt. "And it's
probably shitty of me to do this now. But Grace told
me everything. I'm sorry. I know you didn't want me to
know."

She sits in total silence for a long time, shock unfolding on her face.

"If you ever need . . . to talk, or anything . . ." I cringe. "November?"

She unwinds the earbuds from her neck, places them on the keyboard.

"I should have told you," she says definitively.

"It's okay."

"No one's ever looked up to me before like you. I didn't want to ruin it." She smiles, but it wavers.

My throat closes. "I met Adam my freshman year. I was so used to my dad acting like I was this idiot, and then Adam told me I was smart. It was stupid."

I will never, ever be sad he's dead.

"I thought people would think I was lying. So I didn't say anything. But feelings have to go somewhere, you know? They follow the path of least resistance. Some people turn it on others, I turned it on myself."

She sets her jaw, exhales, and pushes back her sleeve. Scars, underneath the rubber bands. Thin neat lines of them.

"Don't look at me like that. It's fine now," she says quickly. "Every time I get the urge to self-harm, I put a rubber band on my wrist. I just wanted to see some physical evidence that something was wrong. Nobody could see something was wrong."

Crying would definitely be one of the top ten useless things to do right now.

"My dad noticed eventually. You would have thought

I'd done it just to piss him off, the way he reacted." Her voice darkens. "He called it a suicide attempt, had me sent to this mental health place. He was doing it as a punishment, but it was the best thing that ever happened to me."

"I'm sorry," I whisper.

"After what happened to Grace, I didn't . . ." She shuts her eyes. "I didn't want you to think it was my fault."

"It wasn't," I say urgently. "I wouldn't have."

"If I'd told you, she never would've gotten close to him."

"It wasn't your fault." I keep my voice steady. "It was mine."

Her eyes change. "Joy—"

"I thought if I could get Adam to go out with her, she'd love me like she used to," I croak. "I didn't know why we were growing apart. So it was my way of bringing us together. Of helping her."

I'm chained to this truth, and I'm responsible for every single thing it destroys.

"No." She grabs my wrist. "It wasn't your fault."

I pull back. "It wasn't *your* fault."

"It," she says, and stops. "It'd be pretty hypocritical to argue with you, wouldn't it?"

I don't trust myself to say anything.

"I think that it was Adam's fault," she says. "And maybe if we keep reminding each other of that, eventually it'll work its way down to a place we can believe it."

I wipe my nose. "I still look up to you, Nov."

"I don't think I want you to anymore," she says after a

minute. "I think I'd rather just be your friend."

I reach into my pocket for the blackmailer's newest note, to show her. I'll never do it, not this time. I don't care what happens to me. But Nov deserves to know what's been going on.

I'm about to hand it to her when I see it—the headline of her editorial.

"Why I Didn't Tell When Adam Gordon Raped Me"

I lurch back.

"You know what I've learned?" She sounds so calm. "Secrets fester inside people. Things that stay in the dark rot. You can't fix anything until you know what it looks like. And I'm not going to keep quiet anymore to keep life simple for other people."

"You're going to publish this?"

"Eastman was the one who always proofread the paper before it went to print. I can print whatever I want."

I guess the blackmailer is going to get what he wants anyway.

I swallow. "Aren't you scared people will be . . . ?"

"I've been planning on doing something like this ever since what happened to Grace." She stares at the computer screen. "That's why I went to his birthday party. I was going to confront him in front of all his friends. But I barely got through the front door before I ran."

"You don't have to. He's gone." I keep saying that, and every time it feels like a lie. "He's not going to do anything to anyone ever again."

"Maybe he already did. Maybe there's another girl here who thinks she's alone in this," she says. "If so, I want to talk to her."

How could I tell her about the blackmail now, when she's in the middle of doing something so brave?

Maybe there's a difference between keeping a secret for your own sake, and keeping a secret for someone else's. I'll tell her someday. When everything is calmer. In the meantime, I have Preston to help me through it.

And my sister.

"You don't have to do this," I repeat, just in case. "To get back at him, I mean. Revenge won't help."

Even Adam dying didn't help Grace.

"He's not important enough to me for that," she says. "Yeah, I was angry. It's impossible not to imagine doing really sick things when you're angry, things that make you question who you are."

I know about those things.

"Maybe if I did want revenge, it wouldn't look so different from what I'm doing now. But reasons are important. And I'm not doing this because I want to ruin his reputation or whatever. I'm doing it because I feel like telling the fucking truth for once. Even if it hurts some people to hear it."

Like Levi. A jolt runs through me. He'll finally hear the truth about Adam. But will he believe it?

"It's hard to find out somebody you loved isn't who you thought." She smiles at me sadly. "But it's better than believing a lie forever."

"I should be happy," I murmur. "I wanted Levi to know."

"He'll be fine. He's got you to sit next to in movie theaters now."

I shake my head slowly. "I fucked up with him. Really badly."

"Girl," she says. "Repair shit. Don't abandon ship."

She turns back to the computer, saves the file to her desktop, and sends it to the printer.

Maybe it's impossible to be honest without somebody getting hurt. But I think I'm getting better at figuring out when it's not worth it, and when it is.

EIGHTEEN

August 24

Grace

"MAYBE HE'LL JUST LEAVE," JOY WHISPERS. "Transfer schools or something, I don't know."

She opens my window to let the stale air out. The breeze blows my curtains so far into the room they almost brush my forehead. Now all she talks about are the ways Adam could disappear.

"Maybe he'll move across the country and we'll never see him at school again," she says.

I haven't told her yet that I'm not coming back to school. I haven't told her about breaking into Adam's house, either. If I'm silent, she'll fill the empty space with words. She's afraid of my silence.

"He'll graduate early," she says to the window. "He'll do one of those year-abroad programs."

I pull the blanket up to my neck and go still until she thinks I'm asleep.

Then, hours later, when she's asleep in her own room, I leave. Walking at night means the dreams can't find me. That he can't find me. Joy's always so proud of herself for climbing out her window, but it's just as easy to use the front door.

It rained earlier, and my heels catch in puddles on the side of the road. This late, I can walk as far as I want and nobody will see me.

I wonder if November has the dreams. She hasn't talked to me since our night at his house. Which is fine. I don't have anything else to say to her.

One foot in front of the other. Mindless movement, for the rest of my life. That's all I want. Like a zombie.

Music thumps halfway down the street. It's coming from Cassius's house, where he once painted a girl who looked like me. I step closer. I'm a shadow watching normal people, all their details brightly lit up, making them garish, frightening. They spill onto the lawn and lounge against the porch.

I dart through his front door. I want to see the finished painting.

I half slip in a spilled drink as I wander through the throngs. His parents aren't home. I don't see Cassius anywhere. Somebody says something to me, but I trickle away like water. I recognize a few people, sophomores, juniors, but they're as distant in memory as characters from cartoons Joy and I watched when we were ten.

Did Cassius invite his musician best friend to this

end-of-summer party?

Someone bumps into me, and I stumble into the basement door. It's closed. He probably didn't want all these drunk people messing with his precious art.

I open the door and slip into the dark.

Nobody notices anything I do, these days.

I turn on a light. It's too bright, so I turn it off again, using my phone flashlight instead. His paintings on the walls have changed. Some of the clouds are more ominous now, darker, pouring rain over the naked people floating beneath them.

It doesn't take me long to find what I'm looking for. The painting is finished. It's set up on an easel right in the middle of the room, like it's the one he's most proud of.

There are plants growing out of her. Vines and flowers. Most just buds, some blossoming, some barely poking out of her skin. She's gazing straight up and there's a look in her eyes like she sees something beautiful in the distance, just out of reach.

I grab the painting and try to tear it, but it's canvas, and I'm not strong enough. I try to punch through it instead, hitting it so the paint flakes and cracks, and then I throw it to the floor and grind my heel into it.

"Grace?"

That name belongs to the girl in the ruined painting. She can keep it.

"Grace, what are you doing here?" It's Cassius, standing on the stairs. He turns on the light. Suddenly everything in the room is too sharp. Like knives.

"My painting," he says, shocked.

"I'm sorry, I—" I choke on my apology, on his sadness and confusion. I shove past him, run up the stairs, back into the real world. I have to get away. I can't look at him and see an old version of myself reflected in his eyes.

I head for the front door, but Cat and my old friends are standing in front of it. I don't want to hear them call my name. I don't want to know if they'd bother to say it or not.

I cross the living room to the kitchen and stare out the open window, my heart pounding. The backyard is much smaller than the front, and fenced in. Someone's arranged a circle of old tires for people to sit on. Two girls, a guy, and—

Him.

"Let me try," one of the girls says, reaching for the guitar balanced on his lap. "I took lessons."

"Yeah, uh, no," he slurs. "This thing cost like two grand. My hands only."

To them, he's normal. Person shaped.

He lights a cigarette. "Anyone got a joint?"

"We can roll one upstairs," says a girl.

The guitar slides to the grass as he stands, wobbling a little. He hasn't changed like me. He looks exactly the same.

The girls climb the porch first and I watch him study the length of their shorts, almost clinically, before following.

I wander onto the back lawn, gulping lungfuls of night breeze.

His guitar's in the wet grass. The wood's pretty, swirly, expensive, like coffin wood. I pick up a cup on the ground and sniff it. Whatever type of alcohol it is, it's not mixed with anything. I dump it all over his guitar.

That's almost the end of it, except that he left his cigarette lighter.

I look around. Nobody at the kitchen window. In one of the upper bedrooms, a light comes on and several outlines crowd together. He's taller than the others. He talks with his hands.

I'm so tired.

I bend down and pick up the lighter, flick it on, and stare at the flame for a moment before I touch it to the guitar. The fire catches so quickly that I stagger back. Immediately, the wood warps black, flashing in the gold and orange glow.

I drop the lighter, then wind back through the house, curving away from drunken limbs. Once I'm outside, I walk in the coldest puddles.

"Grace, wait!"

It's meant to be a shout, but Cassius's voice is too soft. I don't get very far before he's behind me in the road, still in his sweatshirt even though it's a summer night, all the patterns on his skin hidden.

I force myself to calm down. He's not going to do anything to me. It's Cassius.

Unless he was scheming with his best friend this whole time. Maybe that's why he wanted to paint me. Maybe they laughed about it together. Nightmares swirl together in my head.

"I thought I saw you leaving. . . ." he says uncertainly, his hands in his pockets. "Can I walk you home?"

Boys always think silence means yes.

We walk in the road. No cars this late. If they do come, maybe I won't dodge fast enough. How easy is it to die? Sometimes it seems really easy, and then sometimes it seems unreasonably hard.

"I'm sorry you didn't like the painting." He's looking at the stars, shoulders hunched sadly.

"I don't know why I did that," I burst out. "I'm really sorry."

"It's okay," he says.

None of this is okay.

"Were you at that party to see Adam?" he asks. My stomach turns, but he keeps talking, oblivious. "He's the one who put it together. I told him my parents would be gone for the weekend. He wanted to practice throwing a bigger party, since his birthday party's coming up, I mean. I didn't really expect it to be so big."

My skin feels like paper, like it's not holding me together very well at all.

"I was gonna try not to bring up that night," he says after a minute. "Adam said everything went fine, that I shouldn't be weird about it, but I feel weird about it."

One step in front of the other. Listen to the gravel beneath my feet. I am a collection of small practiced movements.

"I hope . . . I, um," he starts. "I hope . . ."

"Do you love him?" I ask. "Like in a best friend way?"

He looks confused. "Who?"

"Adam. Do you care about him, as a person?"

"Um," he says. "Yeah, for sure. He's the reason I have friends at this school. I know he can be a jerk—sorry—but I owe him."

"Did he ask you to ask me if you could paint me?"

He stops in the road. "You mean as some wingman thing? No. Painting someone is . . . very personal for me. It's a thing I want to do with some people, and not other people, and I don't know why, but I definitely wouldn't do it for him."

The problem with good liars is that you can't tell that they are. The only safe people are the ones who lie badly to your face. At least then you can tell.

"Have you guys talked?" he asks.

"No." The word burns.

"Joy and I haven't talked." He nudges a bottle cap aside with his foot. Joy would have kicked it. "I was worried you were mad that I hadn't called her. Adam said I wasn't supposed to."

I shrug. I have nothing to give him.

"Is it okay if I tell you something that I probably wouldn't tell you if I wasn't drunk?"

He's going to tell me no matter what. Sweat collects along his hairline. I hadn't even noticed he was drunk.

"I tend to keep everything to myself until it spills out all at once, and this is one of those times, and I'm sorry for that. But I haven't stopped thinking about that night we talked at the quarry. Haven't stopped thinking about . . . you."

I look straight ahead, toward my house at the end of the street.

He pulls the neck of his sweatshirt up over his mouth so his words are muffled, like a little boy's. "I really like you, Grace. I feel like we're the same."

The moon's a flat silver disk. If I stare at it long enough, it blurs into a blob of light. I close my eyes and the shape of it glows on the inside of my eyelids. "You slept with my sister."

He winces. "Adam kept telling me to do it, and then she was so . . . she was really into it, and . . ."

"Did you sleep with her because she looks like me or because she's hotter than me?"

I have become a horrible person.

He takes a scared breath. "I slept with her because I knew you wanted me to like her. I wanted to try. Adam kept talking about twins, how hot it would be to hook up with twins, and it was gross, and I should have said something to him, but I didn't. I wanted . . ."

He clears his throat. "I wanted the four of us to fit together. But I didn't fit with Joy. I fit with you."

Maybe the girl that he painted would have fit with him. But this girl doesn't fit with anyone. Even the parts of me that used to interlock with Joy are closed up now.

"So you knew." My voice sounds so dead. "You both planned it. The sex."

He flinches at the way I say it. "No! No. He pulled me aside, said there was this energy, that I needed to live in the moment. Break out of my shell."

I close my eyes again. I want to see how long I can walk without seeing anything.

"It didn't mean anything to me," he says a little desperately. "It was a mistake. So I was thinking, maybe it didn't mean anything to you that you slept with him, either."

The longer I walk with my eyes closed, the more it feels like floating. I veer away from his voice. The darkness behind my eyes yellows and there's a rumbling noise in the distance.

"Car!" I hear him cry, but I don't move. The car can move. The whole world can move, if it wants, and I'll stay still.

A honk, long and blaring. A hand yanks me hard to the side. I open my eyes.

"Are you drunk?" he pants, terrified.

"Just tired."

He doesn't say anything the rest of the way home. His silence is painful. He misses that girl he talked to at the quarry.

I don't. This smooth nothingness is much better.

"Is that your bedroom window there?" he asks timidly when we reach my house. All the shades are still drawn. Nobody noticed I was gone. "Did you sneak out by climbing down that tree?"

"That's my sister's room. She's the one who does that."

It's a chance for him to say something about her. Offer to call her, give me a message to pass along. But he doesn't.

It's not important. I don't think Joy thinks he's beautiful anymore.

I don't say good night. I just walk up the front steps and leave him behind. I can feel him watching me, there on the sidewalk, his shoulders tucked in, trying and failing to disappear.

August fades away. I become nocturnal. The later I stay up, the less I have to sleep, and the less I sleep, the less I dream. I get up early once, to meet with Principal Eastman. He agrees to my independent project as quickly as my teachers do. I keep forgetting what I tell them I'm going to be working on.

I start scheduling normality. Two days a week I'll have dinner with Mom and Dad and Joy. Once a day I'll come downstairs and ask Dad how his new exercise routine is going. I give them just enough evidence that everything is fine. They accept it. It makes them feel good.

This week's big normal event is grocery shopping with Joy. Traumatized people don't go grocery shopping. If you can get a cart and select cereal, you're fine. You're alive.

Everyone here is ordinary. A man talking into his phone, a college girl checking the ingredients on a bag of trail mix. I want to crack them all open like eggs.

Joy hates raisin bran, but she eats only things she hates now. She's putting a box in our cart when she drops it. It slides across the floor. She doesn't pick it up. She's frozen.

I look up and see why. He's walking past our aisle.

He doesn't see us, or he's pretending not to see us.

What if he followed us here somehow? My thoughts spin. What if he's laughing about all the time he spends in my head?

"I'm going to kill him," Joy whispers. Her face is white. He's already gone, but she's lunging. I grab her. She jerks away. Hits the wall of cereal. Boxes scatter.

"Come on," I tell her. "Outside."

"I can't, Grace, I can't—"

"Come with me."

We leave the grocery store like refugees, abandoning our cart. I'm too shaky to walk and so is she. We crouch behind the building, next to the loading dock, on the shadowed pavement. Her knee brushes the side of mine. She digs her thumbnail into her wrist.

"I thought I was going to break his neck," she says thickly. "I can't go to school with him. I'll murder him in the hallway."

"You'll be okay." It's a meaningless thing to say.

"I think something's wrong with me." She sits, resting the back of her head against the brick wall. "I have dreams about hurting him, Grace."

Me, too, I almost cry. *Me, too!*

But I don't want her to know about my dreams. Her anger is noble, mine is slithering and poisonous.

"I hate him so much that I—" She grinds her teeth. Her anger's always been a weapon. Stronger than mine, stronger than November's. I remember how November held the scissors, how her hand faltered.

"We have to do something," she begs. "Please let me do something."

Joy's hand wouldn't have faltered.

"Okay," I say. "I'll let you do something."

We spend hours in my room, figuring it out. Mostly she seems relieved I'm talking to her again. We take precautions—we google how to defend, kill, hurt, like we googled how to have sex. There are parts of the body that are shortcuts to death, too.

"It's not like we're actually, you know . . . planning on killing him," she says for the hundredth time, hesitating before saying it like she can't believe how it sounds. "This is all just self-defense stuff we need to know in case anything goes wrong when we confront him."

"Right. Yeah."

There are thoughts I have these days that I can't acknowledge, because if I do I get so scared I can't move.

Like: Joy's not like November. She's not just talk. She *wants* to hurt him. She would've hurt him in the grocery store if I hadn't stopped her.

Like: She won't be able to confront him without hurting him.

Like: I want her to hurt him.

"We'll say we have evidence, pictures proving that . . . he did what he did," she says. "And we'll . . . .we'll tell him that if he doesn't do what we say, we'll go to the police. We'll tell him that he has to drop out of Stanwick High and move out of town. Go live with his mom. Somewhere not here."

I pull my hair over my shoulder, twist a strand around my thumb.

"I'll say it. You don't have to talk." She's on my bed, hugging my pillow. She has a gauzy look. Is her skin getting thinner, too? "You don't even have to be there."

"I'm not letting you go alone."

"Let me do this for you, Grace." She chews her lip. "To make up for . . ."

She doesn't finish the sentence, and I pretend she didn't start it.

There's no way she'd be able to talk to him without tearing him apart. She's always defended me. She punched Ben Stockholm for making fun of my watercolors in third grade. She's stronger than Adam. She lifts weights, she's angrier, she hits hard.

And I want to see it.

"You can't go alone, and you can't talk to him where other people are listening," I say. "I have to go with you."

"I don't want you anywhere near him." She shakes her

head. "His birthday party on September thirtieth. I'll do it then. It'll be loud, people'll be drunk—I won't be alone with him, but nobody'll be listening." She gulps. "It's just—that's a month away I'll have to see him at school."

"You can do it." I lean forward. "Every time you see him, just remember that we have a plan. We'll go to his birthday party together—"

"No!"

She's shouting. We both look toward the door, but Mom and Dad are downstairs.

"I'm sorry," Joy whispers. Her cheekbones are sharper, the bags under her eyes deeper. "I don't want you there. I don't trust myself to protect you anymore."

"I trust you," I say.

I do trust her. I know she'll be able to do what I want, even if I haven't told her what that is. We're twins. She has to know.

She rests her head in her hands. We've always drawn from the same energy source. When she's strong, I'm weak. When I'm strong . . . "I don't feel old enough for this," she says quietly.

We're old enough for boys to take us upstairs. We're old enough for their fathers to look at us and say *nice*.

"It'll work," I say. It won't work. He'll laugh in our faces.

And that will make Joy mad.

"This'll fix things for you?" she asks. "You won't be mad at me anymore?"

I get up from my desk, sit down next to her, and hug her. It's dangerous, hugging her with my skin so thin. It feels like she's going to poke holes through me. Bleed me dry. I tense up. She tenses, too. Our barriers are too high to allow for whatever is supposed to pass between people during a hug.

I let her go. She looks like she's about to cry. I don't feel anything. And the best part about not feeling anything is not feeling guilt.

School starts. It feels like the first September in our whole lives that Mom doesn't drop Joy and me off together. No—there was fifth grade, when Joy had the flu and missed the first two days of school. In the halls without her, I felt defenseless. I wonder if she feels the same way now.

I make her promise not to do anything to him. I want to be there when she snaps. I picture it: she'll break his nose, knock him down, kick him in the face. And I'll see that the person haunting me is nothing more than one more bully for my sister to protect me from.

And then I'll be fine. I'll go back to school, I'll get back on track, I'll go to college, and everything will go back to the way it was before this summer. I'll be worth something again.

A month slides by. Joy gets thinner. I get thinner and fatter and thinner and fatter again. My weight is the only way I keep track of time now.

The day of his birthday, he has thirty-seven well-wishers

on his Facebook wall by the time I wake up. I spend hours getting ready. I put on makeup so thick it cracks. Makeup is important. If you do it the same way every day, people will start thinking it's how you look. But you can never slip up or they'll realize the truth.

Joy is late coming home. Mom and Dad are at work. I'm alone on my bed, watching the sky change from blue to gray. The shadows in my room lengthen. Where is she?

Finally the door downstairs opens. I hear her drop her bag, clatter up the stairs. She looks terrible when she comes in. Like a drowning person.

"Sorry," she says. "I was at Preston's."

When is she going to learn that she doesn't need anyone besides me?

"It's fine," I tell her. "Go get your outfit together."

But she doesn't move from my doorway.

She looked the exact same way on our thirteenth birthday. We'd been planning to get ice cream and go to the movies with Mom and Dad, like we did every year. But she got invited to some water park. She wanted to go, she'd said. She just really really wanted to go.

But she came with me, in the end. In the end, she always does what's right for me.

"I can't do this," she chokes. "I can't confront him, I can't blackmail him with evidence we don't even have. I'm afraid, Grace."

I force calm into my voice. "He won't do anything. Not

at his birthday party. There will be people around."

"I'm not afraid of *him*."

Of course she's not. She's stronger than him. She would have fought him off.

"I'll be okay," I say. "I keep telling you, I feel fine. This is mostly for you. You're the one who kept saying you needed to do something."

"I know." She wraps a hank of hair around her fist hard. "You're . . . you're strong, Grace. I always thought I was the . . . You handled all this fine from the beginning. I thought you just wouldn't tell me, but you've always been fine. You don't need me."

She gives me this hopeless look and it kills me. She's wrong. I need her tonight. But I can't tell her—it sounds manipulative. *I'm hoping you'll snap and beat the shit out of him. Maybe even kill him. I want to watch.*

It is manipulative. I'm manipulating her.

"I'm scaring myself," she cries. "I've only been able to avoid him at school because I keep thinking, he doesn't know. He doesn't know what's coming. That I'm going to hurt him, that I'm going to . . ."

She gasps and covers her face with one arm.

"I think if I talk to him face-to-face I'll kill him," she says into her sleeve. "I think I'll really try to. I can feel it, this tingling when he's around, like this pressure gauge inside me going up, and if it gets full . . . I don't want to know what happens if it gets full. I don't want to know what I'm capable of."

There's something battering on my shields. Guilt.

You wanted to point her at him like a weapon and set her off. You didn't think about what it would do to her.

But there's so much else behind that guilt. So many awful things churning in the dark. If I turn on the light, if I let it in . . .

"I don't like myself anymore, Grace," she says in a wispy voice. "I always thought everything I did was for you. And that's a good way to like yourself, to think you're doing everything for someone else. But you don't need me to do anything to him. You're setting up this plan, going to all this trouble, because you care about me. Because you think *I* need it."

Don't feel it. If I feel the guilt, I'm lost.

"You're looking out for me." She lets go of her hair. "You always do . . . I want to hurt him to make myself feel better, that's all. I think that's what I wanted all along. I never thought our plan would work. I just wanted a chance, a reason to blow up at him. For my own sake. I couldn't let you be okay."

I'm going to break. If I tell her the truth, if I tell her not to go to the party and beg her to know that she's not selfish, that she's beautiful and good . . .

She thinks I'm a better person than I am. A perfect person. I can't destroy her version of me. That girl deserves to live. Joy deserves that sister. And maybe somewhere there's a version of the universe where that sister does the right thing. I wish her well. I hope she's happy.

"You're right," I say out loud. "All of this was for you. I don't need it."

She nods. Her eyes are red. I battle a wave of sickness.

"*You* need this," I say. "I want you to be okay, Joy. That's why we're still going to go to the party. You have to get this out of your system before it messes you up."

She wraps her arms around herself. "I'm already messed up."

"You won't be if you get this chance." I have to step carefully. Weigh everything I say. "If you talk to him . . . You need to see that he's just a pathetic person. That he doesn't matter. Then you can get on with your life."

"What if I attack him? What if I really kill him?"

"So what?" I mutter.

She stares at me.

I backtrack. "You won't. I know you. Everybody has those thoughts. It's natural. People say it: *I'll kill him*. But nobody actually does it. Not normal people, and you're a normal person, Joy."

"I don't feel normal."

"That's okay," I insist. "I know you and I know that you are. We'll go ahead with our plan. We'll confront him, get out your anger, and then we'll leave. You'll feel better. You won't hurt him."

She will.

"I think I would hate myself forever if I did." She shivers. "Knowing how selfish it was."

Nobody realizes how much emotions cloud you until

they're gone. Being empty makes you clear-eyed. You can see other people for what they are. Their emotions, how they're like arrows, pinging them down a little path that they aren't even aware of. If you can see someone's path, you can alter it. Cheat the maze, set up new corners, a new path, the one you want them to be on. A talent I'm discovering.

Is this something *he* could do? Did he set up a little path that led me to his bedroom?

No. I'm nothing like him. I'll only use this power once. So everything can go back to the way it was. I'll make it up to her.

She's wavering. Everything's still going to happen exactly how I want it to.

"No," she says suddenly, startling me. "I'm not doing this. You've done enough for me, Grace. I'm not making you do anything for me ever again."

Wait. No. "I want you to—"

"I have to do what's best for you for once. Not just what's best for me in disguise."

Everything is unraveling. There's a fresh note of resolution in her voice. Panic seeps into me. "This . . . this is important for you to do. I love you and . . ."

"I love you, too." She looks at me for a second with all of it in her eyes, and I have to stop breathing. "That's why I'm not going."

I was wrong. I don't have any control over her. Or anyone. Just like I had no control over him, or myself. I'm still helpless.

If my sister doesn't protect me from my demons, they'll

ruin me. I won't be able to go back to school, I won't get into college, everything that was worthwhile about me—

Will disappear.

"Grace?" she says.

I'm ice. I'll stay ice forever. Cryogenic. Frozen in time before anything can catch up with me.

But Joy's fire. Fire grows and flickers, changing all the time. Devouring other things in order to get bigger. None of this will affect her for long. She'll go on with her life and leave me behind. She's always leaving me behind.

I want her to stay frozen here with me.

"Everything you said this summer about breaking me out of my shell, that was selfish, too, wasn't it?" I say in my new ice voice. "You just wanted me with you so you'd feel comfortable doing the crazy stuff *you* wanted to do. You wanted me in the background so you'd feel safe fucking Cassius."

Her eyes open wide. The part of me that cares is locked outside.

"You never cared about protecting me." I can't stop. "I was just there as a safety net. So you got to be the brave one. That's always been the point of me, being this background that you get to stand out against."

She hasn't moved an inch. Good. Now we're both frozen.

Trying to be different is dangerous. People only change for the worse.

She opens her mouth, shuts it again. Then she backs out into the hallway. It's the first time in her life she hasn't slammed the door after a fight. She closes it so gently it's like she's shutting a dead person's eyes.

I stay in my room while, three miles away, the rest of the world celebrates the fact that Adam Gordon was born.

Then, at two a.m., while I'm lying awake, my phone blows up with Cassius Somerset's name.

> I didn't know what adam was doing that night I swear. I just found out. I'm so sorry.
>
> I am so sorry grace.

My fingers shaking, I text back. **what are you talking about?**

> adam just said.
>
> I punched him and Im going to do worse than that. Im going to kill him.

whatever you heard. forget about it.

> I shouldnt have listened to him. Your sister was there. she should have stopped it.
>
> She should have checked on you. I should have checked on you. jesus Im sorry.
>
> Does your sister even know? is that why she came tonight?

joy is there? joy went to his birthday party?

> She came to his birthday party and got fucking drunk. what is wrong with her?

is she okay? has she talked to him?

cassius answer me. is my sister okay?

don't let anything happen to her.

you have to make sure nothing happens to her.

NINETEEN

October 26

Joy

THE NEXT MORNING, NOVEMBER'S EDITO-
rial is all over school.

I read it three times.

WHY I DIDN'T TELL WHEN ADAM GORDON RAPED ME
When I was little, I thought I knew what strength was.
It was a powerful person, fighting bad guys. Everyone
understands that kind of hero. They're in every story. The
police officer, the soldier, the warrior princess, the rebel.
Heroes protect people, slay the enemy beast, climb the
perilous mountain.

But what happens when getting out of bed in the
morning takes as much energy as climbing a mountain?
When going to school feels like jumping into the villain's
pit of rattlesnakes? When the enemy's nothing you can

shoot an arrow at but a voice inside you, and you can't destroy it without destroying yourself?

We're heroes, too. But we don't look as good on a movie screen. The problem is that we don't know what we are until we see ourselves somewhere. That's what stories are for, except when we don't look like the people in our stories, it keeps us in the dark. Things turn ugly in the dark. And when we don't see our battles treated like real battles, when we don't get to see how brave others are for struggling with the same thing as us, we don't understand that we're brave, too.

If getting out of bed in the morning is as hard for you as fighting a monster, then you're a monster-fighting badass. If going to school makes you want to cry and you go anyway, you're a hero and your story is worth something.

I changed my name to November because that was the month I got sent to a mental health facility after Adam Gordon raped me. I expected therapy to be bullshit. And some of it was. But mostly, while I was there, I realized what I wasn't. I wasn't weak. None of the people I met there were weak because they were sad. People say *don't let things get to you*, but sometimes things just get to you and that's the way it is. And it's okay.

Originally, I was going to write this as a letter to him. But you are so much more important than he is. And I want you to know that wherever you are, whatever you're struggling with, I see you. Your monsters are real, and you're brave, and I'm proud of you.

The newspaper is recalled once Vice Principal Matthews realizes what was printed, but copies are everywhere. People hide it in their lockers, stuff it in their sweatshirts, read it under their desks in class. There's a lot of whispering.

Levi isn't in American History.

When the bell rings for lunch, November's waiting for me outside the classroom door. Half the people passing by stare at her, and there's a nasty comment somewhere in the crowd, but she ignores it.

"Do we really have to do this?" she groans.

"Yes. I'm escorting you everywhere today." I glare at a freshman who points out November to his friend, muttering behind his hand.

"It's cool, Joy. I don't care what they think." Her smile's real. "I thought I would, but I don't. I wrote it for the right reasons."

"Are people being okay to you?" I say over the rush of hallway noise as we walk together.

"Some people are being dicks and some people are not being dicks. But that's life." She hitches her bag higher. "I got a few hugs."

"Hugs?"

"Brodie Simmons said I helped with her depression. That is a nice thing to be told."

"You helped me, too," I say. It's true. I can handle thinking clearly for the first time in forever. I still don't know who the blackmailer is, but I'm going to figure it out. Today I'll be there for November, but then I'm going to find a way to stop this.

November squeezes my arm. I push away my thoughts. I want to be the great friend she thinks I am. "So nobody's harassing you?"

"Joy Morris, I can take care of myself," she says. "The only annoying part of today was Vice Principal Matthews. She kept me in her office all morning. I'm banned from the school newspaper."

"That's bullshit!" I snarl, fuming. "I'm going in there and—"

"Who cares?" She smiles again. "I said what I wanted to say."

We round the corner of the hallway and head into the cafeteria. The cafeteria has never gone silent before, but today it comes pretty close. November snickers as we get in line.

"By the way," she says under her breath, "daily reminder that it wasn't your fault."

"Daily reminder that it wasn't your fault, either."

"Not working yet, is it?"

I shake my head.

"Maybe eventually," she says quietly.

Before we can get our food, there's a commotion by the doors. It's Ben, trailed by Kennedy and Sarah. Ben has a sheaf of papers under his arm. He slams one to the cafeteria wall and tapes it there.

"Don't start shit, Joy," November says to me as Ben whips around and beelines straight for us.

"I thought you might be interested in this," he says loudly. Now the cafeteria really is dead silent. He pushes a

268

flyer toward her. I intercept it. There's a picture of Adam's face and the words *Remember our friend the way he really was.* "We're planning another memorial service for Adam next week. The point is to celebrate what a *great guy* he was. From the memories of people who knew him, not a lying bitch who hated him for no reason."

November puts out a hand in front of me, but I'm not lunging, even though I'm quaking with fury. She's right. She can handle this herself. My anger's not the important thing. Sometimes being a good friend means standing back.

"The amount I give a shit about what you have to say is so small it couldn't be seen with a microscope," she says coolly.

Kennedy and Sarah press in behind us. Kennedy's glaring. Sarah bites her lip.

Ben leans in. He's breathing as heavily as he did the day he fought with Levi. "You can disguise it with fake-inspirational mental health bullshit all you want, but I know what you're doing. You just want attention."

The freshmen at the tables nearest me are motionless, sandwiches halfway to their mouths. It'd be funny if my skin wasn't buzzing. Even the people who were coming out of the food line are still, their trays tipping in their hands.

One of them is Levi.

My stomach jolts. I thought he skipped today. Our eyes meet for a split second. He's not smiling. He looks really tired. There's only an apple on his tray.

Please let him believe her.

"You all realize she's lying, right?" Ben addresses the cafeteria at large. "She said it herself. She got chucked in a mental hospital. She's fucking crazy."

I punched him in third grade. I'm burning to do it again, but November's staring him down like a badass, unflinching, and he tenses.

Levi abandons his tray on a nearby table and walks toward us.

"You're on my side, right?" Ben says to him. "Adam's half bro?"

Levi's cheeks are hollower than normal. His baseball cap is nowhere in sight. "Why don't you fuck off?"

"I should've known." Ben laughs mockingly. "You're way more of a pussy than Adam—"

"Will you shut up?" It's Sarah, trembling. She glances nervously at November.

"I liked your editorial," she says rapidly, looking petrified. "It was—it—I'm sorry."

The corner of Nov's mouth lifts. She holds out a fist. After a moment, Sarah returns the bump.

Levi stares at all of us for a second. His throat works. I can't tell what he's thinking. He backs away, turns, and half runs out of the cafeteria without telling me what it is.

Ben and Sarah are arguing, their voices raised, but I don't catch a word of it.

"Go," November mouths to me.

So I do.

But I hesitated too long. By the time I reach the halls, they're empty.

I take out my phone to text him, even though I have no idea what to say.

There's a new email on my screen from the address tojoymorris@gmail.com.

Instinctively I know who it's from. My heart stops. But it's done that so many times, and it always starts again.

"Joy?" someone says. I turn, and Preston is coming out of the science wing, one of his lunch hiding places. My chest uncoils at the sight of him.

"Perfect timing," I say.

He steps closer, and I hold the screen up wordlessly. He squints at it, then his eyes go wide.

"You think?"

Breathe. I can handle this fear now. "Guess he's entered the digital era."

"We can track the IP address," he gasps.

"Let's read it first." I keep my voice calm, but my palms are sweating. "Not here. Outside."

We slip out through the side door beside the math classrooms and crouch together against the brick wall, next to the Dumpsters. When my hand starts shaking, Preston opens the email for me. We read it together.

To Joy Morris—

I guess I can tell you who I am now.

The day Adam died was the day I found out what he did to Grace. Do you know what it's like to realize that the person you called your best friend was a stranger? A monster?

By the time I followed him to the quarry, everyone else at his birthday party had left. I hid in the trees while he walked, drunk, to the edge. I don't think he jumped. But it wasn't quite like he fell. It was like the quarry pulled him in.

Most of the time, when people do bad things, nothing happens to them.

It all began when I found those pictures in Savannah's room. I don't trust the police—I thought if I brought the photos to them, they'd brush me aside.

If someone caught me putting them up, Savannah would hate me forever. That's when I thought of you. I knew you'd been blackout drunk at Adam's birthday party, that there was no way you remembered that night, and that you must have wanted him dead after what he did to Grace. I was too scared to put up the photos, but you're brave. I knew youd be able to go through with it.

How rationally were *you* thinking after finding out something horrible had happened to your sister?

And maybe part of me thought you deserved to suffer for what happened this summer. It was supposed to end after that. But November invited me to her house one day, and while she was downstairs, I found that security video of Officer Roseby in his room. I went through his closet—I knew he'd had something to hide. I knew if everyone saw it, he'd have to stop harassing me.

And when November and I got closer, when she finally told me what Adam did to her, I knew the school needed to know the truth. November needed them to know, even if she couldn't tell them herself.

I never meant to use you more than once. It just worked so well the first time. But you used me, didn't you, this summer? So we're even.

I don't think you'll show anyone this email. It would mean admitting you were the one who put up the photos and swapped the DVDs. Either way, I'm far away now. If you accuse me, I'll lie. But I thought I at least owed it to you to tell you that it's over.

We made our school a better place. A safer place.

Cassius Somerset

"It *was* him," Preston's face goes pale and then red. "I was right about him, all along. We'll make him pay for this—"

"No. We won't."

"What?"

I lift my face toward the sky. It's clear. The sun cuts around the edge of the building just enough to douse us completely with light. "I'm sick of revenge."

"We can't just let him get away with this," he says, disbelieving.

I lift my hands, examine them. These hands never pushed anyone into the quarry. They're normal hands. I'm a normal person.

There is no secret evil core in me.

"He's gone, Preston," I say. "Getting revenge will just stop this from being over."

"He *blackmailed* you for something you *didn't do*."

I'm never going to get another one of those notes again.

I can sleep. I can eat. I can focus on Grace. I can make everything about Grace again. This time I'm going to do it better.

"How are you not angry? You're . . . you."

Maybe Grace's Joy got angry. But this is my version. And I decide when it's worth getting angry.

"I didn't do it, Preston."

He groans. "We always knew you didn't do it."

"I wasn't sure," I whisper. "I don't think anybody knows themselves that well. The only way to find out is to be in the situation. I was . . . and I couldn't remember what I did."

I only cry for a few minutes. Preston fidgets miserably beside me. I wipe my eyes, because I know what it's like to want to help and not know how.

I stand up, because I still need to be with November today, because I need to find Levi, even if I'm afraid to face him. But my head fills with light and I lose my balance. Preston catches me.

"You okay?"

"No." I sound delirious. "But I will be."

He sighs, but he doesn't put me down. "You're actually going to let this go."

"I want to try letting something go," I tell him.

When I get home that night, I steal into Grace's room first.

"Joy," she mumbles as I slip into bed beside her, like I used to. Like I always will.

"I have to show you something," I whisper.

The invisible force field between us is weaker. Maybe it was only so strong because I needed it to be.

She wakes up, pulling the quilt over both our heads so that we're in a tent. "Did you talk to November?" she says tentatively.

I show her the email. The cold light of the phone screen illuminates every detail of her face. Sometimes the fact that we're identical seems ludicrous to me. She's so different. Her pores are clogged with makeup I don't wear. Her eyebrows are stubbly with plucked hairs that I let live. She's decorated with choices that are hers alone.

There's only the sound of our breathing and the heavy silence of somebody reading something very important.

Finally she looks up.

My phone light fades. I can't see her at all in the dark, but we're so close that the vibrations of her voice shiver along my skin. "Cassius did this to you?" she chokes. "I can't believe . . ."

"Don't hate him," I tell her.

"How can I *not*?" The whites of her eyes shine.

"You're right," I say. "Hate him until you don't need to hate him anymore. But don't do anything about it."

"You can't trust any guy. No matter how they act." Her voice shakes. Her hair tickles my chin. It lies fine and straight on the pillow, any evidence of our curls burned out of it. "Once, I thought Cassius was . . ."

"It's okay."

"I was wrong about November." In the dark, I can hear all her emotion. It's only in the daylight that she hides it.

"The whole school knows that—they know what he did to her now," I tell her. "She wrote about it in the school newspaper. I'll bring you a copy. You can read it if you want."

"Is she okay?" she says in a tiny voice.

"She's okay." And I believe it.

I want to believe it about Grace, too.

"I hoped you'd blame November," she says, shivery. "I wanted you to hate her. I was scared you were leaving me behind for her. I'm always scared you're leaving me behind."

"I never will, I promise." I can center my life around her again.

"I'm sorry I've been so distant," she whispers. "I thought if I could push you away before you could do it to me, it wouldn't hurt so much."

Her body heat soaks the tiny space we share until beads of sweat pop on my cheeks. "Now it'll be you and me again. Just us," I say.

For some reason, I remember what Levi said, about how neither of us have had the chance to find out who we are without each other. My spine prickles strangely.

She clasps her hands together in front of her mouth. "I won't doubt you anymore."

This is all I ever wanted. To have things be the way they were. But now, for some reason, this feels wrong. Like trying to put on an old favorite shirt only to find it doesn't fit anymore.

I swallow. It doesn't matter. I owe her. I'll spend the rest of my life making it up to her.

"You and me," I tell her, twisting my words until there's happiness in them.

"You and me," she repeats.

Us.

I lean my forehead against hers, just to check, one more time if that twin telepathy has come into being yet. If I can read her mind.

But no current of secrets passes between our skin.

That's okay. They don't need to.

All our secrets have been laid to rest.

The next morning, I wake up in my own bed. I don't remember leaving Grace's room.

I push the covers back and then I'm shivering, freezing cold everywhere, in my blood, fingertips numb, head throbbing, popping full of needles.

"You're sick," Mom informs me after she takes my temperature. She sits back on my bed, studying me while a dragon eviscerates my chest. "Did you take ibuprofen?"

I sneeze.

"I'll call you out," she sighs. "But talk to your teachers about any missed assignments first thing tomorrow. Your father and I have to go to work, but Grace will be home."

Us.

Mom leaves and I go back to dying. This sickness feels like an exorcism. Like all the fear from the past month is being drained from my body.

I'm sick for three days.

It's a blur of fever, arguing with Dad about going to the doctor, Mom bringing me soup, Grace delivering glasses of water to my bedside table. Her coming into my room isn't an event anymore. Once, when she goes downstairs, I get up and walk in and out of her doorway five times just to prove I can.

On the fourth day, I wake up and I can see straight.

I'm not sweating anymore. I check the clock—two thirty in the afternoon. There are a couple of glasses of water on my bedside table, Grace's contributions. I chug them both. Someone knocks on my door.

"Come in," I croak. Mom and Dad are gone. It's got to be Grace.

But it's not Grace. It's Levi.

"The front door was unlocked. Dunno if that counts as breaking and entering. I brought you soup," Levi says nervously, a Tupperware container under his arm. "I googled the recipe and I bought dried shiitake mushrooms and I let it simmer for four hours."

Levi?

Levi's in my house.

I'm 110 percent awake. I bolt upright, tissues falling off my chest.

Did Grace see him come up the stairs?

I was wrong. I didn't tell her every secret.

"November Roseby said you were sick. She gave me your address." Levi stares at my posters, at my bookshelf, like they're fascinating. My room's not as horrifying as it was a month ago, but it's still pretty bad. I don't freak out about it, though, or the fact that I haven't brushed my hair in three days, or that I'm wearing one of Dad's old shirts, because if Grace comes in—

"Are you drinking enough water?" he stutters. "Do you need orange juice? I can go buy orange juice. Do you need more tissues?"

"You have to leave." My throat's full of razor blades. This is the one thing left that could mess things up again.

"That's fair. I figured you'd feel that way." He sets the Tupperware on my bedside table and turns to go.

Grace still sleeps so late. She's probably asleep now. I can risk a few minutes.

"What way?" I ask.

"Well." His voice is scratchy, too, but not because he's sick. "I'm related to the guy who raped one of your best friends."

"That's not why . . ." But I can't finish my sentence.

"It is." He won't meet my eyes. "That's why you hated Adam. That's why you didn't want to be around me at first. And that day it rained, that's why you pushed me away, right?"

There's none of his usual humor. Just guilt.

"I didn't want you to lose your version of him," I say weakly.

"Fuck that version. When I read that editorial . . ." He stops halfway to my door. "My first thought was, what's going to happen if my dad sees it? I'm an asshole."

"You're not—"

"Don't." His back knots up. "I assumed Adam was this—perfect person."

I wince away from the self-loathing in his voice.

He twists his earring hard. Then he exhales and forces a smile. "Now I get it. He was never worth knowing, so I don't have to spend my whole life being sad I didn't get the chance. I'm glad I never cried about him."

I blink hard a few times.

"I'll go now," he says. "I get that you probably won't want to be near me, considering genetics."

"Genetics don't mean anything." I sit up. "Just because you're related to him doesn't mean you're *like* him. Don't go, okay?"

"It's okay. You don't have to make things up to me." He swallows. "My mom called this morning. She's been discharged. I'm flying back to Indiana in a couple days."

There's a long silence. "That's great," I croak, but I'm a jerk for not saying it immediately.

"I was always just here temporarily," he says helplessly.

"Right. Yeah. Of course."

"That's all I had to say." He smiles sadly. "Feel better." He turns, and I hear him going down the stairs.

If I don't follow him, I'll never see him again.

I'm not ready to let go.

I run to the kitchen. It's clean, empty. No sign of Grace. But even if she saw Levi, she wouldn't guess the truth. There's no Adam in him.

He's reaching for the door.

"I don't want you to be temporary," I blurt.

"Are you, like . . . mad?" he says in a small voice. "That I'm leaving?"

"Did you think I'd be a jerk about it and not be happy that your mom's okay?" Which is exactly what I'm being. "Did you think I'd flip out? Because, okay, I am flipping out, but that's only because I'm upset that you thought I'd do that, so this is a self-fulfilled prophecy—"

"Other people, they can hide their reactions," he cuts in. "Not you. I knew if you said, 'That's great, Levi! I'm so happy for you!' or any nice thing that a friend would say, that'd be the end of it, that'd be how you really felt."

"I swear, I am happy for you, Levi." I'm a terrible friend.

He runs his hand through his hair. "I didn't *want* that to be your reaction. I wanted you to be pissed that I was leaving."

"What? Why did you want me to be pissed?"

"Joy? Who's that?"

I turn and Grace is standing in the doorway to the kitchen, a cereal-flecked bowl in her hand, one of the heavy clay ones. All my excuses dissolve on my tongue. I realize with sudden absolute clarity that none of them would matter to her.

She clears her throat. "Sorry . . ."

She doesn't recognize him. How could she? She doesn't know.

"You must be Grace." Levi smiles.

She's makeupless. Her shirt's stained. She didn't know I had someone over. But she can't run back upstairs, she's invested in this interaction now. Thirty seconds of half-hearted chat and she'll leave. *Please don't mention Adam, Levi.*

"This is my American History tutor," I make myself say.

"Joy always talks about you." His happiness is genuine.

She gives a tiny smile. Then she edges past us, rinses out her bowl in the sink, and fishes a bag of microwave popcorn from the cupboard. She opens the microwave and sticks the popcorn in. It's all very choreographed. She keeps the bowl tucked under her arm like a talisman.

Two minutes and fifty seconds on the microwave. The timer to a nuclear holocaust.

"I like your shirt," Levi offers.

There are so many unlit fuses in the room.

"Are you a freshman?" She stays on the other side of the kitchen, away from him. "I haven't seen you around."

"Junior. I'm visiting from Indiana."

"I always forget about Indiana," she says, relatively normally. "All the *I* states."

She doesn't suspect.

"How many even are there?" agrees Levi. "Idaho . . ."

This is fine.

"Iowa," she says.

The popcorn's going off like gunfire.

"Anyway," Levi says. "I don't know if you knew Adam Gordon, but I'm his half brother. I came up for the funeral and ended up staying a while. Joy was the first person in town I met—at the funeral, actually—and she's been . . . great . . ."

His voice trails off as horror and confusion are unfolding in Grace's expression, like awful flowers.

It's okay. It'll be fine. I'll send Levi away. I'll explain everything—

It takes only a second. Her arm whips up and there's a crash. The kitchen floor turns into a minefield of clay shards and Levi's half collapsed against the stove, one hand clapped to his forehead, bright neon electric glowing red blood pouring out between his fingers.

"Grace!" I scream.

"What the fuck, Joy?" She cries. "What the *fuck*?"

This is not the Grace I fell asleep next to last night.

This is a Grace I've never met.

I reach for Levi, peel his hand back from his face. There's a thin gash bisecting his eyebrow, blood pouring out of it. The rest of him is milk pale. He pulls his hand from my grasp and looks wonderingly at the blood on it.

"At the *funeral*?" Grace is snarling. "Like, hey, let me show you around? Did you take him to the Ice Cream Palace? I know you took him into *our house*! Where I *live*!"

I can't hold both her and Levi together at the same time. Both of them are bleeding bright terrible colors.

I finally got her mad at me. I didn't know this is what it would look like.

"You have a right to be angry—" I whisper.

"*You* should be angry. But you're not. Not enough." Her bangs stick to her forehead with sweat. She's not making sense. "You never were. You didn't *have* to be."

Levi staggers upright, half his face streaked crimson.

My sister did this.

She lied to me. She's not okay.

"You need help." I straighten as calmly as I can manage. My voice breaks anyway. "We'll get you help, Grace."

"All I needed was for *you* to be on my side," she throws at me.

I grope for Levi's wrist, clutch it tight. He stares transfixed at my sister, then at me. His forehead's still bleeding. "Are you—" he starts.

"Go outside just for a second, okay? Stay on the porch. I'll handle this."

"Now I'm something to be handled." Grace's eyes glint with tears.

Holding a tea towel to his forehead, Levi opens the front door with his free hand and disappears through it.

I'm alone in my bloodstained shattered kitchen with my bloodstained shattered sister.

She starts shaking.

"Oh my God." She's paralyzed with sudden guilt. "I didn't mean—I was scared—I don't know what—"

I want to hold her, but I don't know if it would help or make it worse.

"It was like—" She chokes. "You think every trace of a person is gone from the world—and then part of him is standing in your kitchen—"

"There's no part of Adam in Levi," I say quickly, my heart pounding.

"How do you know?"

"Trust me." But she doesn't. She doesn't trust me anymore. My chest throbs. "Things still aren't okay with us, are they?"

She shies back like a cat. "This is about you, not me. This is about *you* betraying *me*."

"It's okay to need help, Grace." Calm, calm. I know what path she needs to take now. "Therapy helped November—"

"I don't need *that*," she snarls. "I'm not that kind of person."

"It's nothing to be ashamed of—"

"Not me." She backs away. "I'm different."

"Grace—"

But she's already sprinting up the stairs.

Levi reassures me on the porch as I examine his cut. "My forehead's fine. Head scratches bleed a lot, is all."

He's right. It's barely bleeding anymore. It doesn't make me feel better.

"What happened?" he asks.

"I don't know," I lie. Now that she's not in front of me, I'm shaking as hard as she was. Fights never catch up to me until they're over.

"Tell her not to feel bad, okay?" He twists the bloody towel in his hand. "I get it. It's not her fault. My mom's been there."

"She's not crazy!" I snap before remembering he doesn't like the c-word.

But isn't that what I told her when I said she needs professional help? Now I understand why he doesn't like that word. It makes something sound so much worse than it is.

He looks at me with a little bit of pity. "We don't have

to talk about it right now."

"I know that wasn't what you were expecting."

"I'm sure she's a good person." He nudges me, echoing what I said.

We sit in silence for awhile in the cold breeze, recovering. There's a pit in my stomach at the thought of going upstairs and talking to Grace.

"Look," he says. "This isn't the best time, I get that. And I understand if you have to be with her. But everything between us has been about our siblings since the day we met. Tomorrow's my last real day here. That Halloween fair is happening. There's no school, it's a teacher conference day. Let's go together. Let's talk about something other than them."

I'm supposed to be centering my life around her again.

But Levi is going away forever.

"If you're up to it, that is." He flushes. "You were sick. You are sick. And I mean, if I'm feeling up to it, with my excellent new battle scar and all."

One last moment of stolen time. Then he'll leave and I'll go back to being hers alone.

"Okay," I say, ignoring the wave of guilt.

He smiles uncertainly beneath the blood on his face, like he's not sure it's right, either. "Meet you at the ticket booth at noon."

When Mom and Dad get home, the house fills with normal sounds. Pots clattering, cooking noises. Grace's door hasn't opened yet. I've been waiting for her to go downstairs first.

I cleaned up, but maybe I missed a broken shard, a spot of blood. Maybe Mom will come upstairs and ask what happened and I won't have to start this conversation.

But she doesn't.

So I get out of bed.

It's Grace's choice to tell them about Adam, but I still have to tell them she needs help. If they refuse to see it for themselves, I'll make them look.

Before I can do anything, my phone buzzes.

tojoymorris@gmail.com

All my blood leaves my body.

What does Cassius want? He said it was over.

To Joy Morris—

There's one last thing that I need you to do.

I don't bother scrolling down. Preston was right. I shouldn't have let him get away with it.

I open Facebook, find Cassius's cell number, and call it.

He answers on the third ring.

"What the hell is wrong with you?" I don't realize how furious I am until I speak.

"Who is this?"

"I was going to forget about it, Cassius. I was going to chalk it all up to some kind of temporary insanity after what went on with your sister. God knows I understand that feeling. I even felt *bad* for you. But do you seriously think you can pull this shit when you already told me I didn't kill him? What part of your brain made you think that would work?"

"Is this Joy?" His voice is tinny, terrified.

"I'm not playing this game anymore."

"What are you talking about?" he stammers.

"Everything you said in your email—"

"What email?"

"What do you mean what email?" I bark.

"I never sent you any email. I don't even know your email address."

Why is he lying? There's no one else it could have been.

"This is . . . about Adam?" He gets very quiet. "You mean . . . you remember what happened that night?"

There's something in his voice.

Nausea chews at my stomach. "Remember what?"

"You blacked out," Cassius whispers. "By the time we got you back in your bed, you didn't remember any of it. You were so drunk."

"Who is we?"

"I have to go, Joy."

"Don't hang up—"

"I don't want anything to do with this anymore!" he cries. "I started over. This is my new life. Leave me alone."

The line goes dead. Cassius's name vanishes from my screen, and the email pops back up. My eyes finally settle on the rest of it.

To Joy Morris—

There's one last thing that I need you to do.

Either you tell Levi that you killed his half brother, or I'll send him, and the police, this video.

Attached file: adamsbirthdayparty.mp4

TWENTY

September 30

Grace

GETTING DRESSED IS HARD. MY FINGERS won't move. I maneuver into my sweatshirt with my wrists, elbows. Yank on shorts. I never washed off my makeup.

Don't be scared. Be something else. Empty isn't working.

I can't hold on to the handlebars of my bike, so I abandon it in the dew-wet grass of our lawn, dropping it softly so Mom and Dad won't hear. I don't need it. We walked the last time, too.

She wasn't supposed to go alone. I was supposed to be there, a safety net in the background. *Joy, don't do anything without me. Don't go anywhere without me. It's not safe for either of us to ever be alone.*

Only two cars pass me on the way there, the headlights

slicing through the darkness.

As I get closer, I hear the bass down the deserted road, past all the trees. Fast, like the people are dancing to my heartbeat.

There's a bonfire in the yard, barely controlled, but nobody's watching it. This is the kind of party I thought we'd find that night. The kind of party where everyone is hungry, but it's okay, because everyone is overflowing with themselves. When people take, there's enough to go around. There's still soemthing left behind.

I slip inside like I did at Cassius's party, like a ghost. The furniture's shoved to the side. A rotating black box spits blobs of colored light at the walls. I wind through laughter and screams. Underneath it all, there's the quiet hungry growl of the quarry. Nobody else hears it.

There's a hundred people packed together, one body with a million limbs. The house drinks me into the walls. An elbow knocks the breath out of my chest. Light moves dizzyingly over faces mashing together in front of me. I try to disappear, but there's too many hands and everyone is so starving and there's not enough left of me to feed anyone. *Find Joy.*

And there he is, detached from everyone, in the center of the mass, the hungriest of all, staggering to the beat. In the darkness his shape is feral. Flashes of red light illuminate every drop of sweat, his mindless, drunken grin.

He'll look. He'll see me. He'll take what's left. The fear

knocks all my walls down at once and I feel everything. Everything.

I run. I fight through a jungle of people, and then a jungle of trees. There's no moon, no stars. I lose myself in the dark. Branches snag me, trip me, cut me. I fall. My knees bleed more than when Joy shaved hers. I'm on my stomach in the dirt and dead leaves, just like when November and I broke into his house. I'll always be running, running in circles. I'm in a cage made of my own bones and skin.

Some part of me sits back and watches me sob. *Get over it.*

I was wrong about being empty. I was always full. I just couldn't see it.

People turn off the light when they don't want to know what's in the dark. Everyone's afraid of the dark. They should be afraid of the light.

Pine needles scratch my cheek. Slowly the cold of the earth soaks into me, the truth with it. Tricking my sister into hurting my rapist was never going to help me. There was never an easy fix, a secret shortcut to being okay. I've always been screwed up, and now I'm screwing up Joy, too.

I stay, I don't know how long, until I stop making noises. Then I realize the house isn't making noises anymore, either.

I leave the woods.

The sky's a different kind of blue now. The cars that were in the driveway are gone. I was in the woods for hours.

I left Joy alone for hours.

The house is full of beer bottles, pizza boxes, spilled liquids, but no people. In the silence, my heartbeat is deafening. Did Joy go home? Did she find him first?

"Grace, is that you?"

Cassius is stumbling toward me in the dark, hitting the edge of the dining room table. One of his eyes is bloodshot and swollen. His phone sticks out of his shirt pocket. He stops far away from me and stretches out a hand, like he's reaching over some impossible distance.

"Where's Joy?" I ask, my voice too loud.

"I . . . don't know."

"I asked you to find her."

He sways, still drunk. His cheeks are crisp with dried tears. "Grace—I'm sorry—my head is always in the wrong place and if I'd been thinking right that night, it never would have . . ."

I'm so tired of having to reassure people that what happened to me wasn't their fault.

"Cassius, shut up. Tell me when you last saw my sister."

He blinks his uninjured eye. "I think it was . . . everyone left, right before I passed out in the kitchen. I saw them before that—"

"Them?"

"Joy . . . and Adam."

All my blood jumps. "What were they doing? Where did they go?"

He's staring at me with a horrible apology in his eyes.

"Tell me where they are," I shout.

"They went into the woods . . . I think they were going down to the quarry."

The quarry that I almost fell into. What if Joy falls this time and I'm not there to catch her?

What if Adam pushes her?

"Why didn't you stop them?" I choke.

"I'm sorry!"

I sprint out the door, into the woods again. He follows me. All the times people've walked through the woods to the quarry, and no path has ever formed. You have to fight through branches every time.

If I can get there in thirty-three steps, nothing will happen to Joy.

"Let me talk to you," Cassius pleads in the dark. His steps are loud, crashing. It makes it impossible to count mine. "Please. I need to."

I don't care about what he needs. I care about my sister.

"Please, Grace."

I keep running, branches cracking under my feet. We're almost to the quarry. I can see it through the trees. And the sky, a dim bruised blue. The kind of night that has sun in it, but it's so faint you can barely tell the difference. All you know is that the light's coming. And it's going to show exactly what was in the dark.

Joy's voice slices through the trees, high and hysterical: "You *raped* my *sister*!"

My feet stick to the earth. I never gave her that word to use.

Cassius stops behind me, in shadows. I see Joy's silhouette wavering through the branches. She's barely upright. Adam is standing between her and the edge.

"What the fuck are you talking about?" There's a drunken edge to his voice.

"You know what I'm talking about!" She's blind drunk angry. Her pressure gauge is almost full.

Am I going to find out what she's capable of?

"Is this why you dragged me down here, some bullshit accusation?" Adam says.

Am I going to find out how much she loves me?

"You girls love to stir up drama," he slurs. "Like I was telling Cas, she called me, she probably felt like a slut and decided to cry rape. Prude like her. Her type, they say no because that's what gets them off. It turns them on. I was doing her a favor. People like her are easy as fuck to read."

I'm no longer ice. I am fire. Finally Joy and I can burn up at the same time.

"How can you . . ." But Joy is crying. She's not fine, not now. "How are you like this?"

"Chill the fuck out," he says, disgusted. "She had a crush on me, so I was nice to her because I'm a good guy. Usually I stick to hotter girls." He steps closer to her. "I would've gone for you—you actually have a personality. But I left you for Cas because he's such a charity case. He needs someone to take the reins, like your sister does. Those two never would have gotten anywhere. But you and I are the same. We go for what we want."

"Fuck you." It sounds small and sick and pointless.

"Is that what you want, why you made me come down here?" he asks, smirking. "Does this turn you on? You want me to 'rape' you, too? You and your sister, you're both repressed fucking freaks, you know that?"

"I'm going to kill him," Cassius whispers hoarsely behind me.

Everyone says that.

But nobody does it.

Adam will live a nice, long life not ever believing he did something wrong. He's going to play music and party and rape other girls and teach his kids to be like him. He's going to spread through the world like a sickness.

Normal people can't kill other people. But I'm not normal. I never have been.

Maybe that's my value. I could make the world safer for everyone else.

I could be worth something again.

"Stay away from me," Joy sobs, bringing me back.

"Get over yourself. Spend your time on something that matters. Look up." Adam waves an arm at the fading stars. The effort unbalances him. "We are so small, don't you realize? All this, this doesn't matter. It's petty, not worth it."

I wanted November to kill him for me. Then I wanted Joy to do it. Some part of me always knew it was the only answer. The true secret shortcut to being okay.

Maybe I'm the only one with any perspective. But I'm

the only one who can do it. I'll only be okay if it's me.

He's so close to the edge of the quarry. Unsteady. So close. One push. One easy fix left.

If I jump out of the trees, right now, and do it—

It'll be like he never raped me.

"We'll go to the police unless . . . you leave," I hear Joy mumble.

"Yeah. Sure. Sayonara." He laughs, like I knew he would.

"You." She shivers, totally weaponless, grasping. "You . . . I'll . . ."

She doesn't love me enough to do it. That's fine. If she did, I realize now, my last hope would be lost. I'd be in the cage forever.

I'm the one who needs to do it.

"I'll . . . I'll . . ." he mimics. "Believe whatever you want to make you feel like you had an interesting day. You and your sister, you're both crazy bitches. Clearly getting laid did not help like I thought it would."

My fury expands and then contracts, slamming together into a hard ball of cold iron. It fits inside me. It fits right in my chest. I forget about Cassius, about my sister, about everything. This is the moment. Before and after.

I was always capable of this.

But before I can do anything, there's a movement by the quarry. Joy lurches forward. She slaps at him uselessly. She shoves him a little. I freeze, but she's not trying. She's just drunk.

He stumbles back, his foot scraping the edge, but he's laughing. Neither of them seem aware that they're on the edge of oblivion.

I'm quivering, stuck. I can't push him when she's so close. She could fall.

"What are you trying to accomplish?" he snorts. "You know you're the only reason I hooked up with your sister, right? You practically threw her at me. Mainly I fucked her because you seemed to want me to do it so bad."

No. Don't say that to her. Don't say that.

Joy makes a strangled noise and shoves him again. It's a frail motion. It barely affects him. He's still smirking. All it does is make him take a tiny step back.

Except there isn't anything left to step back onto.

I can just barely see his face, in the bit of light bleeding into the sky. His expression contorts with a stupid bewilderment. His arms swing forward, groping for my sister, but she jolts back. She doesn't grab him like she grabbed me.

And then he drops out of sight.

The sounds of the crack and Cassius screaming thinly mixes with the rattle of the trees in the sudden wind, canceling each other out until my ears ring with silence.

The quiet, hungry growl of the quarry vanishes from the back of my head.

I leave the trees, walk up to the edge, and look down.

He's motionless, spread-eagled on the flat rock. His face is turned sideways, in shadow. A black stain pools beneath his head. It spreads slowly, the darkness eating up the stone.

"Jesus, oh Jesus . . ." Cassius is stammering from the edge of the woods.

The stain keeps moving.

But Adam doesn't.

"Grace?" I hear Joy mumble. I turn just as she sits down hard in the dust. Her eyes are unfocused, her mouth hangs open. The sharp smell of alcohol slaps me.

Something horrible settles inside me, along with a strange calm.

I look back into the quarry, but he's not there anymore, even if his body is. He's gone somewhere else. He's the new weight inside me.

She stole my only chance.

"Please don't tell, Grace." Tears leak down her face.

Because of her, I'll be like this forever.

"Grace . . ." She's barely conscious.

You practically threw her at me.

I wasn't afraid when I was running through the woods, I wasn't afraid when I saw them at the edge—but I'm afraid now.

What if I hate her forever?

"The police." Cassius finally looked over the edge. He's gasping. "We have to call . . ." He fumbles with his phone, drops it. I pick it up.

"It was an accident," I say robotically.

"What?"

"He was drunk and he fell in. Everyone's always saying how somebody was going to fall in."

"You . . ."

"She didn't mean for him to fall. You saw it. She wasn't thinking." I don't know why I'm protecting her. Because of her . . . "If you don't tell anyone, I'll forgive you for that night."

His mouth opens, but nothing comes out.

"It's not that hard, not saying something." *Come on, Cassius.*

"I'm . . ."

"For me," I say.

"I . . ." He won't look at Joy. "I . . . okay."

"Do you promise?"

He's sobbing. "Y—yes."

I move to give him back his phone. Then I notice a tiny green light above the screen, next to the camera.

"Is that recording?" I hear myself say.

"Adam wanted me . . . to film his birthday party." He digs his fingers unfeelingly into the front of his own shirt.

Joy mumbles something incoherent.

Before I delete the video, I hesitate. I highlight the last few minutes and email the file to myself.

Just in case.

"I need you to help me get her home," I say.

Joy's head tips forward onto her chest and then back up again. "You sound so mad," she slurs. "Are you mad at me, Grace?"

Then she leans forward and vomits.

She won't remember any of this.

"You're dreaming," I tell her. "We're going home."

Cassius doesn't say anything. And he won't. I'll make sure.

It's not that hard, not saying something.

TWENTY-ONE

October 30

Joy

I LIE RIGID UNTIL THE SKY CHANGES COL-
ors. Sunset. Sunrise. The broken-off shadow of the
severed tree branch moves over me and across the room.
There's a new stain on my sheets. My wrist is bleeding.
There's red on my fingernails.

Then Mom's in my doorway. Somehow it's the next
morning. I haven't moved since I watched the video. I tell
her I'm fine in an even voice. But she asks if I'm still sick.

"You don't sound—" She frowns. "Maybe you should
get more sleep."

I can't.

I have to meet Levi.

I have to tell him what I did.

Levi's Tupperware of soup is still on my bedside table.

I forgot to refrigerate it. I'll have to throw it away.

I shower, drown in steam, scrub, shave, pluck, blow-dry. Nails—wash off the red. New red, painted on. Band-Aid on my wrist. Makeup. Foundation, powder, kohl, until my eyes pop from pools of black. Hair straightened. Lipstick. Clothes.

If I look human, nobody will know. There's nothing inside me. I've emptied out. I don't want anything to do with the girl I was or what she did. I'm glad she's gone.

I set myself step-by-step plans: *Go downstairs. Walk downtown. Tell Levi I killed his half brother.*

Words don't have to mean anything if I don't let them.

Nothing has to mean anything if I don't let it.

"Joy," Dad yells. "Breakfast!"

My sister's door is closed. She's asleep. She always sleeps so late.

She knew.

Dad chokes on his orange juice when I walk into the kitchen.

"I have a date," I hear myself say. My chin quivers stupidly.

"You look beautiful." Mom glares at Dad. "You could just use a little blending. Can I help?"

"Yes," I whisper.

She brings me to the bathroom and pulls out tissue after tissue, dabs and rubs until my face looks real again. What would she do, if I punched the mirror and it shattered?

"I'm not used to you with straight hair. You look like

your sister." She lifts the edges of my hair. "Who's the date with? That boy who's been tutoring you? I know. I know what it would take to get Joy Morris to spend an extra instant on American History."

I'm glad she knows me. I'm glad she has a version of me to hold on to. She deserves her.

She looks at our faces next to each other in the mirror. "The bad thing about you girls being twins is that nobody tells me you look like me. The only thing anybody says is how you look like each other. Sometimes it feels like you brought each other into the world and I was only marginally involved."

She laughs, then points at my reflection's forehead. "Oh, but see that little mole right by your temple? I have one by my ear. Family moles."

I don't know why she's talking so much, for once. Maybe she senses something.

"I was always looking for evidence of myself in my sister. I made her compare our big toes once, to see if we both had that wonky nail. I could never figure out if we had anything in common."

"Mmm," I say.

"You and your sister, you've never had to do that. You've always been the same."

No. My sister isn't capable of the same things I am.

But if the blackmailer isn't Cassius, and the email came right after she found out about Levi . . .

Shut down. Turn off. Don't look. Nothing's there.

I need to tell Levi the truth anyway. I need to scare him so badly he won't try to stay in contact with me once he moves. He'll stay in Indiana. Stay safe.

Mom's waiting. But I can't find anything to offer her.

"All right. I get it. 'Stop rambling, Mom.'" She sighs, disappointed. "I'll give you a ride wherever you need to go."

She drops me off at the fair.

They have it every year in the middle school field, the one where we got high. I've come here, almost every year, with my sister. Booths are arranged on the field, blazing white against the grass that's still green, despite the cold air. The air smells like onion rings. Everyone's dressed up. Monsters and mummies and ghosts. You can't see anyone's face.

I stand by the ticket booth until he finds me.

He lights up when he sees me, that sudden bright smile. He's freshly shaven, his clothes ironed, a scarf around his neck. There's a scabby bruise on his forehead.

I lose control, just for a second, but then I win it back.

"I love the costume," he says, jogging toward me.

"My costume?" His face is so open and good. He is so good.

"You're Grace, right?"

I killed your half brother.

"I considered dressing up," he says. "But then I was like, what if we take a selfie, and it's the only picture we have together, and months later you think about flying out to visit me, and then you look at that picture and you're like, I am not dropping ticket fare on some asshole who can't even pull off a David Bowie wig."

He never had to be Adam's Levi. He's Levi's Levi, all the way.

"Hey." He takes my hand. "You okay?"

"Just tired. A little sick."

Tired. Sick. The best ways to explain everything away.

"Are you sure you're up to this?" he asks worriedly. "Maybe you should be in bed. You can rest, I'll pick up some medicine and juice and whatever. Are you a movie person or a book person when you're sick? I can go to the library."

I pushed your half brother into a quarry.

I pushed your half brother, and he fell into a quarry.

How different are those sentences?

It doesn't matter. The end result is the same. And it starts with *I pushed.*

"Sorry." He blushes. "Mom Levi makes a stunning appearance."

"I'm fine. How's your forehead?" I structure the words, syllable by syllable, building them, little houses of normality that we can live in.

"My forehead's fine. I got it checked out."

"Good," I tell him. "Let's go."

I want him to have a nice day before I tell him.

I spend as much money as I can—tickets to the pumpkin race, hot cider, rides. He tries to pay for things but I won't let him. I focus all my energy on being normal. Normal is delicate.

Levi makes all his usual jokes, but he's distracted today.

He keeps starting to say something and then cutting himself off, muttering *idiot* under his breath.

Once I catch him looking at me sideways, a lingering gaze, and even though I pretend I don't see it, there's so much warmth that I feel it. But that warmth isn't for me. It's for Levi's Joy, his imaginary girl. All I'm doing is stealing a taste of what would be hers.

Eventually he stops me by the craft booths. He's sweating. "Joy, listen—"

"Oh, hello, Grace!" a woman calls.

Is she here? I twist to look, but instead I trip backward and shear the skin off my elbow on a stone somebody used to reinforce one of the craft booth poles.

"Oh, my goodness. I'm sorry. It's Joy, of course, isn't it? The hair threw me off." It's our sixth-grade teacher, Ms. H something, standing beside the craft booth filled with mountains of identical crocheted dolls.

She's not here.

"I always do like seeing you and your sister. You two were never trouble like other twins. You never switched places," Ms. H. chatters, oblivious to my bleeding elbow. "We had a little joke in the staff room—the one with her mouth open is Joy, the one with her mouth closed is Grace."

Blood's darker on stone.

"Oh dear." Ms. H. peers over the dolls. "Are you all right?"

Levi pulls off his scarf and wraps it around my elbow. I

stare at the dark spot I left on the rock.

"Did you hear me? Joy?" he says.

I struggle upright, draw him away from Ms. H.'s booth. "What do you want to do now? Let's go get caramel apples. Do you want anything else? I've got a lot of money left."

"You don't have to keep buying me things."

"I just want today to be nice."

"It's nice." He cups my forearm tenderly, inspecting my elbow again. "Joy, it's nice."

What will he say when I tell him? I deserve his anger. I want to feel it.

He can even call the police. Prison's where they put people to keep everybody safe.

We walk. I say things and forget them seconds later. We watch a costume-judging contest. We pass a face-painting booth. Everyone's having so much fun.

"All right," he says suddenly, stopping so that I almost bump into him. "Okay. Gotta just do it. I wanna tell you something, Joy."

Tell him now. Don't make him go through with this.

"I was trying to decide how you'd react, but I don't know you well enough yet," he says nervously. "I say a lot of stupid shit but none of the brave shit."

Stop talking for once.

"You're brave," he stammers. "That's the main thing I know about you. And the main thing I know about me is that I wish I was braver. I think sometimes we fall for the people we wish we were. Not that I've *fallen* for you, what a stupid phrase. But I think I could. I don't just like who I am in the context of you, I like *you*."

No, no, no.

"I don't want you to be some fantasy of a girl I met once, I want to know you for real. I don't want you to be an ex-maybe."

The reality of me is going to break his heart, just like the reality of Adam did.

"It's probably wimpy of me to tell you this right before I move back to Indiana," he babbles. Then he stops. "Actually, you know what? I am not a wimp. I'm dealing with the fact that my dead half brother was an asshole, and I told you about my mom—you're the first person I've ever told about my mom—and those were really hard things for me to do. So I'm a badass, as a matter of fact. A super cute and funny badass who you should probably make out with or something."

I can't move or breathe or I'll lose it.

"Oh, God. Okay." He stares at me, terrified, misinterpreting my silence. "Can you just pretend I didn't say any of that? Just, uh. Forget it."

The thing about feelings is that they're not separated into packets you can open one at a time. They're tangled. If you pull on one, everything comes apart. Levi's pulling hard and I'm about to unravel.

"I have to go to the bathroom," I lie.

I don't wait for him to follow me. I find the Porta-Potties, garish blue. Inside, I reach for my phone to call Preston, but . . .

He believed in me. He thought I wasn't capable of it. I don't want to destroy his version of me, either.

Anybody who gets close enough to find out who I am for real is going to hate me.

The people who love me only do because they don't know the real me yet.

Then I see it, shoved in the corner, one more gross thing abandoned in a Porta-Potty. A bottle of cheap whiskey with two inches of amber liquid left in the bottom. I unscrew it.

People talk about their lowest point like there's some safe distance separating it from who they really are. But this is me. Without my sister, me at my truest self. Hyperventilating in a Porta-Potty, drinking a stranger's dregs.

I'm staring myself in the face, and I refuse to look away.

When I come out, I find Levi again and I smile at him. Now that I'm floating, it'll be easier to put my house of cards back together.

"I'll pretend you never said it," I tell him.

He grins like a maniac. "Great! Selective amnesia is a rare talent. Now I can do anything idiotic that I want around you. I'm gonna make a list of other stupid shit I've said that I want you to forget. Including everything I'm saying right now. I'll have the list on your desk by Monday."

He burns up the silence.

I point at a game where you shoot miniature pumpkins with a pellet gun. "I want to win you something."

He trails after me, his shoulders lowered.

"The more you hit, the better prize you'll get," chants the man at the booth as I hand him my money. I take aim. But it's not a pumpkin anymore. Muscle and flesh sprouts, crawling over bone until Adam is smirking at me.

"You and I are the same. We go for what we want," he says.

The pellet pops his eye and splatters the shelf with gore.

But there's another head beside him, turning. "You and your sister, you're both repressed fucking freaks, you know that?"

This time I shoot him in the jaw. His teeth splinter and a long strip of his pink gums gleams through his shredded skin. There's a wall full of sneering Adam heads now. I hit one in the skull. Chunks of brain slap to the ground. He won't stop talking. He won't go away.

"Joy. *Joy!*"

Levi drags me away as the man at the booth shouts after us. He pulls me into a run until I break away, panting. We're outside the fair now, standing in the wide rest of the field.

He steadies me. "You wouldn't stop shooting. Are you okay?"

"Did I win?" I murmur.

"I don't know." His face is ashen. Then he sniffs and his face changes. "Is . . . is that alcohol?"

This isn't supposed to be what makes him hate me.

"Are you drunk?" he asks, stunned.

"No," I say. "I've been drunk for real. This isn't that."

"You brought alcohol with you today?" He steps back. "You went to the bathroom to drink. You came back different."

"You said . . . at the funeral." The funeral for his half brother who I killed. "You said everyone has something they use . . . to cope."

"That was before I lived with an alcoholic."

I flinch.

"I'm sorry." He closes his eyes briefly. "It's okay—"

"Don't ever apologize to me, Levi. Don't ever."

"You're tired. You're sick," he recites. "Let's leave."

"I want to go somewhere first."

"I'm taking you home—"

"I need to go somewhere with you."

I finally know exactly where I'm supposed to tell him.

It's a long, cold walk. But he doesn't ask where we're going, and he doesn't turn back. He just squeezes my fingers so hard I lose circulation.

The graveyard is as sunny as the day he was buried. The ground's wet from a brief rain last night, the dirt over his grave spongy. The headstone shines. The flowers are fresh.

Levi rubs the toe of his sneaker against the granite. "Why are we here?"

I killed your half brother.

Say it.

"You know what the stupid thing is?" he mumbles to

himself, gazing at the grave. "I'm pissed at him for not living up to my expectations. And that's ridiculous. People don't ever live up to dreams. People are real and dreams aren't."

Something seizes in my body. I turn and throw up beside the grave, horribly, unexpectedly.

"Oh, God, Joy, you're really sick." He sweeps my hair back while I retch. "It's okay," he says over and over again. "I'll take you home."

I scrape words together, put them in a line. "It's my turn to tell you something."

"You don't have to tell me anything."

Acid in my mouth, I say, "I killed Adam."

"What?" He blinks. "No you didn't."

"Yes I did. I killed him."

He's still for a minute. "This is a messed up joke," he says at last, in the saddest voice in the world. "I really pissed you off with that stuff I said back there."

"I was at Adam's birthday party," I say numbly. "I pushed him into the quarry. Because I hated him."

Everything I did for the blackmailer was all to avoid saying this one simple truth.

He covers his eyes. "My mom says things, too . . . when she gets like this."

"I did it."

"I know you don't mean this. I'm not going to be mad at you."

"Levi." I bend down and peel his hand away from his eyes. I hold it tightly. "I killed him. It was me."

"Please stop talking." He presses a palm to my forehead, feeling for a fever. I push his hand away, find my phone, find the video, skip to the moment that matters.

"I'm taking you home," he says, but the video's already playing.

You can see in someone's face when they care about you. It makes their eyes softer, their mouth more gentle. You notice when it's gone. Sometimes you can pinpoint the exact moment it disappears.

He starts breathing fast. Too fast. His chest rises and falls in a shallow rhythm. "It's fake. That video's fake. It's blurry, it's dark, you can't see shit."

"You can see my hair."

He doesn't respond. He's trembling even though he's wearing three layers, his lips bluish-white. He wavers and collapses, grabbing Adam's headstone for support. "I—you—"

I reach for his wrist. His skin's ice-cold.

"Please tell me—this is a joke." He won't breathe normally. "Tell me—that video's not real. Lie about it—I don't care."

"You need to breathe slower."

"Lie," he pleads. "I don't need—to know the truth—about anyone—anymore."

"I'll never stop being sorry," I whisper.

He curls up on Adam's grave.

Let him get angry. Let him call the cops. Anything other than this.

"Go away," he gasps. "Please."

"I can't leave you here—"

"All this time, you . . ." His teeth chatter. "I even—oh, God—how did you keep that inside? Every time we talked—and you never showed it . . ."

And then he's crying for real, yell crying, the kind where you're just making a lot of noise and breathing hard. He folds in on himself to try to get away from the person doing this to him.

Me.

"Look at me, finally crying at his grave." Hysterical laughter bubbles up between his sobs.

Sorry is my least favorite word. It's so insulting.

"Please just go." He leans against the headstone. "Please just go."

So I do.

Mom asks how the date went, what happened to my elbow, is everything okay. I ask if my sister's coming downstairs for dinner.

"She went out a while ago," Dad says from the kitchen. "She said she was going to work at the library."

The library closed two hours ago.

"Why do you let her skip dinner every night?" I ask.

"Grace is independent," Mom says. "You know her."

"Grace needs to see a therapist."

In the kitchen, something falls and breaks. Dad sticks his head in. "What?"

"What?" Mom echoes.

"Why don't you notice anything?" I feel very far away. "All you have to do is look."

"What are you talking about?" Dad asks, bewildered.

"She never comes out of her room. She works out too much. She doesn't eat right. She needs to talk to someone. Maybe go on medication."

"*Medication?*" Dad frowns.

"It's normal to withdraw a little when you're her age," Mom says soothingly. "Everyone goes through it. I did, too."

"She's not you." My chest pulses. "Everyone does not go through what she's going through."

"Why don't you talk to her? I'm sure she'd tell you more than she'd tell her nosy parents," says Dad.

I see it now. They've always made us each other's responsibility so we wouldn't have to be theirs.

They want her to be fine so badly. Bad enough to look the other way.

"I'm going to find her," I tell them.

"You say that like she's missing," Mom says, annoyed.

"I'm just going to look," I tell her.

From now on, I'm always going to look.

She doesn't answer her phone. But I know where she is.

The sun starts setting when I'm halfway to the quarry. The sky is the dusk blue of late evening, just a hint of orange left. I'm cold, I think, but I don't really notice. I walk fast. I don't know how long I have before Levi tells the police and they come for me.

The houses on our street glow with pumpkin lanterns and laughter, trick-or-treaters darting from house to house. I remember having to hold my sister's hand, take her candy for her. She never trusted strangers.

The trick-or-treaters thin out when I hit Adam's road. His house is the only one at the end of this street, up the hill. The trees are different at night. Evil shapes. When we came here together, that night, she held my hand, even though it was the night she decided to be brave.

I push through the woods.

Now that I've seen the video, I remember bits and pieces of the birthday party. My own nausea. Fury, thicker. Stumbling over branches. Him behind me. Telling myself, over and over again, not to run.

They haven't started fencing off the quarry yet. It's still exposed, a raw scar, the rim of the world with the moon shining into it.

And my sister is standing at the edge.

She's not wearing a sweatshirt. Her T-shirt's thin against her back. She's looking at the sky.

People are wrong about twins. I've never had any private window into her head. But everyone wanted me to. They loved the idea of it. After a while, I convinced myself I did.

"Grace," I say, my voice rasping in the silence.

She jumps a little, turning around. The tears on her face are silver in the moonlight. "You found me."

"I looked," I say.

"Are you mad at me?" she whispers.

"No."

"You're lying." Her voice cracks. "How could you not be mad at me?"

She's not wearing shoes, either. Her sneakers are several feet away. She's hugging herself and she looks so fragile and she's standing really, really close to the edge. Closer than I thought. Closer than I want to believe.

The darkness peels back and her closeness sears brighter than everything else, dagger sharp.

"Grace, come over here." My words are suddenly clear.

"You straightened your hair," she mumbles. "You look like me."

"Come here, Grace."

"You can be the one with straight hair once I'm gone."

I lunge. I've caught her before, I'll catch her again. But the distance between us is too wide and she jerks back, *too* close, TOO close, her heels balanced on the edge.

"Don't." The word flies out, a warning.

I'm going to burst into tears and it's not going to help. I don't know what the words are to make this stop. I've never known them, and she's going to fall because I'm not smart enough to know them.

"Please just leave," she cries.

I can't. I'm tied to her more than any other person in this world, and I need to learn how to tie the rope between us in something other than a noose.

"I love you," I tell her.

She shuts her eyes. "If you do, it's only because you don't know me for real."

"I know you, Grace."

"You don't." Her heel scrapes nothingness and *please, please, please*, but she doesn't fall, she just looks at me all shivery in the cold.

"I want to." My mouth is desert dry. "Tell me."

"I don't want you to know who I am." The wind wraps her hair around her neck. "But I'll never be able to be someone else. Not ever in my whole life. Even when I tried to be you, it didn't work."

"Please come here, please, please."

"It doesn't take long to hit the bottom," she says. "It didn't take him long."

Fear leaps everywhere in my stomach.

"It's so dark in there," she says quietly.

Both her heels are on the edge now.

"I'm not scared, though."

She's trembling all over.

I'm crying so hard I can't speak. "Please. Just don't. Talk to me. Stay and explain everything. There's so much I don't understand. Start from the beginning. How did I get home the night—the night Adam died?"

"Cassius helped me carry you." Her eyes slide to a point over my shoulder, like she's watching it happen in the distance.

"And—" *Breathe.* "He knew all along what happened to Adam."

"I made him promise not to tell."

"How—how did you—" I lick my lips. "How did you get those photos of Eastman and Savannah?"

"That part of the email I wrote from Cassius was true." It's like she's in a trance. "He found them in his sister's room. He came to me. He said I might be able to understand what Savannah was going through, wanted to know how to help her. But there's no way to help. All you can do is get back at that person. That's the only way to get the feelings out of you."

"He gave you the photos?" I stammer.

"I stole them from his house." She hugs herself. "After the photos went up, he was so upset. He knew it must've been me. But he felt so guilty about what Adam did. So he didn't do anything."

"So he didn't have anything to do with the blackmail. You sent those emails." I already knew, but shock breaks over me in waves anyway.

She looks away from me. "I have to go."

Keep talking. She can't fall if I keep her tied to me. "I don't understand, but I'm not mad, okay? I love you no matter what, okay? Tell me—tell me where you found that video of Officer Roseby."

"In November's house." She answers readily, robotically. "She invited me over one time, when her dad wasn't home. She wanted to talk to me about Adam. I think she wanted to fix me. I poked around. I wanted to find out more about her. Then I found that video in her dad's room,

321

hidden away like a secret trophy. And I remembered how he arrested us that night, how awful he made everything. Everyone deserved to know what he's really like. Just like everyone deserved to know what Eastman is like. People don't believe all men are like that unless they see it for themselves."

"Grace—"

"I knew it would be bad for Savannah, okay? And I knew it would probably be bad for November, too." She lets out a whimper. "But I have to tell the truth, even if it hurts some! You have to warn everyone about what people have done. Or they just keep doing it forever."

She yanks her fingers hard through her hair.

"Either the person has to die, like Adam," she keeps going, "or everyone has to find out what they did. Those are the only ways. And I don't want anyone to know what I did."

"You're not bad—" I can't breathe. "You're not a bad person—"

She covers her ears.

"I knew people were blaming Cassius," she says. "Officer Roseby started it. I was afraid he'd break. So I had to do something to discredit Officer Roseby before that happened."

There's still the main question—*why*—but I'm afraid to ask it, afraid it'll upset her more.

"Tell me about the third note," I say instead.

"I wanted everyone to know what Adam was. But I

didn't want them to know about me," she says. "I'm sorry I convinced you that November was the blackmailer—I needed you to believe it was someone else. But it made you so sad, and I couldn't tell you it wasn't really her without telling you the truth. I knew if I wrote that last note, you'd realize it wasn't."

"She told the whole school on her own," I say. "I never showed her that note."

"She's stronger than me. Everyone in the whole world is stronger than me."

"No, they're not. I'm not."

She opens her eyes suddenly. "Did you tell Levi?"

"Yes," I manage.

"Does he hate you now?"

It hurts so much to say it. "Yes."

"Good. Now he won't ever be able to do anything to you." Her blue eyes are darker in the evening light than they've ever been before.

I don't bother telling her that he never would have.

"When are you going to ask me why?" she says.

"It doesn't matter." If I ran, could I get to her in time? No. She's too far.

She tilts her head back. "It didn't work."

"I know why you did it." My arms ache from holding them out toward her. "You said it. Getting back at somebody, it's the only way to fix things, right?"

She covers her mouth, clamps her elbows tight to the sides of her chest like she's trying to shrink herself.

"You wanted to get back at me," I say painfully.

She's the only one smart enough to have pulled it off.

She stammers through her fingers. "I didn't . . . I didn't want . . ."

"It's okay." I feel so heavy. "I deserved it."

"No, you didn't!" she sobs. "None of it was your fault! But I couldn't stop blaming you, I couldn't feel different, even when I tried to stop feeling everything—"

She shakes and shakes. She's going to shake herself off the edge.

"And I thought," she says, "if I could make you hurt a little—if I could make you feel it—I could stop feeling it."

"I'm sorry." The worst words.

"I wanted you to think *maybe* you killed him, and then at the end I'd pin it on someone else. When Cassius left, it was perfect. If I hadn't gotten so upset about Levi, it would have been fine. I'd have gotten it out of my system, you'd never have known it was me, and we could have gone back to the way we were."

"Why couldn't you have just told me you were mad?" I whisper.

"If you knew I was the kind of person who'd blame you—"

"Well, now I know. And guess what? I still love you."

"I hurt you on purpose," she says dully. "You're not safe with me."

Maybe I do have a special window into her head. Maybe we've been feeling the same things, but in different ways, for different reasons.

"I have to keep you safe from me," she says.

"Grace, shut up, shut up or I'll say something really corny about how we'll always be together—"

"We would've been. That's why I have to go. I'm holding you back."

"If you fall, I fall with you." As it bursts out, I know it's true.

Her eyes open wide. "Stop."

"I'll dive after you. You know I would. Right over the edge."

"*No.*" She recoils.

"Then come here," I beg. "You're going to get help. I'm going to be with you through every second of it."

"I hurt you," she repeats, faintly.

"People are more than one bad thing they did." I inch toward her. She doesn't move. "We're the ones who get to decide if we want to forgive."

"What if I can't forgive you?" She's so close to me now, almost close enough to grab. "For forever?"

"I trust forever." So close. "I trust you."

"Things won't change." She's a foot away. "They never have before."

"You won't know unless you stay."

I catch her. I catch her, I catch her.

And this is how it ends, sometimes. With nothing feeling good. With all your worst fears confirmed, every nightmare coming true, and the last time you saw the only boy who ever made you smile when you didn't want to, he was broken because of you.

But someone you love is alive and safe, and hurting someone doesn't mean you can't save someone else.

No matter what I say, Grace, I don't believe it yet, either. It might be impossible to believe that things can change when nothing ever has.

But maybe waiting for it anyway means that you're starting to.

November 7

Grace

To Joy Morris—

The food here is exactly as bad as November warned me.

I know you and Mom and Dad are trying to bring it down from three visits a day to one, that you're trying to give me the "time I need." I guess a suicide attempt is what it takes to move them from clueless to helicopters. I'm hoping eventually they'll stop somewhere in the middle.

My therapist told me to write you letters. She said

I didn't have to send them. But from now on, I want you to know exactly what's in my head.

I'm still kind of mad that you told Mom and Dad what I almost did at the quarry. I don't want to be, but that's the thing about feelings. They happen to you.

I told my therapist about Adam. The bare minimum. I haven't been able to talk about it much, but she says that doesn't mean I'll never be able to. Next week. Or the week after. When I'm ready.

She says there are these inventions called Rube Goldberg machines that are meant to do something simple in the most complicated way possible. She says I'm like that with my emotions.

I hope your therapy appointments are going well, too. I'm jealous that you just have to see someone once a week instead of staying in this place, but I guess you weren't the one on the edge.

At first I talked a lot about you. My therapist says that's how you can tell who somebody loves the most, when you ask them about themselves and they start talking about that person. And that you know somebody's family when you love and hate

328

them at the same time.

Thanks for visiting today. I'm glad more people are supporting November at school. I'm glad you're thinking about telling Preston the truth about who was sending you those notes. It scares me, but I think he deserves to know more than I deserve not to be scared.

I guess Levi never did tell the police what you told him. That's the other thing I was going to say. After what you told me about him, I wrote him a letter, too. And I told him about the parts you left out. I told him you didn't know what had happened the night of the birthday party until I showed you the video. And I told him what Adam did. I don't want to stay locked up in my own head anymore. I think telling is the key to getting it out.

And I told him maybe it wasn't really like you pushed him. Maybe it was more like he fell. Maybe he took a step he didn't have to, that he wouldn't have taken if he wasn't drunk.

He can decide how big a difference that is.

We might not ever know the absolute truth for

sure. But maybe there is no absolute truth. Maybe believing what makes you happy is all you can do. Maybe it's just what you can live with.

Choosing to believe something is hard. You have to work at it every single day for a long time before it sinks in. (This is another thing my therapist said.) I still sort of think it's all bullshit. That's how it feels. But I'm repeating the stuff she says anyway, since it's her job to know better than me.

I don't know if I can ever be a different person. Or what that girl would be like. Or if she exists, in this forever we're apparently trusting.

But if she does, I kind of want to meet her.

Love, and some hate, I guess,

Grace

ACKNOWLEDGMENTS

This book has been with me through lots of different phases in my life, lots of terrible haircuts, and lots of wonderful people.

Thank you so much to the amazing, dedicated, and inspiring Sarah Davies, who is the reason Joy and Grace first had a chance to grow.

Thank you, too, to Karen Chaplin, who was endlessly patient and helpful through an intense revisions process. She knows exactly what it means for a book to be at its best, and without her, it never would have gotten there.

And thank you to Dana Levy, Sarah Harian, Rachel Simon, Luvina Jean-Charles, and Michelle Painchaud for reading the earliest version of this book and offering flawless advice.

Thank you to the Freshmen Fifteens and the Sweet

Sixteens—I'm so lucky to know so many wildly talented writers.

To my parents, who rightfully interpreted "I'm writing, you guys" as "I'm on Facebook" in high school, but now for some reason believe me, even though it still usually means "I'm on ~~Facebook~~ Tumblr."

To my best friends from Maine, who are always supportive and never fail to forgive the unreturned calls and texts when I'm on deadline. To my new friends in San Diego, who are all kinds of really awesome—especially Sarah Mack, who chose to believe that the person tweeting "hey I just moved here, someone be friends with me" wasn't a serial killer. To Amit, for convincing me I'm not a failure at everything whenever I decide I'm probably a failure at everything.

Thanks to Courtney Summers, Laurie Halse Anderson, and Libba Bray, whose books about complicated, confused teenagers I devoured as a complicated, confused teenager, and who continue to inspire me as a still-pretty-confused twentysomething.

Thank you to all the fantastic people at HarperCollins—this book would not exist without you.

And thank you to everyone reading this who has dealt with terrible, scary things and stuck around anyway. You make my world better.

JOIN THE

Epic Reads

COMMUNITY

THE ULTIMATE YA DESTINATION

◀ DISCOVER ▶
your next favorite read

◀ MEET ▶
new authors to love

◀ WIN ▶
free books

◀ SHARE ▶
infographics, playlists, quizzes, and more

◀ WATCH ▶
the latest videos

◀ TUNE IN ▶
to Tea Time with Team Epic Reads

Find us at **www.epicreads.com**
and **@epicreads**